I0762639

CITY ON FIRE

CITY ON FIRE

A NOVEL OF HONG KONG

SIMON ELEGANT

PEGASUS CRIME
NEW YORK LONDON

CITY ON FIRE

Pegasus Crime is an imprint of
Pegasus Books, Ltd.
148 West 37th Street, 12th Floor
New York, NY 10018

First Pegasus Books cloth edition May 2026

Interior design by Maria Fernandez

Library of Congress Cataloging-in-Publication Data is available.

ISBN: 979-8-89710-095-8

10 9 8 7 6 5 4 3 2 1

Printed in the United States of America
Distributed by Simon & Schuster
www.pegasusbooks.com

For Nick and Nomi, who were born into it.

"And if we burn, you burn with us!"

—Suzanne Collins, *Mockingjay*

Unofficial motto adopted by the protesters in Hong Kong

ONE
KILLIAN

Light flooded into the room and Killian bolted upright, heart hammering, gasping.

The motion detectors at the front of the station had kicked on the floodlights.

He swung his legs over the side of the bed and leaned over, forearms on his thighs, and breathed. His face was wet, and his throat was scratchy, raw. Had he been shouting?

The wind moaned around the corners of the old building and rattled the roof tiles. It smelled of the mudflat: The sweet stink of rotting vegetation mixed with the briny tang of the sea.

Another slow breath.

Two or three times a week since he'd left the hospital months ago, he jolted awake in the bowels of the night. Heart racing. Panting as though he'd been running. And never a memory of the dream. Only a deep despair that clung like a shroud.

He knew what it must be, of course. What happened on that night would be with him until he was on his deathbed.

Shouting, screams, bodies heaving around him, then the detonation as his pistol fired, the protester who had been swinging a pole at him lay splayed on the ground, arms flung out, the widening pool of blood around his head glistening in the light of the streetlights.

Then another demonstrator was squatting, pulling off the balaclava, a chorus of screams from the crowd at the sight of the blood pouring from his head.

And the face, that deathly pale face, a child's face: He was just a kid, a boy. The horror at what he had done crashing down on Killian, then more screams, this time of anger. The crowd turning on him, seeing out of the corner of his eye a steel fence post scything through the air . . .

Enough. Killian shook his head to clear it. Enough for one night.

He sighed, stretched his back, got up, and went over to the sink for a glass of water.

Outside, the floodlights clicked off. Probably a tree branch.

He took the glass over to the big bay windows at the back and stood for a moment staring at the miles of dimly lit skyscrapers across the bay in Shenzhen. This station had originally been built as an observation post during the Cultural Revolution when hundreds of Chinese had tried to escape the chaotic violence being meted out in Mao's People's Paradise by swimming the three miles to Hong Kong.

Officially, this was called Deep Bay, which it certainly was not. Perhaps if they'd known the original English name—Shark Bay—fewer people would have braved the waters.

Da had been posted to this same station not long after he'd arrived in Hong Kong in 1978. He had spent a year fishing swimmers out of the water, hundreds a night. And not just desperate Chinese. There were still Vietnamese boat people arriving from another Worker's Paradise.

"Spotted a woman, just her head above the waves, unresponsive. Pulled her up by the hair. Nothing there from the hips down. Both legs chewed off. Sharks." It was an oft-repeated story. Told with relish.

Killian turned to go back to bed when a flash of movement on the shore below caught his eye. Instinctively, he reached for the switches on the wall.

The station's huge bank of floodlights would make the entire four-hundred-yard stretch of coastline as bright as day. But he hesitated, then dropped his hand. The area leading down to the sea had mostly been cleared in the seventies to make spotting refugees easier. But since vegetation had returned and it was now covered by small trees and bushes, it had become an unofficial headquarters for Hong Kong's malcontents: the homeless, the dispossessed, a few petty criminals. He could often smell the woodsmoke of their cooking fires drifting up on the shore breeze. They were harmless. He let them be.

He lay down again, the rough cotton of the pillowcase scratchy under his ear.

With the floods off, the only light came from the streetlight at the compound gate, shadows of tree branches played against the ceiling. He watched as the shapes began to leap and twist above him, the wind whistled through the rafters.

A light patter of rain. Another, heavier shower. Then the wind rose to a howl, and the full storm arrived, water battered at the glass of the high windows in the observation room next door, the grumbling thunder almost continuous, seemingly right above the station roof.

A shape appeared in the bedroom doorway. Gau, his head cocked to one side, tail moving in a slow inquisitive wag.

"Go back to bed, boy," Killian said, waving his hand. "It's just thunder and you're not scared of thunder, remember?"

A pause. Another roll of thunder. No reaction except a last, amiable wag of the tail, then Gau turned and disappeared back to his lair under what used to be the station sergeant's desk in front of the main doors.

Gau. An undoggy dog. No canine eagerness to please. Affable, but totally independent. More like a cat than a dog, though Killian had never met a cat that could be called affable.

Killian smiled and rolled over on his side. A sharp jolt of pain came where his weight pressed down on his ribs.

Listen to your body, they said. Listen to your body.

Head. Only a vague, throbbing ache, an echo of old pain.

Ribs. He flexed his back and felt a twinge where the steel pole had hit him, then a jolt of pain. He let out an inadvertent gasp.

The boy had gasped too, after they'd taken off the balaclava. Wet croaks. Teeth black with blood.

Killian sat up. There would be no more sleep.

On the counter, his mobile lit up. The phone, charging from the wall socket, buzzed and twitched on the counter, dancing toward the edge. He took two steps over and caught it just as it fell.

Not a number he recognized. But the first four digits were 5858, so it had to be from police headquarters in Wan Chai.

3:22 A.M. Nothing good ever came from calls at this hour.

"Tong."

"Superintendent Tong?"

"Yes?"

"This is Senior Superintendent Pang. Crime NOIC."

Pang. Not a real policeman. A bureaucrat. A networker. A calculating crawler, making his way up the ladder, currently punching his card as night officer in charge at Crime and Security. Next would be deputy commander of a district. Then district chief. On and on until he held the commissioner's gold baton in his clammy palms. Or so he hoped.

"Yes?"

"I said Senior Superintendent Pang."

They'd been the same rank for years, but now Pang was delighted to let him know he'd been promoted ahead of him.

"Yes?"

"That's 'Yes, sir,' Tong."

"Yes, sir. What do you want . . . Sir."

Killian spoke with his teeth clenched.

Pang grunted. A beat. The rain drummed against the observation windows. "We need you at the New Territories west landfill. A body. Probable homicide."

"You know that's impossible. I'm under strict orders: No active duty until the inquiries are finished."

"This is an exception, Tong. There's no one else available except a couple of baby CID inspectors in the district. This is way over their heads."

"Send someone from HQ. You've got four murder squads."

"Two are seconded to Tactical Unit duty. One in reserve. The cockroaches are going crazy tonight. Demos everywhere. The other unit is already on a case."

Killian didn't reply, but felt the stirrings of hope, long suppressed.

"Come on, Tong, you stubborn bastard. Everyone on the Force knows you would sell your own mother to be back on the job."

He didn't reply, not trusting himself. Pang continued hurriedly, knowing he'd overstepped, almost pleading now.

"There's no one else to send. And you're ten minutes away instead of over an hour."

"Did you clear it with the forty-seventh floor?"

Pang cleared his throat. "Provisionally."

"Provisionally? What does that mean?"

"It means you'll only be on the case temporarily. And advisory only. Stop stalling and get out there."

"If this prejudices my case . . ."

"Tong." Pang sounded exasperated. "We're jammed up all over. Half the city is out on the streets. Demos everywhere. Full callout. Plus, two suspicious deaths in Kowloon east."

"Even if I wanted to, sir," Killian stressed the title, "I can't. As Border Security, I'm under Operations Division now, not Crime and Security, so technically, to be seconded back to CID . . ."

"I told you. You'll only be advising."

"I won't be in charge of the investigation?"

"You'll be senior officer present. We'll make sure Tin Shui Wai understands that. Okay?"

"Operational protocol . . ."

"For God's sake, Tong. This is what you do. It's what you're good at. Stop messing around and get out there, will you?"

Pang was right. It was a golden chance, but Killian hesitated. There were too many ways this could make a bad situation far worse.

"It's messy. Right up your alley."

Translation: No one else wanted to touch it. Killian didn't speak. Pang sighed.

"Alright. I'm giving you a direct order. Are you refusing, Superintendent?"

Pang had been trying to avoid the direct command, which would go on the record. Too bad.

Killian felt his heart rate tick up, the old excitement. And another bloom of hope. If he solved the case quickly . . .

He kept his voice even. "Tell them I'll be there in fifteen."

"Keep a low profile." Pang knew he'd been outmaneuvered. "And whatever you do, don't talk to the media. I've told the locals to set up roadblocks."

"Yes, sir."

"There's a crew of constables working the scene. Some sergeants. Plus three CID inspectors from Tin Shui Wai. The senior officer is Chief Inspector Choi. She's young. And inexperienced."

"That's a lot of babysitting."

He heard Pang curse again under his breath. "Never mind that. Just get out there and don't screw it up."

"Yes, sir."

Killian killed the call and put the phone down on the counter. Gau had appeared from his lair, one ear flopped over, looking up expectantly.

"What?"

Gau's tail moved back and forth in a slow wave.

"You want to go out? Sorry, boy. Not tonight." The wind moaned outside, and the rain lashed against the windows. "You should be glad."

TWO

Thick cords of water plunged out of the darkness into the glare of the halogen lights that lit one corner of the landfill. Twenty constables strung out in a line picked their way through the mounds of garbage, fanning out from the lit-up area.

The rain bounced off the black plastic covers stretched over the policemen's caps with such force that a fine mist seemed to hang above each man's head like a neon-lit halo. It pummeled their shoulders and bent backs and ran off their caps, over their faces, and into their blue uniform collars. The men ignored the rain, heads bent, eyes fixed on the ground, each holding a black rubber service flashlight making a pool of light ahead, the line advancing at a funereal half step.

The landfill was huge, over seventy acres. Most of that was garbage that had already been processed and compacted by bulldozers, after which it was loaded onto trucks, dumped in an excavated corner, then covered with a layer of earth and left to decompose.

This search was confined to the receiving area, not far from the administration buildings. Here, the garbage was still raw and pungent, an obstacle course made up of the detritus of urban life: doorless refrigerators; rusting air conditioners; kitchen cabinets covered in a thick layer of nicotine-brown grease from years of stir-frying; shattered computer monitors; bent bicycle wheels, spokes pointing menacingly outward; plastic sacks of household rubbish crammed in between the bigger items, often ripped and spilling out gape-mouthed fish heads, dead flowers, banana peels, grey lettuce leaves, jagged broken beer bottles.

The piles of garbage sagged alarmingly, sometimes toppling over, releasing a rank, sweet exhalation of decay that penetrated through the full-face respirators the constables wore.

The wind had been nipping at the men, pushing at their caps and capes. Now, a gust exploded from the right side of the dump, billowing up the black slickers and forcing the constables to clutch at their uniform caps. A few were enveloped, capes flying up over their heads.

Two men had already fallen and cut themselves, one gashing his hand badly enough for stitches. Methane gas was a greater danger. New constables were rotated in every fifteen minutes, and two sergeants stood on the lip of the platform, watching the men closely for signs of incapacitation.

Killian stood on a concrete platform that extended out from the landfill administration buildings, overlooking the sea of garbage. The CID investigators huddled under an awning near him. Chief Inspector Lin and Inspector Yeong, one rake-thin, the other plump, both smoking as they gazed out at the scene. The most senior, Chief Inspector Choi, stood apart from the other two, closer to Killian. Her hair was cut severely short and she wore a stern expression, the armor of a woman competing in a male-dominated world like the Force.

Before Choi began to brief him, she offered Killian a tin of Tiger Balm to smear under his nose. "To help mask the smell."

He accepted, but the strong eucalyptus odor made the stench of garbage even more sickly. His stomach heaved, and he clenched his teeth, taking shallow breaths.

They were waiting for the forensic techs to bring the body down.

Getting to the corpse in the first place had been a challenge, Choi explained. The garbage was dumped in haphazard piles that could collapse at any time. Forensics had to send for wooden planks to construct a makeshift walkway, then put up an awning to try and protect the site from the rain.

Choi briefed Killian on the search procedure she had ordered. By the book. Two-meter lanes. Two constables following each other down each lane for redundancy.

Killian sighed. They were probably wasting their time. This section of the landfill covered three acres, Choi said. The chances of finding anything was tiny. But it was procedure. And procedure was a savior. It was what they fell back on when everything looked hopeless. Like now.

He turned to Lin and Yeong.

"Gentlemen."

They both turned. Was Yeong the plump one or the skinny one?

"One of you can start the interviews with the night staff. How many are there?"

"Two," said Yeong, the fat one. "Both were probably asleep."

"Okay. You take care of them, Yeong."

He nodded, surly, and muttered something. Clearly, the judgment that Killian was about to be cashiered or forced to resign had reached even Tin Shui Wai station.

"What did you say, Yeong?" Killian asked sharply.

"Nothing." A beat. "Sir."

"Get on with it, then."

Killian turned to Lin. "Chief Inspector."

No reply. Dumb insolence here too. They probably resented being bigfooted by an outsider. Not to mention one of the few *gweilo* Brits left on the Force.

"You take the remaining constables and start sweeping the road leading into the landfill. Twenty meters on either side."

"It's a mile long."

"Yes, it is. The sooner you start, the sooner you'll be done."

Lin glowered, then spun on his heel. Killian turned back to the scene.

"Any suggestions on what else we should be doing, Choi?" he asked.

"Only the scavengers, sir. We need to interview them too."

"We'll do that once we get a look at the body."

The rain had finally stopped, though the wind was still strong. A blast rattled the lights, the tin reflectors clanging against each other. Several constables rushed to hold on to the bases, but the wind continued to slam the tops together. Another gust. A bulb shattered with a muffled crack, and half the site disappeared into darkness for a moment, only the bobbing flashlights marking the line of searchers.

The lights flashed back on. Two technicians dressed in full white hazmat suits and respirators were bent over the body, preparing to lift it onto a stretcher. It had been wrapped in layers of black plastic, some of which had come loose and were flapping in the wind. Patches of white flesh showed through the rips in the black bags, but not much else. The two figures in white reached down and slowly lifted the body. It was tiny. A child?

The two men clumped funereally down the line of planks, the stretcher swaying until they finally climbed up onto the concrete platform and into the protection of the overhead awning. They lowered the body carefully onto a trestle table set up by their colleagues. Then one of them produced a large pair of shears and began to cut away the black plastic, the pieces falling off with an awful, teasing slowness.

Not a child. A torso.

First, there was the pale swell of a belly, the little knot of the belly button, a sparse triangle of grey hair. But below that, there was nothing but gore, the whole pubic area caked in black dried blood. On either side were grey-red stumps, matching, precise cuts, the white edge of the hip sockets starkly visible, severed tendons hanging in tatters around the joints.

Killian closed his eyes for a moment.

A loud gagging sound came from his left. The sergeant stumbled away, hand over his mouth. Choi, ashen-faced, coughed into her hand, then spoke, her voice rasping.

"Is it a man or a woman?"

No one replied. The technician pulled away more plastic, giving a glimpse of the top of the torso. No breasts. A scattering of gray hairs. It was a man. Or had been.

Noticing a tear in one of his blue rubber gloves, the technician stopped to pull on another pair. Then he picked up the scissors and cut away the last of the black plastic, revealing the ragged stump between the shoulders.

"Why is there so little blood on the neck and shoulders?" Choi asked.

This must be her first murder. The city only had forty or fifty a year, most of them domestic.

"The cuts were made after death," Killian said. "The heart had stopped, so no blood. That's why there's so much around the groin. The victim was alive."

Choi shuddered, her hand covering her mouth.

"How long has it been . . ." She trailed off.

"We won't know until the autopsy."

A silence followed as the technicians worked. Choi glanced at Killian, regarding him quizzically.

"Something else on your mind?" Killian asked.

"I'm wondering what you think. So far, I mean."

"It's too early to say. No point in speculating."

"Yes, sir. But surely . . ."

Killian held up a hand.

"Sorry. Just a second."

The lead technician had shuffled over to them. Even with his face shield misted up, Killian recognized the heavy black glasses. It was Chan Wai Lik, one of the better forensics people, though permanently gloomy even for someone in his line of work.

"The pathologist is stuck in traffic, Superintendent. A protest in Yuen Long. She told us to go ahead with the fingerprinting."

"Thank you, Mr. Chan. Do what you have to," Killian said.

Chan nodded, then slouched away again, the thighs of his nylon suit swishing as he walked.

Two more technicians arrived, also wearing full hazmat suits and respirators. They set up four telescopic aluminum poles around the body, slotting them into metal rings in the plastic sheet that lay under the trestle. Then they draped a clear plastic sheet to the top of each pole, forming a small awning about a foot above the torso. With the ease of long practice, they unfurled the plastic sides and zipped them together to form an enclosed tent.

One of the technicians put a small boxy machine shaped like a large teapot into the space, flipped a switch, and pulled the last zip down so the body was completely enclosed. Wisps of steam puffed from the spout.

Chan shuffled over and leaned in toward Killian.

"You need to stand back while we open the tent. The gas is toxic."

Choi and Killian retreated to the wall of the single-story office building that housed the landfill administration.

The technicians lined up at the corners of the tent and rolled up the zips, the wind blowing away the pink vapor. Two others carried handheld UV lights from the trestle table and began to scan the torso, one at each end, a centimeter at a time, the yellow light of the scanners reflecting off the plastic of their face shields and giving their intent faces a sickly, jaundiced sheen.

When they finished, the technicians huddled together and conversed in low voices. Then one of them leaned over the lower half of the torso and passed the scanner over it again. Chan looked over to Killian and shook his head. No fingerprints.

Choi and Killian watched as the team turned the body over and went through their routine again.

After a few more minutes, Chan looked over and shook his head again, emphasizing with a thumbs down. Nothing on the back. The other technicians began to dismantle the tent. They had returned the body to its original position, facing up.

Killian stepped forward.

"Before you finish, can you lift the body, please? So that I can see the back?"

"Yes, sir."

The two technicians leaned down, each grasping the torso with their gloved hands, one sliding his hand under what was left of the left shoulder, the other under a buttock. They glanced at each other.

"Three, two, one. Lift."

They could have been nurses moving a patient from stretcher to bed. Killian leaned forward, dropping his mask and wiping away the Tiger Balm from his top lip. He bent so that his nose was an inch from the body.

The back was startlingly white in the harsh light of the arc lamps, unmarked except for a spray of moles. There was some light red coloring around the small of the back and the top of the buttocks. Lividity. That meant the body had been on its back after death, though with this amount of blood loss, it was only a faint coloration.

The skin of the buttocks was almost completely covered by crisscrossing scars. Fresh.

Killian bent closer.

"These are antemortem from the pink color. The killer must have used something very thin. A switch of wood. A branch maybe."

"Like those rods they used to use in school?" Choi asked, still standing back, glancing down at the body, then looking away.

"Maybe," Killian replied.

He remembered the whip of the cane from his schooldays. The explosion of pain on the palm, traveling right up the arm like an electric shock, cringing as he waited for the next blow. But it had been designed to sting, not maim. Barely a centimeter wide. What kind of force would you need to draw blood with one of those?

The scars were concentrated on the upper part of the buttocks. Below that dried blood covered everything, clotting the groove between the cheeks.

One of the technicians said something in a low voice. A snigger. Killian looked up, frowning. The technicians looked down at their feet.

"This was done while the victim was alive too?" Choi asked.

"Probably. We need confirmation from the autopsy," Killian said.

He snapped on a glove and leaned forward, pressing his right forefinger on the livor.

No blanching, as expected. The body had been there longer than the six to eight hours it took for lividity to set in.

Killian pulled off the glove and threw it in a trash bin next to the doors.

"Let's go and talk to the scavengers."

* * *

The garbage pickers were a washout.

Four of the ten turned out to be illegal immigrants from China. All but one were over sixty. The exception was a woman of twenty with a baby strapped to her back that wailed incessantly. They all stank of garbage and sweat, their hollow eyes and gaunt frames betraying their desperation and poverty.

Killian watched them shuffle up to be interviewed, his gaze lingering on an elderly woman visibly trembling with fear. He couldn't help but wonder what had happened to his city. For years, it had been ranked as one of the richest in the world. Yet, more and more people scavenged through garbage to find something to eat or trade.

Two decades under Communism, and the number of Hong Kongers the government classified as living below the poverty line had surged to 20 percent of the population. Another one of life's little ironies.

The last scavenger was a man in his sixties whose few remaining teeth were yellowed from nicotine. He had a boil the size of an orange bulging from his shoulder, his grey T-shirt soaked with pus.

"Has anyone looked at that?" Killian asked the sergeant who had escorted them into the room, nodding to the man's neck.

The sergeant frowned. "Why would anyone want to look at it?"

"Because he's a human being."

The sergeant shook his head, unimpressed. Sarcasm never worked with his type.

"Have someone drop him at the Tin Shui Wai Hospital A&E when we're finished."

The sergeant stared at him blankly, understanding perfectly well, but unwilling to acknowledge it. The whole of Tin Shui Wai station seemed to have decided he was a lame duck. Or a dead one.

"Just do it, Sergeant," Killian said. "And send me a copy of the admissions form, understood?"

The man finally nodded, then stomped out, slamming the door behind him.

Killian shook his head and glanced at his watch. Eight thirty. He turned to Choi. "Come on, then, Chief Inspector. We have an autopsy to attend."

THREE

Choi and Killian walked into the car park of the MTR where Killian had parked his patrol cruiser. They had agreed to ride together into town for the autopsy. Assuming the cross-harbor tunnels weren't more jammed than usual, it would take about an hour.

As they neared the bottom of the ramp leading to the car park, Choi tapped Killian on the arm.

"What?" he asked, looking up from typing a message to Chan asking about the objects the searchers had recovered around the body.

She pointed ahead. Someone had thrown a metal garbage bin onto the hood of the patrol car. The wire meshing protecting the windshield was intact, but the hood was covered in rotting cabbage leaves, sodden newspaper, and other trash.

They pulled the garbage bin off the hood and pushed it behind the car. A deep gouge marred the white paint, and the reek of decay hung in the air. The stench of the landfill flashed into Killian's mind, quickly followed by the image of the torso encased in flapping black plastic.

He unlocked the door and switched on the windshield wipers. They swiped back and forth, smearing slime across the glass. He pressed the water jet, holding it until the screen began to clear.

"*Lapsap gingchat*," Choi muttered.

"Garbage police?" Killian asked as he turned the wipers to their highest speed.

"It's one of the things the protesters shout. Maybe someone thought this was a pun."

"They don't like us much, that's for sure."

"Sometimes they have good reason," Choi said before hastily adding, "I mean, when the PTU units are on the rampage . . ."

"The Tactical Units do their job, which is to intimidate the protesters when things get out of hand."

She nodded doubtfully. Killian had heard the hollowness in his glib reassurance too.

"We just have to get through this, and we'll be back to normal, Chief Inspector. Never fear."

The screen was finally clear, and Killian put the car into gear.

For the first part of the drive, Choi was silent. She wasn't on her phone, just staring out at the passing streets, likely contemplating her first autopsy.

After half an hour driving through the New Territories and Kowloon east, they reached the near-permanent traffic jam marking the entrance to the second cross-harbor tunnel. Choi's phone pinged.

"Yeong and Lin say we've been allocated space at Tin Shui Wai station for the operations room, sir. They'll set it up today," she said.

"Good," Killian replied, inching the car forward a few feet. Not even a siren would help in the tunnel queues.

"There's one other piece of business we need to deal with, Chief Inspector," he added, turning toward her with a concerned expression.

"What's that, sir?"

"Would you please stop calling me 'sir'? My name is Bogong. Or Killian. Or boss, if you prefer. At least when we're with other ranks."

She nodded.

"Dumb *gweilo* would probably work too, if I've done something particularly foolish. I'm sure the rest of our colleagues call me that."

A hint of a smile tugged at her lips. "That would be racist, sir . . . Sorry, boss. And call me Blue, please."

"Blue, like the color?"

"Yes, boss. Blue like the color."

"Good name for a police officer."

She looked puzzled for a moment, the association was less obvious in Chinese, though it had grown stronger as the protests continued. Yellow for protesters. Blue for the government and police.

"Blue like police, right. But I just liked the color. And one of the characters in my name is blue, so . . ."

"Makes sense. Better than calling yourself Glacier."

"Or Chlorine. I saw a server at McDonald's with that on her name tag."

"I guess it sounded nice to her."

A pause, and then Blue spoke again. "So, boss, can I ask you something?"

They crept forward another ten meters.

"Sure, as long as it's not about politics."

"Actually, I was wondering why your Cantonese is so good. Not just for a *gweilo*. If I closed my eyes, I'd think you were . . ."

"My birth mother was English. She died when I was a baby, so I was raised by my dad's second wife. She's from Guangdong and doesn't speak much English. And then I went to government schools like everybody else. So no choice, basically."

"You're a real *heunggong jai*, then?"

"Yup. Hong Kong boy, born and bred." Killian ran his hand over his close-cropped russet hair. "Except for the hair. And the rest."

Another ten meters but now at least they could see the tunnel entrance.

"What about you, Blue? Why did you join the Force?"

"How did a nice girl like me end up in the police?" She grinned, transforming her usual severe expression. "That's easy. Civil service jobs are an iron rice bowl. Everyone knows that. Plus good benefits. And I was told the hours were regular."

Killian snorted.

"I was misinformed."

"A little."

"What about you, boss?"

"The usual reasons. I was young and idealistic. I wanted to contribute to Hong Kong, not just be some investment banker leech. The Force was the best in Asia. A fantastic community policing program. A crime rate lower than Japan's. One of the lowest in the world." He sighed. That was only a few years ago, but it felt like a century. "Anyway, my father had been a cop, one of the last British recruits pre-handover to China in '97. So I knew the Force. It was a logical choice."

Blue studied him curiously. "And now that you're old . . . er, older?"

Killian glanced at her, smiling. "You mean, do I regret it now that my career is in the tank?"

She blushed, and he immediately regretted speaking to her that way. It was nothing to do with her. "No, sir. I didn't mean that. I . . ."

"Relax, Blue. I just wanted to get it out in the open. And for the record, no. I don't regret anything except what happened to that boy." *Mealy-mouthed vagueness*, he thought. "I mean, the boy I shot. Shek."

She nodded, face carefully neutral. Instead of bringing the issue into the open, he'd probably made it even more taboo.

Killian turned back to the road.

They had finally reached the tunnel entrance. There had been a small demo here last night, a flying squad of protesters attempting to block the flow of traffic at rush hour to cause maximum disruption. Fully geared up riot police had marched down the emergency lanes while their colleagues had chased protesters through the lines of waiting cars. A few gasoline bombs had been thrown at the officers in the emergency lanes and the piles of hastily swept up shards of glass glittered in the gutters while the concrete walls were smeared with swaths of black carbon.

No arrests were made according to the morning briefing circulated among officers of superintendent rank and above. The protesters had sprinted ahead of the encumbered officers and jumped on the backs of waiting motorcycles, then sped away through the tunnel, weaving between the halted cars. Killian had felt a wash of relief. Every time he read the briefings, he scanned the lists of those arrested for Jun's name. But she hadn't been caught yet, though it was just a matter of time if she kept going to protests, as she seemed determined to do.

Killian had called her repeatedly. And texted. Then she had blocked his number. And Mother wouldn't get involved. As ever.

He sighed and saw that they had finally edged through the tunnel mouth, leaving the chaotic snarl of the entrance ramp behind, the road opening ahead. Killian hit the accelerator, and the cruiser leapt forward.

FOUR

KILLIAN

A body from the northwest would usually have gone to the Kwai Chung mortuary, which was closest to the landfill. But this was a murder, so the remains had been sent to the main Victoria mortuary on Hong Kong Island. And it had priority over everything else.

"This is your first?" he asked as they walked through the front doors of the squat, two-story building. It was ugly even for a government building, with electric wires and pipes crisscrossing the peeling façade, air conditioners poking out of the first-floor windows like a row of broken teeth. Ugly as death.

"Autopsy? Yes, sir."

"You don't have to stay for the whole thing. To maintain the chain of evidence, we need two of us to confirm the remains are those we saw in the landfill. You're free to go after that."

Blue shook her head, her chin thrust forward.

"I'll stay, sir."

"Fine. But stand well back from the table, okay?"

"Why should I . . . Oh, I see." She smiled weakly. "You're worried I'll . . ."

"Faint and contaminate the evidence? Yes."

An attendant led them to a small side room where they put on gowns, gloves, masks, and plastic face shields. The room stank. Not of death, but of formaldehyde so strong it made his eyes sting.

Blue turned even paler behind the clear plastic shield.

"There's no need to come in now. Take a break and join us in ten minutes."

"I'm ready, sir."

He shrugged, then nodded to the attendant.

There were six stainless steel dissection tables in the autopsy room, each equipped with a hose and sink at one end and a hanging scale. At the rear of the room stood another table, the jointed arm of the X-ray machine poised over it like a vulture waiting for its next meal. Behind the X-ray, a line of stainless steel refrigerated cabinets ran the length of the wall.

The pungent stink of disinfectant was overwhelming here too, catching at the back of the throat.

A suited and masked tech was hosing down one of the tables. Pink liquid spouted out of a steel pipe that ran down the side and into a floor drain.

Only one of the tables was in use, a short figure in a lab gown bent over the remains, his masked face only inches from the body. An assistant stood behind him.

The Victoria mortuary was the preserve of Hanson Poon, the territory's chief pathologist. Single, mid-fifties, garrulous, Poon was known for insisting that homicide detectives remain for the whole procedure. And for his bow ties. Today it was royal blue with yellow polka dots, poking jauntily out of the top of his gown.

"The victim was a Chinese male in his mid-sixties," Poon spoke without looking up. "And he wouldn't have lasted much longer if he hadn't been murdered."

He straightened up, holding the glistening russet mass of the liver in two hands, then made a clucking sound of disapproval before dropping it onto the scale with a plop.

"Advanced cirrhosis. He must have been a very heavy drinker. Smoker too, from the state of his lungs."

He heard an intake of breath and turned to look at Blue. Her face was white, beads of sweat on her forehead.

"You've done your duty, Chief Inspector. You can go now."

She didn't argue. Poon didn't notice Blue's departure. Or pretended not to.

"Fascinating."

"What is, Doctor?"

"Now, now. Don't be so impatient. I'll brief you once I'm finished. Scissors."

Most of the organs were already weighed and packed, ready for refrigeration. Flaps of skin hung down the sides of the torso. The assistant handed Poon the scissors. He reached into the cavity and snipped at something twice, grunting with satisfaction, then handed them back and began pulling out a loop of intestine, grey-brown and covered in leprous patches of bright yellow fat.

"You are, of course, eager to know the precise time of death. And, as always, I must repeat that forensic pathology is as much an art as a science. But I can tell you that this gentleman ate a meal of rice and black pepper chicken no more than an hour before his demise. He died on a full stomach, which is something I suppose. Scalpel."

He made a few cuts, held up a kidney—rosy, fresh—then flipped it into the scale pan.

"But that only establishes how long the interval was between the man's last meal and his demise. Not how long ago that demise was. Left kidney, 93.2 grams."

Poon reached in again. "What about rigor mortis, you ask? Fair enough. Well, in this case we have no evident rigor."

He looked up, grinning expectantly. Killian raised his eyebrows.

"No limbs, no rigor, eh Superintendent?"

Killian nodded, too tired to humor the man.

Poon smirked and turned back to the table. "From other indications we can make a broad estimate, however, that death occurred somewhere between thirty-six and forty-eight hours ago." Poon turned again, lifted his scalpel, streaked with blood, and pointed it at Killian. "But remember, young man. Even that broad window is subject to variables such as humidity and temperature. And individual variation."

"Okay, Doctor. What can you tell me for sure?"

Poon regarded him with amusement. "Patience, Superintendent. We're coming to the interesting part." He tapped the tip of the scalpel on the bloody mess that had once been the man's groin. "He was castrated, obviously. We have identified what appears to be small pieces of oxidized iron in the two main wounds. From that and further microscopic analysis of the cuts, which showed tissue was torn instead of sliced, we can say with confidence that the castration was performed with a blunt-edged instrument. Some sort of tool, perhaps."

He waved to the two lab assistants, twirling his scalpel as though it was a conductor's baton. The two men came forward and gently turned the torso over. "Because we found matching deposits in the anal region, we can say with a high level of confidence that the same tool was used there, repeated stabs."

He looked up, smiling. "The evidence is beautifully clear."

"Was the victim alive when this . . . when he was being cut?"

"Possibly. Although he would have been in the process of exsanguination from the blood loss caused by the castration. In shock too, obviously. But as we are missing the complete cadaver, we have no way of judging what other wounds might have been inflicted. If the victim had sustained a substantial head injury, for example, he would have been unconscious."

"So he sawed off the poor bastard's parts while he was alive, then turned him over and stuck the rusty knife up his backside?"

"As you say. Quite an intriguing puzzle for you, eh, Superintendent?"

Killian nodded and turned to leave. Poon's jaunty air amid carnage had always rubbed him the wrong way. But this time it seemed worse than ever, disrespectful to the suffering this man had gone through.

Blue had gotten rid of the robe and mask and was sitting on a bench in the corridor, bent over, hands on her thighs. She looked up as the doors swung shut behind him. Her eyes were rimmed with red and her face sagged with fatigue. He went into the changing room, stripped off the protective gear, then reemerged.

"Is that it, sir?"

"Finishing up. He'll send the full report later tonight. It's the most vicious thing I've ever seen."

He told her what Poon had said about the wounds. She nodded, then frowned.

"I'm sorry I couldn't stay."

"I'd be worried if you hadn't reacted that way."

"Still, I should have . . ."

"No, you shouldn't. What you should do is go home."

"What about the landfill? The constables are still searching."

"I called them off. We can start again in the afternoon."

She nodded, then yawned, covering her mouth with her hand. "Sorry, sir."

"We both need to go home and sleep, Blue. We're no use to the investigation like this." He wagged a finger at her. "And for God's sake, don't call me 'sir.'"

"Yes, sir." She smiled, then yawned again.

"Funny."

"I mean, boss."

"Go home, Blue."

She nodded a third time and stood to go.

FIVE

Killian paused to catch his breath halfway up the hill, wishing he'd taken the escalator. He'd forgotten about it, even though it had been installed many years before. It wasn't in his mental map of Sheung Wan, which had been laid down when he was a schoolboy, walking back and forth to school each day. Up and down. Down and up.

Sheung Wan. Once a working-class neighborhood, clinging to the side of the mountain that reared up over the harbor, hundreds of four- and five-story walk-up apartment buildings, narrow alleys full of shops selling bolts of cloth, barrels of rice, Chinese medicine, the bitter reek of the medicinal teas catching at your throat as you passed.

But the district abutted Central and its office buildings, as well as the bars and restaurants of Lan Kwai Fong so beloved of the expats. Inevitably, foreigners had colonized the area. Invaded, really. An initial trickle had turned into a flood: Twenty- and thirty-something bankers and traders who brought their preferences along with them. Shops that had once sold dried sea slugs, sea horses, shark fin, and bird's nest had been replaced by bistros, fromageries, and boutiques selling silky frocks.

He stopped where an alley crossed the steep stairs. On his left was a familiar wet market. He recalled shopping there with Mother. It was small, just a series of stalls: pork butcher, two vegetable sellers, a florist offering rows of purple orchids in pots, a fresh fruit vendor. Biggest of all was the fishmonger, wares displayed on ice: red snapper, horse mackerel, porgy, whitebait, squid.

He caught the eye of the young woman in yellow Wellington boots standing in front of two large tanks in which whiskery grass carp swam back and forth, her arms crossed over her rubber apron. She looked vaguely familiar. Could she be the daughter of the original owner, someone from whom his mother had bought fish?

The woman glared at him, turned her head, and spat deliberately, muttering something. He had forgotten he was in uniform. It would have been one of the usuals: *Hak ging. Dong gau.* Gangster police. Communist Party dog. Maybe even *Lapsap gingchat.*

He sighed and turned to continue his trudge uphill. Past the Man Mo Temple, incense smoke drifting out its gates. Mother used to bring him there every day during exam time to light incense. And when his results came, she would say: "You see. It worked. The gods were listening."

Onto Ladder Street, the steepest part of the climb. There was a new coffee place on the corner. New to him anyway. La Tazza D'Oro. The caffeine would give him a boost on the last and steepest part of the climb.

The barista was a skinny White girl behind a hulking Gaggia coffee machine. Jet-black hair. Tattoos. Bandana. Addict chic.

"Espresso, please."

She nodded, smiling. "*Un café. Subito, comandante.*"

Comandante?

Paola from Catania. She had the characters for Hong Kong tattooed on the inside of her forearm. Nice running script. He complimented her and she told him the name of the tattoo shop. Around the corner.

"You should get one."

"Thanks, but it's not really an option." He gestured to indicate his uniform and she shrugged and threw out her hands: What are you going to do? Very Italian.

He walked up past the two huge banyan trees clinging to the top of a wide brick wall, their thick roots entwined like lovers' entangled legs. When he finally turned into the narrow alley and stood at the door to Happy Fortune Mansion, he paused. The doors of the apartment building were behind a steel gate, a huge, upside-down red-and-gold good luck character pasted on top of the bars.

He keyed in the passcode and started up the narrow, achingly familiar stairway.

When Mother married her new husband, Sammy, six years after Da's death, she had moved into Sammy's townhouse on the south side, taking Jun with her. Killian had already joined the Force by then and was living in junior officers' quarters. Sammy was rich and wanted her to sell the family place in Sheung Wan. But she had insisted on keeping it, even though it was a pokey, two-bedroom walk-up. And on the unlucky fourth floor as well.

Now she was back in Sheung Wan. They weren't divorced. That wasn't done. And Sammy still kept her in clothes and jewels and lunches at the Mandarin Oriental. But for practical purposes, they were separated. He must have had a *jinaai*, a number two wife. Killian had once asked what was going on between them and had been told sharply it was none of his business.

At the entrance to 4E, there's another steel gate in front of a door fitted with three locks: You'd think this city was crime-infested instead of one of the safest in the world. Or used to be. He reached for his keys, then remembered he no longer had any and pressed the bell. A long silence, then the clunk, clunk of the bolts being drawn.

"Ma."

"It's you. At last. I thought you'd been delayed again."

She swung the door open and turned to walk back to the kitchen.

"The food's been ready for an hour already."

"The food is always ready hours beforehand," he said, putting a smile in his words. "You're just too well organized."

A sniff. But he could see from the set of her shoulders as she picked up a dish of stewed mushrooms that she was mollified. A little.

Impeccably dressed as ever. No shoes in the house, of course. The Manolo Blahniks and the Jimmy Choos were lined up in her bedroom cupboard, color coded. But the rest of her outfit was pure *taitai*. Turquoise slacks. Raw silk, by the looks of them. Chunky gold necklace. The Piaget with the diamond bezel. None of your vulgar Rolexes.

The usual rings. And a hip-length printed silk shirt. Butterflies. Lots of white and black and yellow, so presumably Versace.

Ma. Or Mama. Not Mother. "Don't call me that," she'd snapped the first time he'd tried as a teenager, copying something he'd seen on Nickelodeon. "Your mother is dead. She gave her life so you could be born." That had shocked him into silence, as she meant it to.

So it was always Ma. Or Mama. But in his head, she was "Mother," filling up all the space there, no room for anyone else. Certainly not some English lady who he'd never even seen. Whose touch he'd never felt. Whose family hadn't wanted to know he existed.

Maybe he should get a tattoo as the Italian barista had suggested. *Mother* written over a heart with an arrow through it. He smiled.

"What?" She put the mushrooms on the table and glanced over, brows furrowed.

"Nothing. Just looking forward to dinner."

She frowned again.

"Did you have to come in that?" She gestured to his uniform.

"I'm not a detective anymore, Ma. You know that. I have to wear the uniform when I'm on duty."

"At least take off the jacket. I suppose I should be glad you aren't wearing a gun."

He sighed. "Not this again, Ma. Please. We don't carry guns everywhere. It's Hong Kong. Not a war zone."

Sniff.

"Hard to tell these days. And anyway," she said, straightening a pair of chopsticks, reversing one that had been laid down with its broad side facing up, "I don't know how you could think of carrying a gun again. After what happened to that poor boy."

"His name is Shek, Ma. And it was an accident. A tragic accident."

"It was inevitable, that's what it was, the way your precious police have been waving their guns around, beating children half to death."

She adjusted the table mats, squaring them to the edge of the table.

"And then they humiliate you by putting you out in that abandoned station. You're obviously not wanted. You should resign and do something sensible."

"It's just temporary, Ma. Until the shooting inquiry is done. Then I'll be back full time."

She didn't reply.

"And I'm not alone," Killian said, filling the silence. "I got a dog."

Mother shook her head.

"A dog. For heaven's sake, how pathetic. You should have had children when you had the chance. But your career had to come first, didn't it?"

"Can we not do this now, please?"

"You should at least ask for help from that man Tsang. He was your father's deputy. And his closest friend. That counts for something, doesn't it?"

Eddie Tsang, deputy commissioner for operations. Number two in the Force and probably the next commissioner of police.

"I've told you, I can't do that."

These were well-worn grooves. In fact, he didn't really need to be there: she could hold the whole conversation without him.

"I never liked him anyway. A politician."

The ultimate put-down.

He turned and sat down on the couch, wondering if there was anything to drink in the house. Probably not. Unless he'd left it on his last visit.

Mother was still talking.

"I don't want you and Jun bickering tonight." She had changed the subject with a veteran interrogator's dizzying deftness. "You're ten years older. Please make sure you act like it."

Jun. His little sister. Half-sister, technically.

"I'll try."

"She worships you, you know. She always has."

"Even if that was true once, Ma, Jun has made it clear she doesn't have a high opinion of me anymore."

Mother waved a dismissive hand in the air.

"She's just going through a phase. It's normal for her age. Ignore it. You're more like a father to her than an older brother. It's normal for her to resent you for . . ."

She was interrupted by the doorbell. The same wheezing, muffled clang. How long had it been like that? Twenty years?

"That will be her."

Jun's only reaction when she saw him was a small frown. She must have known he'd be there. No hug. Certainly no kiss. She'd consider that far too Western. All moot anyway since she had stopped talking to him or answering his messages.

Jun favored their mother, even though she was Eurasian. People mistook her for pure Chinese, which was something in this race-conscious city.

Killian felt just as much a Hong Konger as Jun was—even if he had green eyes and skin like a dead fish, as a ten-year-old Jun had once said. Mother had raised him with no thought to the fact he was Caucasian, ignoring the stares and comments when they were together. By the time he'd been old enough to notice, the neighborhood knew exactly who they were, and nobody batted an eyelash.

Jun put her pack on the floor next to the door and hung up her coat. Under the green down jacket, she was dressed all in black: jeans, polo neck, even the Nike swoosh on her sneakers had been blacked out with a marker pen. Black was the protesters' color. Even wearing a black T-shirt could get you arrested if you were stopped after a demo.

"You look exhausted," Mother said. "You both do."

And Jun did, heavy circles under her eyes, skin blotchy. What did it take for a twenty-four-year-old to look like this? Her eyes were bloodshot. Faint red lines on her cheeks. From the gas mask? She reeked too.

"Is that petrol? Jesus, Jun, were you . . ."

But Jun had anticipated him, as she often did.

"Did you have to come in uniform? Some of our neighbors have kids in prison. You should show some consideration."

He started to reply, but she walked past him to her bedroom.

"I'm going to change."

Mother went into the kitchen and emerged with two more dishes. Gailan. And steamed chicken.

"Get the rice, would you please, Ah Gong."

She never used his English name. Family legend had it that when she and his father got married and she inherited care of him, she had insisted on having his birth certificate changed, inserting the Chinese name she had picked. He was British and didn't need another name, his father argued. To no avail.

Jun had followed her own path, of course. She'd changed her name by deed poll when she turned eighteen, adding Mother's family name, Tong, and wiping out everything non-Chinese: Siobhan Deidre Riordan. That had left the two of them with the same legal last name: Tong.

Mother had gifted Killian her name early on, filling out school forms and the like with it because it was so much easier than using his Anglo name. Then after Da died she'd had his name changed, making him: Tong, Killian Conor Bogong Riordan.

It was a mouthful. But Killian liked having two names, Chinese and English. It felt like a reflection of his bifurcated self. When he'd signed up for the Probationary Inspector Exam, the form had a space for English or

Chinese names. He'd filled in both. No one ever used his English name in the Force. It was easier for everyone, even if it did give him a false sense of acceptance.

"Don't mind her," Mother said, putting the dishes on the table. "She probably hasn't slept."

"You know she's risking arrest just by wearing that outfit? And God knows what she gets up to at the demos."

"I don't know what you're talking about."

He wasn't going to say anything about the petrol. Not yet. He needed to talk to Jun first.

"You said she hadn't slept. There was a demonstration last night that didn't finish until . . ."

"I meant she was probably out clubbing with Kelvin."

He opened his mouth to reply, but Mother pointed to the kitchen.

"He'll be here any minute now. The rice, please."

He went into the kitchen, lifted the aluminum bowl out of the rice cooker, and put it on a plate.

"What are you thinking? In a real bowl, please. And don't use the plastic scoop. There's a proper spoon in the drawer. You know where."

He turned and did as she said, the doorbell wheezing as he came back out. Mother had disappeared into her room. To freshen up.

Kelvin. Razor cut above the ears. A wave of waxed hair sticking up from the top of his head like a shark's fin. Half the men under thirty had that cut these days. Shiny silk suit, polished brogues, though with the absurdly long skinny toes that made him think of clown shoes.

"Jesus Christ, what are you people actually doing?"

Kelvin was out of breath and visibly shaken. Killian raised his eyebrows.

"You people?"

"The police. Out of control. Those apes from the riot squad. They made me kneel against the wall with my hands on my head like, like a criminal."

"For what?"

"For nothing. I was just walking on the pedestrian bridge over Queens Road. Bastards."

"What happened to you?"

"They were going to arrest me. I told them I was just leaving the office."

"Nothing else, Kelvin?"

"Of course not."

"You just meekly showed them your ID card? Nothing else?"

"I . . ."

"You didn't ask them if they knew who they were dealing with? How dare they ask you for your ID? That kind of thing."

Kelvin's face reddened. Killian shook his head.

"I ought to arrest you myself."

"What for? I didn't . . ."

"For being a bloody idiot, that's what for. I've warned you over and over not to mess with these boys. They're exhausted. Full of adrenaline. And rage. And they're younger than you are, for God's sake. You're the adult."

"I can't believe you're defending those riot squad pigs." Jun had come out of her room.

"I wasn't defending them. I was telling Romeo here that if he wants to stay out of jail, he should have some common sense."

"You're defending rapists. Murderers."

Killian frowned.

"No one has been murdered. And the allegations of sexual abuse are being investigated."

"Being covered up, you mean."

"Do you think I would still be in the Force if for one minute I thought . . ."

"Why did you even join in the first place?" Kelvin said, still upset about his encounter with the PTU. "Most people who join are sadists. Inadequate personalities who get a kick out of ordering people around. Everybody knows good people don't join the police."

"Hou zai m' dong caai."

Mother, standing next to the dining table, repeated it yet again.

Hou zai m'dong caai. Good children don't become police.

Killian ignored her.

"That's childish, Kelvin. Most people who join want to contribute something to Hong Kong."

"Bullshit."

"Enough!" Mother slapped the table with her palm. "No swearing at my table."

"Sorry, Mrs. Tong. It just came out." Kelvin hung his head like a schoolboy.

"And no more politics in my house."

Silence.

"Fascist." Jun muttered under her breath, audible only to Killian.

"Now," their mother took a breath, patted her hair, and pulled back a chair. "Let's sit down and eat like civilized people."

* * *

When Kelvin and Jun left, Killian followed them out into the corridor, pulling the apartment door closed behind him.

"Jun."

She kept walking. Kelvin turned his head and smirked, then stabbed at the elevator button.

"Jun, please."

He spoke loudly enough that this time she turned.

"Could you please tell me why you aren't answering my messages or calls?"

She shook her head with disbelief.

"You know why."

"Is this something to do with what happened in Wan Chai? The boy, Shek? That was an accident."

The elevator pinged, doors opening behind her.

She didn't reply.

"Jun," he said, stepping forward and reaching for her, then dropping his hand when she glared at it. "Seriously, you've got to stop going to the protests. If you get arrested, I might not be able to help you."

She replied without turning around.

"Thanks for the advice, Superintendent."

Jun walked into the elevator followed by Kelvin, still smirking.

SIX

JUN

The first time Jun saw her was at a play. An open-air mixed-media performance staged way out in the New Territories. The stage was the forecourt of an abandoned factory near the Fanling golf club.

It was called 海/生, the characters for "sea" and "life," separated by a backslash. There were no seats or stage, the audience standing in a semicircle around the actors. Half the performers were a kind of Greek chorus, separate from the main action, walking freely among the actors and the audience. They were all women, wearing papier-mâché fish heads, cotton tops, and sarongs covered in shiny printed scales.

The one-page program said the chorus represented the amphibian ancestors of the Hong Kong people. The story, if it could be called that, was supposed to be an origin myth with parallels in the present day.

At one point, when all the fish figures were dispersed among the audience, they began chanting:

The net is coming!
The net is coming!

Each figure turned slowly as they chanted, staring briefly at the audience members around them.

Tell us how to escape the net.

She was standing next to Jun, rivulets of sweat sliding down her neck from under the heavy mask.

Tell us how to escape!

She leaned down to Jun's height, her voice hoarse, muffled, eyes staring out of the holes, black and intense.

Tell us how!

Then she whirled and slid away, undulating through the crowd, her movement smooth and controlled, full of coiled power.

That was what caught Jun's eye at a demo two weeks later—her third since she decided to start attending the protests again—that way of holding herself, of moving, a slender figure at the front of the crowd, swaying from side to side, balletic. Her height too, of course. She was taller than most of the women and many of the men.

She was dressed all in black, of course, plus a yellow construction helmet, elbow and knee pads, chest protector, full-face gas mask, and gloves. That level of equipment marked her out as one of those who led the demos, the so-called frontliners, the ones the government labeled rioters, arsonists, thugs.

Could it be the same woman, Jun wondered, pushing through the crowd to get closer. She was giving orders, twenty or thirty protesters clustered around her, looking up. The voice sounded the same, raspy tones muffled by the gas mask. Then she glanced around and Jun caught a glimpse of those piercing eyes behind the plastic lenses of the mask: It was the same woman, for sure.

The crowd heaved and shifted and Jun lost sight of her. Then, a few hours later, she saw her again, loping through the protesters, umbrella in her left hand, a shield fashioned from a red-and-yellow bodysurfing board strapped to her right.

A single protester had tripped and fallen in the center of the road while retreating from a baton charge. Two cops had pounced on him, one pinning his head to the ground with a boot while the other struggled to pin his arms to put on plastic cuffs.

A blur of running figures from the protesters' side. Two of them crashed into the policemen, knocking them both to the tarmac, then spinning around and retreating. Two others grabbed their comrade's arms and began to drag him away, the PTU officers in pursuit. Then she appeared, darting in front of the retreating protesters and their fallen comrade. She danced from side to side, jabbing at the two cops with the umbrella, using the board to protect herself from their batons.

After a backward glance to confirm that the others were safe—the crowd applauding—she bowed briefly, then whirled around and loped away. The two police, weighed down by their gear and padding, round shields strapped to their backs, lumbered after her. But it was too late. The crowd closed around her and the two policemen turned back to a chorus of jeers and whistles.

An hour later, when the protest was dispersing, Jun saw her yellow helmet bobbing above the heads of the other protesters and pushed through the crowd to follow.

She must be part of the leadership, Jun thought. *She would be the one to talk to.*

The lanky figure ducked into an alley full of restaurants. By the time Jun turned the corner, her long strides had taken her a couple hundred meters ahead.

"Hello."

No reaction.

"Yellow helmet! I need to talk to you!"

She glanced back, but didn't slow.

"Hey! Dancing Fish. I want to talk."

The playbill had listed the chorus as "Dancing Fish," numbers one to twelve. No names.

This time, she stopped and waited for Jun to catch up, hands on hips.

"What do you want, rich girl?"

"I'm not rich. Why do you say that?"

"Clothes. Accent. Attitude."

"Well, I'm not. And I don't see what difference it would make anyway."

"This is a class war too. The fat cats are all cowering in their apartments on the Peak, afraid we'll turn on them."

"Will you?"

She snorted. "Of course not. Even though most of us are working class. Unlike you."

She turned to walk away. Jun grabbed her elbow.

"I want to do more. To help organize."

"You think it's so easy?"

"I don't know. That's why I'm asking."

"How do I know you're not a spy?"

"Because I'm not."

"So, you aren't a member of the police force?"

Jun shook her head emphatically. "Of course not."

"And you're not being paid by them to be here either? Or blackmailed?"

She thought of Killian, but shook her head again. "No and no."

"And what is it you think you'll be doing if you join?"

"Organizing. Planning. Raising money. Something more than just marching, over and over with no result."

She considered, then nodded. "Find me on Signal. Wellington2020. Say you're the rich girl."

Jun opened her mouth to protest, but Wellington2020 was already walking away.

SEVEN
KILLIAN

Killian spent the night at Mother's flat. He was too exhausted for the trek back to Tsim Bei Tsui and had a morning briefing at HQ, which was a mile away from Sheung Wan instead of twenty-five.

He couldn't remember the last time he'd slept in his old room. Fifteen years?

He dropped his bag on the floor, kicked off his boots, and lay down on the lower bunk.

He and Jun had shared the room once.

She spent much of her time at Kelvin's apartment these days, Mother had said. But it was still very much her room. Where once he had hung a poster of Coldplay—embarrassing to remember—there was now a huge black protest banner.

FREE HONG KONG. REVOLUTION OF OUR TIMES.

Red letters dripping blood.

A poster next to it bore the image of the eye patch girl, the medic who'd been hit with a rubber bullet and lost her sight in one eye.

AN EYE FOR AN EYE.

Killian grimaced. A constable had lost an eye in the early days, poked out by one of those innocent-looking umbrellas. Then, when the medic had been blinded in turn, the lower ranks made it their mantra for a while: An eye for an eye. And the protesters began saying the same thing. It was a microcosm of the whole mess, two sides locked in a dance of the damned, neither willing to change.

Jun.

She was practically a stranger now. How had that happened?

The age difference had made him more like an uncle when she was small. Maybe even a father figure, as Ma said. She was only three when their actual father had died. Killian had always assumed her conception was an accident. Unless their parents were trying to do that impossible thing, save a marriage by having another child.

When they'd started sharing the room, she was too small to climb the ladder on the bunk bed, so Jun had slept in the bottom bed. Later, she'd climb up and lie next to him, ask for a story. Or simply to cuddle.

The last book he could remember reading to her—with her by then—was *The Little Prince*. It was just before he'd gone to university, so she would have been eight. When they came to the part about the baobab trees and their roots that threatened to eat up the Little Prince's asteroid, she had nodded in understanding.

"Like that big tree I pass on the way to school. On Ladder Street next to the temple."

"The banyan?"

It was an ancient monster towering above the narrow alley, trunk perched atop the wall, roots as thick as boa constrictors slithering down over the bricks and into the pavement, hammering through the concrete into the earth below.

Jun had shivered.

"I don't like to pass it in the dark. It's scary. Like a monster trying to eat the wall. Is that what the Little Prince meant?"

"I think so. But there's no danger of banyans eating Hong Kong. The Public Works Department cuts them down if they get dangerous."

She had nodded, but he could see that she didn't understand.

"They're people in the government whose job is to protect people. Like our father."

"The man who was married to Mama before and died?"

"Yes."

"He cut down trees?"

"No, silly. He stopped dangerous men from hurting anyone."

"He was a policeman?"

"Yes."

"Did the bad men kill him?"

"No. He was helping people during a storm. He drowned."

Jun had frowned and nodded, then looked back at the book. It was ancient history to her.

A few days later, they reached the end. The Little Prince was bitten by the snake and died. Jun had clutched at Killian, sobbing, inconsolable. He could still feel the warm tears, the sharp, brittle bones of her shoulders, her heart beating rapidly against his chest like a small bird's.

How had he let her drift away? It seemed a blur, the years melding together. He'd been at university. Away on internships two summers. Then he'd joined the Force and moved into single officers' quarters, working, working, always working. And if not working, he'd be out drinking, blowing off the stress in the Wan Chai bars.

Then, suddenly, it was 2014 and Jun was seventeen and marching with all the other protesters. He remembered once, after things had gotten ugly, they'd met at the house, at a dinner just like this one. She'd glared at him, told him she was ashamed to be related to him. But she'd still talked to him. Until four weeks ago.

Killian sighed, his eyes drifting around the room. Some things hadn't changed, despite his long absence. The crucifix over the door, which he had hung when he was at his most fervent, before university. There were also a few knickknacks of his that Jun had left on the bookshelf. *Lord of the Rings* figurines Mother had bought for his twelfth birthday. Frodo. Gandalf. A rearing Balrog. And, of course, the framed photo of Da in his probationary inspector's uniform, stiff and proud, chin up, still self-conscious, Sam Browne belt across his chest, the revolver on his hip, khaki shorts, white knee socks, black lace-ups. Schoolboyish, really. So young.

And next to it, the leatherbound, blue-and-gold box. Inside, the silver medal and its red, white, and blue ribbon. The queen's face on one side: ELIZABETH II DEI GRATIA REGINA F.D. The obverse read: THE QUEEN'S GALLANTRY MEDAL. The citation was there too, folded neatly, paper brown and brittle.

Killian remembered wondering if his father had been drunk when he dove into the sea, then feeling ashamed. Sean Riordan was a hero. Would he have done the same thing? Probably not.

More ancient history. Pointless to think about it. He had more than enough problems in the present day to worry about.

He reached out to switch off the light, then rolled over.

EIGHT

Umbrellas?"

"Yes, sir. Three umbrellas. One from ParknShop and a large blue golf umbrella. Both appeared to be brand new. And both types have been widely employed by protesters."

Chan, the chief forensics officer, looked even paler and more exhausted, the circles under his eyes like bruises. He must have been up all night preparing his report.

"And the third?" Senior Superintendent Weng, the head of CID, kept his tone neutral. Killian's old boss was seated at the head of the conference table. Whip-thin from running four miles every lunchtime, even in August when humidity was in the eighties, the air like wet cotton wool. Weng had a beaky nose, the reason for his nickname, *futau*, The Axe. Also because officers who got in his way ended up on the chopping block.

Killian had found a curt email in his inbox that morning from one of Weng's deputies: We need Chief Inspector Choi to brief the meeting this morning. Make sure she's ready.

Weng had ignored Killian when he swept into the conference room. Not a good sign.

"The third was a black, folding-type umbrella, well used. Several of the ribs broken. This was discounted."

"But you are classifying the other two as, what?"

"Possibly political."

"Possibly political. Better you stick to telling us what you find, Chan. We'll decide what it means."

Next to Weng were two men in suits. They hadn't been introduced, but everyone knew they were mainlanders. Ministry of State Security liaisons.

Spies.

The rest of the table was made up of a couple of chief inspectors Killian didn't know. Weng's sidekicks, presumably. Blue was there at the end of the table, of course, Chan next to her.

"Yes, sir," said Chan, looking uncomfortable.

"Good. Anything else?"

"We also found a copy of the *People's Daily*." Chan glanced at the mainlanders. "The front page was . . . defaced."

"Defaced by what?"

"Dog feces, sir. It was smeared on a photograph of the president."

A long silence as the table considered this. Killian, leaning against the wall along with a couple of inspectors, raised his hand. Weng pretended not to see him.

"Excuse me," Killian said. Heads turned. "How was this material connected to our body?"

"The objects were found in the same vicinity as the body," Chan said. He consulted his notes. "The newspaper was found approximately half a meter away. The two umbrellas about a meter away."

"But didn't you say yesterday that the body could have moved a few meters after the scavenger found it and fell over?"

"Yes, sir," Chan said.

"It could be just a random series of objects. Paper someone used to clean up after their dog. Umbrellas thrown out by mistake? Or . . ."

Weng interrupted curtly.

"We have to err on the side of caution when it comes to possible political angles, Superintendent. You know that. Now," Weng turned back to the table. "Anything else, Mr. Chan?"

"We've covered the main findings. The fact that the cyanoacrylate fuming failed to show fingerprints on the body. Similar lack of results from the plastic rubbish bags used to wrap the body. All detailed in our report. Plus there's a list of other potentially relevant objects found in the area around the body. The attachment is at the end of the report."

A rustling in the room as everyone flipped to the back of the report.

Killian skimmed the first page:

Child's slipper, blue
Plastic water bottle marked Spritzer
Green plastic kitchen bucket
One golf ball, Spalding
One chopstick, wood
Lower half of a Bic brand ballpoint pen
Spring from the same pen
One bead necklace with cross
Torn black T-shirt labeled "Metallica"
One student's notebook, Chuntzse Primary School, Sha Tin
A bronze compass in a wood box, top broken off
A bodhisattva head, two inches high, cast iron
A brown-colored toy bear, no eyes

The list went on for pages.

Weng gave a low whistle. "You listed everything?"

He flipped forward, turning over a flurry of pages.

"Everything within a one-meter radius that could be relevant. We excluded large items such as air conditioners, bicycles, automobile tires," said Blue.

"So how many altogether?"

"Four hundred and fifty-two, sir."

Weng nodded.

"About what I thought."

He dropped the list and nodded to Blue.

"That's going to take some legwork, Chief Inspector. Can you update us on the other aspects of the investigation?"

"Yes, sir. You've already heard from forensics that they have come up dry on the crime scene. And Doctor Poon also pointed out that without the head, feet, or hands, the remains give us very little to work on as far as identification is concerned."

"Yes. I saw the report. Anything else?"

"We are also reviewing camera footage from the landfill."

"That will be hundreds of vehicles."

"They only keep a record for three days, so not that many, sir. But a further complication is that the remains could have been placed directly into an EPD dump truck."

"What is EPD?" Weng frowned.

"Sorry, sir. Environmental Protection Department. They operate the landfill and the garbage collection as well . . ."

"Right. Go on."

"Thank you, sir. I was saying the remains could have been placed directly into a garbage truck. Or a dumpster on a construction site. Or at a hotel. Or a restaurant. The landfill is the sole waste collection facility for the whole of the western New Territories and Kowloon. That's about three million people. There are over seventy EPD trucks there every day, so . . ."

Weng waved his hand for her to stop again. "I think we get the picture, Chief Inspector. What else?"

"We plan to continue the detailed search of the landfill area open to the public, sir."

"That's a lot of manpower, Chief Inspector. Explain why."

"Superintendent Tong and I believe the fact the murderer deposited the remains in a public location like the landfill means it has some special significance to him. He could have dumped them at sea with far less chance of being observed, for example. We feel the rest of the body could be at the site too."

Weng drummed his fingers on the table, considering.

"I see the logic. But this is a huge use of manpower when we're already shorthanded. Let's hope it's not a wild goose chase. Is that all?"

"We are hopeful our review of missing persons will turn up something. If that draws a blank, we'd like to broadcast a public appeal and a reconstruction of how the body was found on RTHK's Police Report."

"Not yet, Choi. And make sure you clear that with me before you go down that road."

"Yes, sir."

"We need to keep this out of the news as long as possible."

Killian stepped forward a pace. "Why is that, sir?"

Weng frowned, but Killian persisted.

"Appealing to the public for witnesses or jogging someone's memory about a relative or friend who disappeared could be critical. Especially when we have so little else."

"You may not have noticed, Tong, but things are a little sensitive right now. Having this kind of case splashed all over the papers would make things worse. Much worse. You remember Prince Edward. There were stories for months afterward that we killed protesters and took away their bodies."

Weng waved a hand in Killian's direction to dismiss him, then turned back to the table.

"To reiterate, I don't want even a hint of this case in the media. Is that understood?"

"Yes, sir," they chorused.

Weng stood, and the rest of the room followed suit.

"Good," he said. "Let's get to it then."

He caught Killian's eye and held up his forefinger to indicate he should stay.

When the door closed and they were alone, Weng waved Killian over. He picked up a stack of blue files, dropped them in his briefcase, then snapped it shut and placed it upright on the conference table. Only then did he look up at Killian, standing stiffly in front of him.

"As I said in the meeting, the situation is delicate, particularly in Tin Shui Wai."

Delicate. The way a powder keg was delicate. Three weeks earlier, three dozen men in white T-shirts had descended on the Tin Shui Wai MTR station late in the evening and attacked crowds returning from a demonstration in Central. They used iron bars to break bones and crack heads. One woman was still in a coma.

Despite thousands of 999 calls, officers had not appeared until forty-five minutes after the attacks started. Public anger had grown after video appeared online showing constables outside the station before the attacks started, smoking cigarettes and chatting with the attackers, who were widely believed to be members of the Triads, organized crime gangs.

Since then, angry crowds had gathered outside the police station at Tin Shui Wai almost every night. Gasoline bombs had been lobbed at its walls and the external sidewalk barricades so often that they bore heavy scorch marks.

"Yes, sir. Delicate."

Weng looked up sharply. But Killian's face was expressionless.

"That's what I said, Tong. And that means you're off the case as soon as we find someone else. In the meantime, advise Chief Inspector Choi. Tell her what to do if you must. But keep a low profile. I do not want the media getting wind that you are on active duty."

"Sir, I . . ."

Killian started to speak, but Weng held up his hand.

"You're still waiting for the decision by the shooting tribunal, correct?"

"Yes, sir," Killian replied, his tone clipped.

"And there's the CAPO thing too, correct?"

"The Complaints Against Police Office? I haven't been told anything about that."

"It's the boy you shot, Shek. The family has filed a complaint."

Killian shook his head. "With respect, sir. I wasn't aiming at him. My . . ."

Weng interrupted, holding up his hand again. "I have no interest in hearing your excuses. There's also the announcement coming on Saturday. I suppose you don't know about that either?"

"No, sir."

"That's what comes of being stuck out in the wilds of Mai Po."

"Tsim Bei Tsui, sir. What's the announcement?"

"It's political, and it's big. That's all I can say. So we have to ensure news of this case doesn't get out first. The last thing we need is headlines about a headless body found in a dump. Some idiot will claim it's a cover-up for a protester we killed, and then all hell will break loose. That's why it's doubly important you make sure there are no leaks."

"Yes, sir."

"Remember, this is about wrapping this thing up before the announcement Saturday. If there's no result by midnight Friday, put it on ice until the fallout is over. Understood?"

Weng was already reading an open file, his eyes down. Killian took a deep breath.

"Yes, sir. Is that all?"

Weng looked up again, eyes cold.

"Don't question me again in public, Tong. Ever."

"Yes, sir."

Whatever it takes, Killian told himself. Whatever it takes.

"Good. Now get your backside to Tin Shui Wai and start doing your job."

Killian snapped a salute, spun on his heel, and walked out.

NINE

The neat rows of wisteria shrubs that had bloomed in front of the entrance to the Tin Shui Wai station in more peaceful times were a mass of blackened branches and trampled earth. The sidewalk adjoining the flowerbeds was blocked off by a wall of three-meter-high blue and white blast barriers that encircled the front of the station. Made of thick, hard plastic and filled with water, most bore scorch marks from Molotov cocktails, as did the front wall of the station.

The protesters had started using makeshift slingshots for extra distance. But it was a tricky process: Two had already been taken to the hospital after their gasoline bombs detonated in their hands.

There had been a gate in the barrier wall in the early days of the protests. It was removed after protesters pried it open with crowbars. All entry was now through the heavily guarded rear of the station, one hundred meters down a side street.

Even though Killian was in uniform and driving a patrol car, the constables standing guard outside the station's high steel gates insisted on seeing his police ID card, then carefully scanned up and down the street before hitting the button that slid back the gates. Nervous.

There was a soccer pitch and a large concrete parade ground behind the station, along with a parking lot. Today, Killian saw that the PTU constables—the riot squad—were doing a training exercise in the parade ground. He stood for a moment, watching.

They were practicing snatch and grab, some of them in plain clothes acting as protesters, the others in riot gear. The idea was simple: Three or four plainclothes officers would infiltrate the protesters. After identifying a leader, they would swoop in, tackling and cuffing him or her, then drag them away before the crowd could react. The regular riot police would only intervene if the team got trapped.

Today, Killian saw it wasn't ordinary policemen putting in their mandatory three months every five years in the PTU. These were STS, the Special Tactical Squad. The unit was created during the Occupy Central demonstrations in 2014 when regular riot squads couldn't cope with the enormous numbers of protesters and their shifting tactics. Officers were picked for their size, speed, and above all, their ruthlessness. They dubbed themselves the "Raptors" and soon got a reputation for brutality. When the STS went in for an arrest, there would be blood and broken bones.

For this exercise they were fully geared up: helmets and face shields, chest, knee, and elbow pads. Gas masks, of course. And, as well as their Smith & Wesson service revolvers, they carried truncheons, jugs of pepper spray, and Tasers. Three had Remington shotguns loaded with beanbag rounds or rubber bullets. Another four had Federal Riot Guns strapped to their backs for launching tear gas canisters—or tear smoke, as the Force insisted on calling it.

A tall man stood on the edge of the parade ground, barking orders into a megaphone. He was in his forties, wearing a white T-shirt and blue shorts, his body thick with muscle. His head was shaved, and his bald pate gleamed in the morning sun.

Kwok Lai Meng, founder and patron saint of the STS. Everyone knew his face. He'd been photographed during a demonstration, bareheaded, mouth open in a shout, face twisted in rage, shotgun at his shoulder pointed directly at the photographer. The image went viral on the mainland, where he was lauded as a hero, someone finally standing up to Hong Kong's rioters.

Kwok looked around, seeming to sense Killian's gaze. Rivulets of sweat ran down the side of his face and into his T-shirt, molding it around his bulging deltoid muscles. His eyes were small in that big, glistening head, flat, black shards. Killian nodded. Kwok didn't acknowledge him, looking away and swinging the megaphone up to his mouth.

"Get it right this time, you lazy pricks or I'll come out there and put my boot up your arses."

This was the first time Killian had seen Kwok in person. But they'd bumped heads before.

Not a memory he wanted to dwell on.

He turned to go into the station.

***

"You're second-guessing me. Sir."

Alex Tse Wai Mun, senior superintendent and head of Tin Shui Wai district, sighed. His face was gray with exhaustion, the skin of his face waxy. He could have been on the autopsy table. A coffee mug that read Hong Kong Disneyland sat steaming on his desk. He reached for the mug and took a sip.

"It's not second-guessing. They're there to review the same material and see if they can find something you and your people missed. It's called a Red Team."

Killian shifted in his chair. "I know what a Red Team is, sir. I've just never heard about one being used on the Force before. And especially for a murder investigation."

Tse waved his hand dismissively. "Innovation, Tong. Keep up with the changing times and all that."

He swiveled his chair to the left, his eyes on his computer screen.

"Can I ask who ordered this? I was specifically told there was a very tight deadline on this case and having two parallel investigations will slow things down badly."

"It came from the top. That's all you need to know." Tse looked up from his computer, frowning. "We need to get this solved as soon as possible, Tong. And if you get taken off the case, there'll be someone there, fully briefed and ready to step right into your shoes."

He reached for the keyboard.

"Anyway, don't you have to appear at the CAPO inquiry?"

Killian nodded. "Yes, sir. Tomorrow."

He had received the email that morning. A case had been lodged against him, it said. The officer should present himself at the Complaints Against Police Office, Caine Building, Police Headquarters, at noon on May 19.

"Are you sure you have time to work on this case?" Tse asked, his tone skeptical.

"I'll be fine, sir. My point is, a second team means everything will take twice as long. And the longer we take, the more likely it is to leak. It's a miracle it isn't in *Apple Daily* already."

"I'll worry about *Apple bloody Daily*, Superintendent," Tse flapped his hand toward the door. "Now stop being such a prima donna. Go away and solve this thing."

"Yes, sir. May I ask who's going to lead the Red Team?"

Tse had turned back to his computer and was pecking at the keyboard. "Hmm?"

"Who is going to be the lead on the Red Team, sir?"

"Superintendent Kwok. You probably saw him on the way in."

"Kwok? But he has no experience in this kind of investigation. He's . . ."

Tse swiveled around, his face flushing. He spoke deliberately. "Listen to me, Superintendent Tong. Who is Assistant Commissioner Shum?"

"Head of NT north district, sir."

"Very good. And AC Shum says he wants this. And he says it's what the deputy commissioner wants. So for God's sake, just do what you're told."

"Yes, sir."

Tse shook his head wearily. "Christ, Tong. You used to be known for being reliable. What the hell happened to that person?"

Killian didn't answer, and Tse waved him away again, swinging back to his computer.

Killian could feel himself flushing with anger as he walked to the elevator.

Anger and shame.

Kwok.

Of course it was Kwok. Karma.

* * *

The operations room they had assigned to Killian and his team was in the basement. Barely big enough for the four desks and the three whiteboards. When he opened the door, Killian was enveloped by a cloud of cigarette smoke, mold, and body odor. Yeong was stubbing out a cigarette; Lin was lighting a fresh one. Both were seated in front of computer screens, Yeong with a game of solitaire running.

On the central whiteboard, the Lines of Enquiry section hadn't been added to since the previous day. And on the Assignments board, one of them had scrawled "dump" next to Blue's name. Both of their names were blank. Killian's shoulders tightened, and a flush of heat washed into his face.

"There's no smoking here," Killian said sharply.

Lin looked over at Yeong, who shrugged. Yeong lifted the cigarette to his mouth and took a drag, then ground it out in the overflowing ashtray on his desk.

Killian strode over to them. "On your feet. You too, Lin."

They stared at him, not moving.

"Now!" Killian barked. "Up!"

They both stood abruptly, Lin's chair rolling back and smacking into the wall.

"I've had a bad few days, gentlemen. Some might even say I've had a bad year. But if you think that means you can sit here, picking your noses and playing cards until this investigation fails, you are wrong."

Lin, the smarter of the two, kept his face rigid. Yeong was still gaping.

"There are plenty of people in the Force who owe me favors. If this investigation goes down in flames, I will make sure you go down with it. Dismissal from the Force. Prosecution for willful negligence. The works."

Both men stared at him.

"Is that clear?"

"Yes, sir," they shouted.

"Good."

Silence followed. Killian spoke again.

"One other thing. This case is juicy. Very juicy. Headless body found in a landfill. You can just see the headline, can't you?"

Neither man replied.

"Me neither, because no one will be printing them. You know why?"

A head shake from Yeong.

"There are only four of us with access to the files. If I read so much as a hint about a dismembered corpse in *Apple Daily* or the *Oriental Daily News* or in some random post, I'm going to blame you two. And that means prison time. Automatic. No appeal. Is that clear too?"

"Yes, boss," Lin said quickly.

"Yes, sir," Yeong added, all the fight gone.

"Good." Killian walked over to one of the empty desks, dropped his backpack on it, sat down, and swiveled to face them. "Now, let's get back to what we're here for—the investigation. Lin, you were reviewing the license plate lists from the landfill, correct?"

"Yes, Superintendent. We've reviewed the three days before the body was discovered, which is all they keep. The memory is written over after that."

"I know. What have you got so far?"

Lin hesitated. "Apart from the EPD, there are a lot of private vans and pick-ups. Contractors. Landscapers. Interior decorators. There were also a fair number of institutions. Schools. Hotels. That kind of thing. Fewer individuals. Nothing suspicious."

Killian nodded. "The TSG said the same thing."

Both men looked blank.

"The Technical Services Group. They do facial recognition, that kind of thing."

TSG was a shadowy tech-focused group set up inside the Force a few years before. Killian would never have heard about it except that one of his oldest friends in the Force had transferred there: Ngam Man Lik, or Zen, as he insisted on being called.

Zen was American-educated, unlike most people, who went to the United Kingdom if they ventured overseas. Computer engineering at Caltech, no less. While there he learned to code like a demon. And speak like a bro. He came home to Hong Kong, but instead of going to a start-up, he signed on with the Cybersecurity Division. They promised all the perks they could muster. And that he'd never have to wear a uniform.

Killian smiled at the thought. The recruiting officer hadn't mentioned that Cadet Officer Ngam Man Lik would have to do the nine-month police training course in Aberdeen, like everybody else. Not only was wearing a uniform mandatory, but so were 6 A.M. runs up Brick Hill, long hours on the firing range, and even longer hours in the classroom with classmates who'd barely managed to get a pass at Hong Kong Poly.

Zen had come to dinner at Mother's flat regularly during their time at the academy, and had even taught twelve-year-old Jun to play chess. Killian could see them, the two heads hunched over a foldout board, moving the plastic pieces. Very analog.

Soon afterward, Zen had disappeared to Cybersecurity, which was based in some hideaway in Mongkok, of all places. Later, Killian had heard he was posted to an even shadowier outfit under the wing of the Crime and Security Division, the Technical Services Group. It supposedly reported directly to the deputy commissioner for operations, none other than Eddie Tsang.

Zen was careful to the point of paranoia, so it was no surprise that when Killian called him out of the blue for help with the landfill videos, he had refused.

"Call the TSG duty desk number directly and get their help. And don't call me at work again," he'd said, then hung up.

Killian, used to his peculiarities, made the call. It went right through to an efficient-sounding woman who didn't identify herself. He sent the video files to a generic email late that afternoon. She left a voice message on his phone at 4:30 the next morning. Six words: "This is TSG. Nothing suspicious found."

Zen had popped up again a couple of hours after Killian got the voice message. It was an invitation to connect on Telegram, the most secure comms app there was. End-to-end encryption and a feature that deleted messages thirty seconds after they were opened. For an added layer of security, Zen instructed Killian never to send any messages directly on Telegram. Instead, he had to send a luxury designer's name first over the app ("no one will suspect anything if there's Versace in the message; this is Hong Kong"), then look in the draft messages box in a Gmail account Zen had set up.

Killian messaged Zen asking him to review the tapes himself. He came back a few hours later. Three of the names from incoming car license plates were flagged by the system as politically suspect, he said. That meant they were involved in the protests, but there was no evidence of any relevance to the case. Two brothers in their late twenties who owned a landscaping business. The third was a teenager who worked part-time at a youth hostel.

Killian turned to the whiteboard and gestured.

"TSG only gave me a verbal answer. No actual file. But mark it as investigated and dismissed anyway."

"We have to trust a bunch of nerds?" Yeong asked.

"No choice," Killian replied. "Now, what about Missing Persons?"

Yeong explained that three thousand people went missing each year in Hong Kong. Most of them—95 to 98 percent—turned up within a week. Wives and girlfriends running from abuse. Teenagers running away from home, usually getting ensnared by the Triads—the girls as prostitutes, the boys as low-level enforcers, runners, drug couriers.

There were a few older people too. Often dementia cases who wandered off. Also the odd husband ditching a family, though Hong Kong was so small it was hard to disappear and start over. But out of the few dozen disappearances that remained open, no one matched the profile they were looking for—a mid-fifties to mid-sixties male.

"Not a single one?" Killian asked.

"Not still missing," Yeong replied. "There were plenty in the right age category. But they all turned up. Dead in the harbor. Or in Vancouver with the wife's money and a new family. That kind of thing."

"How far back did you go?"

"Five years."

"Okay. Sounds like another dead end. Follow the drill, please. Written report, then put it on the board."

"Yes, boss," Yeong replied.

"I'm going to join the Chief Inspector at the landfill," Killian said.

* * *

The door to the parking lot whipped open as Killian walked toward it, banging into the wall, sunlight flooding into the hallway. A burly figure in shorts, silhouetted. The door swung shut. Kwok.

Killian moved to step around him. Kwok put out an arm.

"You're Tong."

"Let me pass, please," Killian said.

"I'm Superintendent Kwok."

"I know who you are," Killian said.

"And I know who you are."

They regarded each other in silence.

Killian felt the acrid taste of shame in his throat, the urge to smash a fist into Kwok's smirking mouth. But he had to try and work with the man.

"I know we had a disagreement . . ." Killian began, but Kwok started speaking at the same time, raising his voice and talking over him.

"I'm running the Red Team for the dump murder. You need to brief me on where the investigation is. I'll need full details of each line of . . ."

Killian put up a hand and interrupted him. "Lin and Yeong are in the ops room. B7. They'll brief you."

"I prefer to get my briefing from you," Kwok insisted.

"I'm on my way to the crime scene," Killian said.

"Then I'll come with you."

"No. I can't have you backseat driving on this. You're supposed to be reviewing our findings, not reinvestigating every lead."

"That's not what I was told."

"That's what SS Tse told me, and that's the way it's going to be. Now let me pass."

Instead, Kwok stepped in closer, his face inches away. His breath stank: rotting pickles.

"You *gweilo* leftovers all have a monkey on your back, don't you? Trying to prove you're better than the rest of us."

"Move aside," Killian said through gritted teeth.

"Oh, I get it. You're having a little seller's remorse about those girls, are you? I can see why. It was stupid to think I'd do anything for a washed-up has-been like you."

Killian shook his head. "Don't take out your problems on me, Kwok. It's your own fault you've been stuck at superintendent for eight years."

Kwok flushed and stepped closer.

"Nostalgic for the old days, are you? When even the stupidest White man could get promoted?"

"Let me pass."

Instead, Kwok took another step forward and shoved Killian so that he banged into the wall behind him, nearly falling.

"We're going down to the briefing room now, *gweilo*. And you'll . . ."

Killian leaned forward and jabbed his right fist into the other man's solar plexus. Kwok doubled over, clutching his stomach, and Killian stamped on Kwok's right foot, trapping it, then grabbed his ear with his right hand, twisting it viciously.

Kwok howled and bent over even further, desperate to loosen Killian's grip, arms flailing.

Killian pulled hard on the ear, then leaned down, his mouth inches from Kwok's right ear.

"Let me pass, prick, or I'll rip it off."

Behind him, the door banged open and light poured in. Killian let go. Kwok, face purple, one hand pressing on his ear, straightened and took a step toward him.

"What is going on here? Are you two fighting?"

A senior superintendent Killian didn't recognize was staring at them incredulously.

The two men glared at each other, then Kwok spoke up.

"It was just horseplay, sir. The superintendent and I were practicing a new arrest routine. It's a move the STS uses when arresting protesters."

The senior superintendent frowned, obviously unconvinced. "I'll let it go this time. But you should be ashamed of yourselves. Brawling like schoolboys. What kind of an example is that to the lower ranks?"

"Yes, sir," they chorused in unison.

Kwok stepped back inside to let the senior officer pass and Killian brushed past him, following the senior officer out into the sunlight.

TEN

It was almost midnight by the time his headlights lit up the barred steel gates of the little station at Tsim Bei Tsui and Killian was struggling to keep his eyes open. Choi—Blue—and he had spent what was left of the day with three teams of constables, scouring the thick woods surrounding the landfill.

They hadn't expected any more discoveries at the landfill, and all they got for their pains were blisters and a sweet, sickly garbage stink that penetrated clothes and clung to the skin even after repeated showers. But the work had to be done. More process.

Once night had fallen at the landfill, Killian went back to the Tin Shui Wai station. The parade ground was empty: No sign of Kwok and his Raptors.

The operations room was also empty, only the lingering smell of cigarette smoke hanging in the air. The whiteboards were mostly blank too. No faces or names. No picture of the mangled torso, of course. Just a box marked with the date and time of its discovery, no arrows to connect it to anything. Yet.

The Lines of Enquiry column at least had a few entries: landfill search, review of gate video, missing persons, staff interviews, scavenger interviews.

But they were probably dead ends too. It reeked of failure, and Killian was happy to pull the door shut behind him and leave for Tsim Bei Tsui.

He parked the Land Cruiser in the shallow bay in front of the blue station gates. The road continued eastward, dead-ending in the marshes at a little-used Marine Police pier. There was almost no traffic except for the odd wrong turn. And the occasional family of boars. A mother with three little piglets the last time. Small red eyes glaring at him through the headlights as she escorted her brood across and into the trees on the far side of the road.

The smell of roasting meat sometimes drifted up to the station from the encampments below. It was, of course, illegal to catch the boars but no one was going to enforce that rule all the way out here. Certainly not him.

The floodlights kicked on as Killian trudged up the incline, dazzling him, and he fumbled the keys, dropping them and cursing. A low whine came from the other side of the door.

Gau stood a little way back from the door, giving Killian room to come in, tail swishing back and forth. Killian ruffled his ears as he passed, dropped his backpack, and went through to the kitchen. Half a bowl of dried food and a can of the good stuff—Trippett New Zealand Lamb Tripe.

He put the bowl down on the floor, and Gau ambled over, looked up at him.

"Go ahead. Please."

Gau put his nose down and began to chew, almost silently. Polite. Definitely no Labrador blood in him.

Killian carried the brown San Miguel bottle out into the observation room. Strictly against regulations to have alcohol in the station, much less drink it. Circumstances were exceptional.

The skies were clear that night. Rank upon rank of Shenzhen office towers glittered across the bay, fully lit up in their evening glory. In the space of a few decades, the obscure Chinese county town had transformed itself into to Hong Kong's upstart younger sibling.

Now it was *daaigo*, the elder brother. The boss, though most Hong Kongers hadn't clocked that yet. Shenzhen had surpassed Hong Kong's economic output for the first time the previous year, an event that was little reported in Hong Kong. Maybe the protests, the clashes, and the speeches were too distracting. But people should have paid attention. It was the end of an era. The beginning of the end of Hong Kong, some people said.

He took another grateful swallow, savoring the familiar sweet, hoppy taste.

San Miguel. Once practically the official beverage of the Force. No one drank it anymore. It was all Carlsberg. Or Tiger. Or, more likely, Tsingtao from the mainland.

Da, of course, had been one of the faithful. A San Miguel lifer. Had probably sat in this exact room. Scanning for heads in the water. And, yes, probably drinking a bottle of San Mig.

The observation room probably hadn't changed since then. One hundred and eighty degrees of glass. The radar screen glowing in the left corner. The Zeiss 20 × 120 binoculars on the right atop the old-school mahogany and brass tripod. Next to them an old night vision monocular, a Starlight Scope, fading silver letters proclaiming its manufacture by the Optic Electronic Corp. of Dallas.

It had been a long, long time since anyone had bothered to try and slip across the border. No midnight swims across the bay, the children pulled along atop inflated inner tubes. How Mother had come in 1976.

What would his father have thought about this blazing metropolis? What would he think about his son being posted out there? Not posted. Exiled. Not much, probably. Not much at all.

Glum thoughts. Pointless. Killian put down the beer bottle on the windowsill.

But Da would have understood about the CAPO inquiry, the danger of being ground down and spat out by the bureaucracy. Or, more likely, that of being served up by the top brass as a scapegoat, a public example of the Force's ability to police itself.

Whatever the case, Killian would continue to fight. Because, even now, when everything around him was crumbling—Hong Kong, the Force, this investigation, even Jun—he still knew one thing with utter certainty: He wanted his old life back, longed for it with a fierce urgency that sometimes shocked him.

Eyes on the prize. That had always been his mantra. It had worked until that terrible day in Wan Chai when he shot the boy. And it would work again.

He took a sip of beer, made a face. Warm. He put the bottle down on the sill. Movement behind him caught his attention.

Gau trotted out from behind the reception counter, heavy shoulders inherited from some big-boned ancestor. A big dog. Frightening even, or would have been except for the eyes. Wary but not threatening, lively. And the one flopped-over ear, the long blue and pink tongue lolling out. The blue tongue would be his Chow Chow genes. A fellow mongrel. Killian's genes might be pure *gweilo,* but in every other respect—culturally, linguistically, maybe even morally—he'd always been mixed-blood, as the Chinese said. An outsider to all.

"Finally finished, are you?"

Gau gazed up, head cocked to the side, then made a low noise in his throat. Questioning.

"I know. A walk, right?" Killian said.

The steady gaze didn't change. But Gau's tail swung back and forth. Once.

"Okay then. Let's go."

In a single smooth motion, Gau flipped around, landed neatly, and trotted away toward the front door.

* * *

There was a path down to the water he had taken a few times with Gau. But even though the campers kept their tents and belongings inside the cover of the trees, there were always a few wandering around near the path, clearly living rough. Standing police orders said he needed to stop them. Check ID. Take them to the station for booking, if needed.

So now Killian and Gau stuck to the roads. Avoided the pointless paperwork.

They turned right at the Tongmeng Garage, onto Laufashan Village Road. Two dogs were guarding a heavy steel gate. A nasty shit-brown creature on a chain who yowled as they passed and an older, jet-black fellow with a grey muzzle. He trotted out, inspected them with a rheumy eye, then went back inside, duty done.

If they had turned left instead and gone up Daisu Lou—Big Tree Road, a testament to the stunted flora on the peninsula—they would have passed by the Kelly Animal Shelter where he and Gau had met only five months ago. He'd been still at the late puppy stage, scrawny, big feet. Now he'd filled out. Not surprising, given the amount he ate, even if he did have good manners.

"Don't take him unless you have the space," said Doris, the girl in her twenties who had introduced them. "Or the time."

"Don't worry," Killian said, extending his hand. Gau—still laboring then under his shelter name of Adolph—inspected his hand but didn't move. "I'll be out here for a while. I'm just down the road. At the police station."

Doris had visibly recoiled at the mention of police, which Killian ignored. He extended his hand again. This time, Gau leaned forward and gave it a sniff. He looked up, eye contact, seemed to nod his head. And that was that.

Laufashan was a dead end. Empty buildings. Dead village. The end of the road.

They turned back and made their way back up Deep Bay until they got to the lookout point with its little pagoda-topped gazebo and deserted car park, the glow of the station lights beckoning just over the hillcrest.

Then Gau barked once and broke to the left, ducking under the railings and disappearing into the scrub.

"Gau! Gau!"

Killian cursed and trotted over to the railings. He pulled out his flashlight and swept it back and forth. Nothing. The slope plunged toward the marshland below, the steep hillside choked with low shrubs, foxtailed rushes bobbing above them, and clumps of sugarcane run wild. Beyond that, low trees clustered together, acacia and casuarina, growing denser as they descended, a thick band of mangrove at the water's edge.

The fecal reek of the marsh below drifted up, with it a hint of woodsmoke.

"Gau!" he called again.

A far-off bark. Killian cursed again, vaulted the rail, and swished through the scrub grass. After a few minutes, he saw a glow of lights through the trees ahead. How had they managed to get electricity down here?

Killian pressed forward, pushing past the spindly trees, the lights growing brighter until he came to a clearing where a string of bulbs had been hung from tree branches. A red, white, and blue shipping container sat in the middle of the clearing, doors wide open, a sofa and a pile of bedding visible inside. American President Lines. It looked weirdly out of place, as though it had been dropped from the sky.

Behind the container, the ground had been cleared and tilled for a large market garden. A fire burned in front of the container, surrounded by a ring of stones. Close-up, he identified the sweet smell under the wood smoke: manure. The patch was fertilized the old-fashioned way.

A row of fish hung by their tails on lines strung between two trees, butterflied, heads wrapped in salt-filled wax paper. Old school salting. A tarpaulin was tied to the corners of the container and propped up by two branches. A couple of red plastic chairs, pied white with age, sat in front of the fire. More were stacked drunkenly on the right side of the container.

Gau appeared from the trees on the other side of the clearing, trotted over to Killian, and sat down at his side, watching.

"Idiot. Where the hell have you been?" Killian muttered.

Gau kept his eyes fixed on the far side of the clearing and made a low sound in his throat.

Killian switched the flashlight back on, playing it over the trees. "This is the police. Show yourself, please."

Nothing.

"Come out and show yourself. I'm a police officer," he called again. That wouldn't reassure anyone these days.

Killian took another step forward.

No sounds in the clearing. Just distant lapping water and bullfrogs croaking.

Movement. A shadow on his left.

"Help you?"

Killian swung the flashlight around. A man stood next to the container, five yards away. Mid-thirties. Sinewy. About five foot five. His bare torso was the color of mahogany, hair buzz-cut down to bristles. He had high cheekbones and a sharp nose. Features more like a northerner than a Cantonese.

Killian was still pointing the flashlight at the man's face. He put an arm up to cover his eyes, waved the other as if shooing away a fly.

"Do you mind?" he said, then squatted down and called to Gau. "Here, boy."

Gau loped over and submitted to having his head stroked. A first.

"ID card?" Killian asked, holding out his hand.

"Too friendly to be a police dog. What's his name?" the man asked, ignoring Killian's request.

"Okay if I ask the questions?" Killian said.

"Right. Sorry. Not a lot of visitors. Especially not foreigners. I thought the White policemen all left in '97 when China took over." The man walked over to one of the plastic chairs, picked up a gray T-shirt, and pulled it on, the ropey muscles of his back moving under the taut skin.

"Can I see your ID, please, Mr. . . . ?"

"I'm called Wong," he said, frowning. "Don't have an ID."

"Everyone has one. It's the law."

"Not me."

"You must have had one once." Killian waved his arm at the clearing. "Before you moved out here."

Wong squatted and put a blackened kettle on the fire, a smile on his face as though he was humoring a pesky child.

Killian frowned. Could he be autistic?

"Listen, Mr. Wong, I need to see your ID card. If you can't produce it, the law says I . . ."

Wong shook his head doubtfully. "I have something from years ago."

"An ID?"

Wong nodded.

"Let me see."

He nodded again and disappeared into the shipping container. Killian stretched, his ribs feeling loosely knitted together, as though they might pull apart again.

Gau's bobbing tail was visible as he trotted around the site exploring the smells. At least someone was having fun.

Wong reappeared, holding a folded brown envelope. "It's inside," he said, handing it to Killian.

Killian tipped the envelope, and a piece of plastic fell into his palm. It was an ID but an ancient one. No embedded chip. The plastic cover was half peeled off. The black-and-white photo was smeared and blurry, but the sharp features were recognizably the same person—twelve or thirteen years old, impossibly young, his face full of hope. The whole section where the name should have been was stained dark brown, nothing visible except the date of birth: 23.11.1985.

"Is that what you wanted?"

"It'll do for tonight," Killian replied, putting the ID back in the envelope and handing it to him. "But you have to go in and get it renewed. Tomorrow."

Wong nodded obligingly and pointed to one of the cracked plastic chairs, smiling again. "Do you want a coffee? You can sit on one of those if you like."

A chair. Everyone in Hong Kong knew that foreigners couldn't squat.

"No need. Thanks." Killian frowned. He should do his job, pull Wong in, and get him fingerprinted. Wong could be anyone—illegal immigrant, a criminal on the run.

"Sure?" Wong gazed at him, patiently waiting for an answer, a mug in one hand, a sugar jar in the other, his head cocked to one side. Like Gau.

"Just go in tomorrow and see about the ID, okay?" Killian said.

Wong nodded.

"Good. Have a nice night then, Mr. Wong."

"Goodnight, Mr. Policeman," Wong replied.

ELEVEN

Yeong and Lin were both at their desks when Killian walked into the operations room the next morning. The smell of old cigarette smoke still hung in the air, but underneath there was a vague scent of something else—floral. Blue had placed an electric air freshener next to her empty desk and from time to time it gave a little sigh, exhaling a cloud of lavender.

Killian had dropped off immediately when he and Gau got back to the station. And though he'd only had a few hours of sleep, he felt refreshed, energized. He'd woken once in the night, but he'd been so exhausted that he fell back to sleep almost immediately. After that, nothing but a deep pool of sweet, rejuvenating blackness.

The sharp features of the fisherman, Wong, popped into Killian's head. That sweet, dopey smile on his face. Killian wondered again whether he should have brought Wong in, then dismissed the thought. He had enough distractions already—CAPO and the formal inquiry into the shooting, not to mention Kwok and his bloody-minded determination to use the Red Team role for his political advantage. It would be a miracle if Killian could find a few hours for actual police work. For the investigation that was supposed to be his ticket back to normal life.

"Morning, boss," Lin said, giving his best attempt at an ingratiating smile. "Chief Inspector Choi is up at the landfill. We're taking it in shifts."

Yeong stood up as well. "I'm going up there in a few minutes."

"Good," Killian said. "Put me on the roster. I have to go to Central this morning but should be back after lunch."

"Got it," Yeong replied.

Killian had decided with Blue the previous day that they'd have to limit the search to the top layer of earth. There was no point in going deeper. They'd need a backhoe to break up the next layer of compacted garbage the EPD officer had told them. And that would destroy the evidence they were looking for.

"If my calculations are right," Blue had said, "it will take a team of ten constables about twenty minutes to sort through every fifteen yards of earth the bulldozer plows up."

Killian had winced. The pit they were searching was the size of three football fields, the layer of earth somewhere between five- and ten-feet thick. It would take . . .

"About five days, unless we get more uniforms," Blue had said. She was showing a slightly irritating ability to guess what Killian was thinking.

Lin said something, and Killian turned. "Sorry. What?"

"I said we found some of those sieves . . . nets? I don't know what you call them. They use them in construction. Crossed wires on a wooden frame. You prop it up and throw the dirt against it. Anything we're interested in won't go through."

"Good. That might speed things up. Anything else new?" Killian asked.

Lin shook his head. "Nothing. Yeong and I have been rereading the interviews with the onsite EPD guys. And the scavengers. But there's nothing there."

Killian's phone buzzed. "There is one other thing, sir," Lin added.

Killian looked up from his phone. "What's that?"

"When we returned the video files to the EPD, they said they'd forgotten to mention that the guardhouse kept a logbook. License plate numbers."

"They forgot?"

Lin nodded glumly.

"What the hell? We asked them specifically about car plates."

"Yes, sir. Not the brightest bunch. It's better than nothing, but the numbers are recorded by hand, obviously. Never changed their procedures even after the camera was installed. We have three constables transcribing them into a digital list, and we're feeding the numbers to the Transport Department as they come in. It's a mess, but we should have the full list within a couple of days."

"So long," Killian muttered.

"Yes, sir."

"All right. Keep on them."

"Yes, sir."

"In the meantime, write it up on the board."

Lin nodded, and Yeong raised his hand like a schoolboy.

"What is it, Yeong?" Killian asked.

"We really have no other leads at all?" Yeong frowned. "Then, if the landfill is a washout, the only thing we have left is to appeal to the public."

"There's a ban on that for the moment," Killian said.

"From HQ? SS Weng?"

Killian nodded. "Is that all?"

"One other thing, sir," Lin said. "Superintendent Kwok was here yesterday while you were at the landfill."

"He's the head of the Red Team, as I'm sure he told you," Killian replied.

"Yes, boss. I gave him a full briefing."

"Good. We don't want to give him an excuse to say we're not cooperating."

"No, sir. But he still wasn't happy. Kept saying we were hiding things from him."

"What things?"

"It was vague at first. Just suspicion. But he latched onto the landfill videos. Refused to believe that we hadn't seen anything worth following up. I told him we'd even sent them to the face recognition people. PSG or whatever it's called."

"TSG. Technical Services Group."

"Right. Anyway, he wanted to see their report. I told him you didn't have it."

"That's fine. Let him waste his day trying to get it out of them. At least he won't be in here bothering us." Killian's phone buzzed. Blue.

"What have you got?" he asked, answering the call.

There was the sound of male voices in the background. "We've found another body part, sir. An arm," Blue reported.

"Where?" Killian asked.

"A truck driver at the landfill saw it. It looks as though an animal dug it up."

"The same body?"

"Almost certainly. Wrapped in the same black plastic. There are some other items too. Found in the same area as the arm. They look random to me, but forensics will see if they can find a link."

"Good news. Or at least I hope it is."

"Yes, sir. But I can tell you now the arm won't be much help in IDing the body."

"Why is that?"

"I'll send you a picture."

The phone pinged as Blue ended the call. Killian opened the attachment.

The image showed the hand, palm up. Three fingers and the thumb were curled up, the forefinger sticking out. The first joint of all four fingers and the thumb had been neatly clipped off.

* * *

A gate barred entry to the courtyard of Caine House at Police HQ. "Police Old Comrades Association," read the top sign. Underneath, a smaller, faded sign stated, "This Way to Report to the Complaints Against Police Office." Killian shook his head. A sense of irony was not the Force's strong point.

The reception desk at B Block was staffed by a constable who took his name and asked him to wait. Two superintendents strolled past, heading toward the elevators. One did a double take when he saw Killian, nudged his colleague, and they both snickered. Killian turned his back.

"Please go up to the sixth floor, sir. Room 610. Someone will come and get you when the inquiry is ready."

Room 610 was a small space equipped with a worn lime-green IKEA sofa and a couple of battered armchairs. A set of fluorescent lights overhead bathed everything in a white glare. Killian leaned back and closed his eyes.

Should he be nervous? He hadn't bothered to contact the Superintendents' Association about having a representative sit in with him. CAPO was mainly used to handle small complaints at the lower ranks—attempts to extract a bribe, unnecessary use of force. That had been until the protests started in 2014. After that, the panel was deluged with complaints about police conduct during demonstrations. But those had dwindled to almost nothing in recent years. A total lack of success by any of the thousands of complaints was one reason. Another was that the police often lodged countercharges against complainants.

The waiting area was part of the main inquiry room that had been partitioned off with plasterboard. Killian had registered the low murmur of voices from the main room when he'd entered. The voices grew louder. He strained to listen. A single man was speaking, reciting something, the individual words indistinguishable.

A shriek interrupted the droning voice. Silence, then the second voice, shouting.

"An accident! How dare you? Was it an accident they ground his face into the concrete so hard they shattered seven teeth and his jaw? Was it an accident that he lost sight in his left eye? A sixteen-year-old boy on an innocent date with his girlfriend. Was it an accident they . . ."

Another voice interrupted, soothing, low.

"Calm down! Calm down!" a man interrupted. "Was it an accident when they pissed on him? Was. That. A. Damn. Accident?"

The sound of a fist striking a table punctuated each word. Bang! Bang! Bang!

Killian shuddered. The endless protests were turning them into brawling cavemen. Each cycle of violence would spiral, getting worse and worse until someone died. And then all hell really would break loose, especially if it was police officer. A police riot to end all riots. No mercy.

The shouting abruptly halted, then Killian heard shuffling footsteps in the corridor.

He forced himself to think about the upcoming hearing. What would he say if questioned? He had already told the story as best he could recall three times for the shooting inquiry, material this board would have.

Parts of that night were crystal clear. Other parts hazy and dreamlike. The doctors had warned him the memories might never come back. Concussions were tricky, and different people—different heads—reacted in wildly different ways.

The moment he shot the boy—that was etched in his mind forever. He could see the pole the boy was swinging traveling through the air in slow motion, the gun pointed up to the sky, then someone knocked into his side, pulling his arm down, the gun going off, enormously loud, the shock as the bullet hit the protester and he was knocked backward onto the ground.

Then he heard the swelling rage in the roar of the crowd, baying like dogs at the kill and swiveled to face them, raised the pistol.

After that, it was a blur. The doctors said he'd been hit in the ribs, probably with one of the railings they ripped up from the pedestrian fencing that lined Nathan Road. That put him on the ground. Then came a blow to the head, and lights out. He'd been rescued by the PTU almost immediately after that, apparently, the gun still clutched in his hand.

For a while, he had been in the same hospital as Shek, Queen Mary. On the morning of the day he was discharged, Killian put on the street clothes Mother had brought and walked down to the nurses' station.

"The boy who was shot, is he here in the hospital?" he'd asked.

The nurse looked at him a little oddly but said, yes, he was one floor down in the nonresponsive ICU. The coma unit.

It was a single room like Killian's. The same spectacular view of the southern harbor entrance, Stonecutters Island, Lantau just visible to the left.

An older constable in a seat by the door, reading the paper, a thermos on the floor. Killian showed his ID. The man didn't recognize him. Or pretended not to.

"How is he?"

"The same."

The door was open, three nurses inside, clustered around the bed. Shek was naked. They were washing him, one doing long strokes with a wet glove down his limbs, the other dabbing at his face, wiping the mucus away from his closed eyes. They stopped, then rearranged themselves on either end with quick, practiced movements. A quick "one, two, three" and they turned him so they could do his back, which was striped with long red creases.

When they turned him, his scrotum got caught between his legs, bulging out obscenely under his buttocks. One of the nurses noticed. She reached down and lifted the top leg casually, like a piece of meat, used her other hand to flip the scrotum through, then let the leg drop.

I did this to him, Killian thought. *I pulled the trigger.*

Months later, when he was already well into his exile in Tsim Bei Tsui, Killian took the MTR from Tin Shui Wai to Sha Tin, another of the satellite towns scattered across the New Territories, but on the east side, the opposite coast. It looked almost exactly like Tin Shui Wai, as did all the new towns. Clusters of ten to twenty tower blocks sprouting out of the countryside, the government-mandated low-cost housing estates distinguishable by how closely the buildings were packed together, the tiny windows, the drab cookie-cutter exteriors.

It took him fifteen minutes to walk from the MTR station to the estate, then another ten to find the right building: Block 24. Killian got out on the thirty-third floor and found 3307. The usual steel gate, the red-and-gold character, *fuk* for wealth, inverted.

Behind the door was the smell of incense and the low sound of a woman's voice chanting. He listened for a while. A Buddhist sutra from the cadence. Someone knew it well. No stumbling or hesitation. The sutra was supposed to help the soul of the deceased find its way to Nirvana. He began to catch repeated words: Amitofo. Sakyamuni.

A door opened down the corridor and a head poked out, stared at him. A middle-aged man.

"What do you want?'

"Police. Go back inside please."

"How do I know you aren't a fake? Show me your police ID."

Killian already had it out, waved it in the air. The man moved to come closer. But Killian held up a hand to stop him.

"I said this is police business. Go inside immediately."

"Police business. At that house? You've got to be joking."

He shook his head, then closed the door.

Killian took a breath, another, then pushed the doorbell. The "William Tell Overture" blared out so loudly he nearly jumped back. The chanting stopped. An indistinct shout, a young voice. The door banged open and a boy of sixteen or so peered out.

"Yes?"

"Is this the Shek family house?"

"Yes. Who are you?"

"Are your parents home?"

"Only my mother." He examined Killian, frowning. "Who are you? You look . . ."

Realization dawned.

"You're him, aren't you? The pig who shot my brother."

Killian held up his hands to try in a gesture of placation. "I wanted to talk to your parents, if that's okay. I'd like to . . ."

"It's not okay," he hissed. "It's not okay at all. Just fuck off and leave us alone. You've already . . ."

"Who is it, Ah Pek?"

"It's nothing, Ma," the boy said, not turning his head, continuing to glare at Killian. "Only a salesman."

There was the sound of movement behind him and a moment later a woman appeared. She had an orange shawl of some kind draped over her shoulders. She must have been forty or more, but her face was unlined and her eyes—dark, liquid—shone.

"You don't look like a salesman to me," she said with a gentle smile.

"I'm a policeman, Auntie."

Her expression didn't change.

"And what can we do for you?"

He licked his lips.

"You see, Mrs. Shek, I'm the policeman who . . ." He faltered and her expression changed as she understood what he was saying. But instead of hate, he saw pity in her eyes.

"You are the one who shot my boy?"

"Yes, Auntie. I'm sorry to disturb your prayers. I wanted to say how sorry I was. It was a terrible, terrible accident and I . . ."

He hesitated. She didn't say anything.

"Tell him to go away and leave us alone, Ma."

"Hush, Pek. This man is trying to atone for what he did. He has been granted the courage to come here and seek forgiveness." She addressed

Killian. "But I cannot give you that forgiveness, young man. There is only one person who can."

Killian thought of Jun. Would she forgive him? Could she?

"You mean your son, Auntie?"

"No. I mean you. You must show compassion for yourself as well as others." She waited for a reply, but Killian had nothing to say. "Thank you for coming," she said finally. "It is time to go back to my sutra. I need to finish this cycle."

The sound of heavy footsteps in the corridor outside the CAPO waiting room brought Killian back to the present. The door opened, and the constable looked in.

"The panel won't be needing your testimony after all, Superintendent. The senior superintendent says your written testimony will be enough."

Killian opened his mouth to say something, but the constable had already ducked out and pulled the door shut.

What a farce, Killian thought. He could only hope it didn't turn into tragedy.

TWELVE

It was raining when Killian came out of the high steel gates of Police Headquarters and stepped onto Hennessy Road, heading for the MTR, which cut the time for the return journey to Tin Shui Wai to forty-five minutes. Not the lashing, roaring storms of the past few days, but a constant, melancholy drizzle. What Mother would call long-life rain, *coeng meng jyu*. The office towers in Central had disappeared under a blanket of mist. Even the brutal Bank of China tower was invisible except for its first ten stories, the clouds drifting lower as he watched, as though the sky itself was sinking, the city about to be crushed between heaven and earth.

A tram rumbled past, the clanging of its bell muffled. In a city where everything changed by the minute, the trams were one of the few constants. The fares had barely edged up since Killian was a boy, and it was still possible to travel the breadth of the island for pocket change.

He walked as fast as he could manage in the crowd, past the old police headquarters on Gloucester Road, a four-story colonial building with high ceilings for the fans and wide, airy verandas. It was now awaiting redevelopment, which meant someone would fill it full of swanky stores—or just knock it down and put up an office building.

Killian had visited Da there once, when it was Police HQ. His father had pointed out the huge crest hanging in the lobby: Royal Hong Kong

Police. A crown on top. In the middle, a painting that looked as though it had been done by a child. Sailing ships. A wharf. Two Chinese men with their hair in long ponytails, wearing gowns. They were talking to another man in a top hat, European. White bales lined up on the dock.

"Opium," his father had said, pointing to the bales. "One of your English traders selling opium to the Chinese." Da always talked about "you English," as though Killian was the one who had been born in Liverpool, not him. In his head he was pure Irish. "Tells you a lot about what foundations the Force is built on."

Killian cut through a back alley and emerged onto Queen's Road East, six lanes of traffic. Mercedes and BMWs. The odd Bentley. Past Pacific Place: Ferragamo-Hermès-Gucci-Prada-Coach. Huge ads. The usual pouty models.

When Killian reached the entrance of the Admiralty MTR station he stopped and stood there for a moment, the throngs of post-lunch workers flowing around him like a river around a rock. He should go straight back to Tin Shui Wai and the case. But he needed some peace, maybe even a sympathetic ear. It felt like a long time since he'd had that.

He raised his hand for a taxi.

"Saint Joseph's," he told the driver.

A questioning grunt from the man.

"The big, blue *gweilo* temple. Cotton Tree Drive. Central."

The driver nodded and put his foot on the accelerator.

* * *

Killian stepped into a pew at the rear of the church and knelt. The space calmed him, as it always did. Or used to. Sacred and ordinary. The muted orange and blue from the stained glass windows, the faint scent of incense. Sounds were muted too. The faint shrieks of children from the school next door. The hum of traffic outside, a low grumble as a double-decker charged down.

Was this why people took up the priesthood, became nuns? To always have this space away from the gnawing chatter in their heads? Away from the sounds people made living. And dying.

This had once been the center of Killian's life. He had been there every day after school. Sometimes twice a day. Then he had gone to the United Kingdom to study. And when he came back, it had seemed small. Irrelevant. A little ridiculous.

Now he was back. After how many years? Was that pathetic, or what? Running back to . . .

A movement in his peripheral vision, a familiar black shape moving behind him toward the confessional booths, flash of steel-grey hair, ramrod posture. Declan O'Halloran. Father Dec. He would listen.

Killian stood impulsively. Why not? The psychiatrist who had done his mandatory sessions for the shooting investigation had seen from his file that he was Catholic and had said, "By all means, go see your priest if that helps." The patronizing air—witch doctors are fine if you believe in them—had irritated Killian, and he hadn't replied. But the principle couldn't be denied. A sympathetic ear.

Killian smiled to himself as he walked over toward the confessional booths.

Inside, pulling the curtain after him, Killian knelt. The familiar smell of incense, dust, sweat.

The wooden slat slid open with a clack, a shadowy figure visible through the wickerwork lattice.

"Bless me, Father, for I have sinned," Killian said.

A murmur.

"It's been . . ." he started, then fell silent.

A chuckle.

"I know it's been a very long time since your last confession, lad. No need to fret over that."

Still, Killian didn't say anything. Another chuckle followed.

"Come now, Killian. It can't be that bad. I've heard worse. And so has God. Much worse," the priest said reassuringly. "If it's about the shooting . . ."

"No, Father Dec. It's not. That was an accident. My conscience is clear."

"I never thought otherwise, of course."

It was glib, but Killian believed him.

"This is something that happened when I was on riot duty. Last month."

"Alright. Go on."

"It's a fairly long story, Father."

"That's what we're here for, my boy. To listen."

A creaking sound as Father Dec made himself comfortable on the bench on the other side of the wooden barrier. Killian cleared his throat.

"It was early morning. The demo was dying down. Most of the protesters were going home. I was trying to remember where I'd parked my patrol car when I saw a small group of demonstrators huddling around a streetlight, a ring of STS encircling them. STS are special riot police, Father. They call themselves Raptors and they're very . . ."

"I'm aware of the Raptors, Killian. Go on."

"Okay. So, these Raptors, a dozen maybe, were clustered around three young girls. A small crowd had gathered to watch, mostly ordinary civilians. Then the girls started to sing. The tune was "London Bridge is Falling Down":

All you cops are stupid pigs,
Stupid pigs, stupid pigs,
All you cops are stupid pigs,
Party arse-lickers

"Provocative."

"Idiotic. The Raptors were about to charge, and there would have been blood and broken bones, teenage girls or not. I ordered them to stand down.

For a moment I thought they might refuse, especially when someone at the back shouted something about ignoring the *gweilo*." Killian stopped. "Sorry, Father, I . . ."

"It's alright, Killian," Father Dec said. "I've heard the word before once or twice. Continue with your story."

"Right. I talked to the sergeant, and he eventually ordered his men to back off. But he radioed for a van and made me promise I would take the protesters to be booked myself. The girls huddled together in the corner of the van, one of them sobbing quietly, dabbing at her nose to try and stem the flow of blood.

"I asked them why they came out on these demos, knowing that they could be arrested and convicted, ruin their lives. They looked at me as though I was speaking a foreign language. Finally, one spoke up, a bookish-looking little thing who still had the red marks of the gas mask across her cheeks. 'We have no choice,' she said. 'Of course you do,' I said. 'There's always a choice. Just stay away.' She shook her head, frowning. 'No. We must protest. It is our duty.'

"The other girls nodded in unison. Solemn as owls. It was bizarre. I remember wondering where this crazy idealism came from. My generation would have said their only duty was to themselves and their families. It was then I realized how much Hong Kong had changed. It wasn't the money-grubbing, materialist refugee city that was our default image of ourselves. Somehow, we'd become a people who were ready to fight for their freedoms. Ready to sacrifice. And until that moment in the back of the van, I had failed to notice any of this. It was as though I'd been sleep-walking for years and . . ."

Killian trailed off.

"No need to be embarrassed, my boy," the priest said. "It's the power of the confessional at work."

Killian cleared his throat. "Right, Father. Anyway, I asked to see their ID cards. They were classmates. All born in 2003. According to regulations, I should have scanned the IDs and booked them into the system. Instead, I handed the cards back and ordered the constable to pull over. I asked them to promise they wouldn't come out again, but they refused. Then I let them go."

Killian halted again. After a moment, Father Dec spoke.

"I don't see the sin in that, Killian. You broke your promise, and your standing orders I suppose. But surely you took the honorable path in letting them go."

"There's more, Father."

"Ah. I see."

"The next day I got a call at my desk. It was from a Superintendent Kwok, head of the STS. He's quite . . ."

"Yes, I know who he is."

"Of course. He asked if I took the girls to Wan Chai station for detention. I said I hadn't. They were underage and obviously not a threat to public order. Kwok said he didn't believe me, that I never had any intention of having them detained. That kind of thing. We argued for a while, and then he threatened to have me up on disciplinary charges. I told him to go ahead."

Another pause.

"And then?"

Killian sighed. "And then he changed his tone. He said he could help me. That he had two million followers on Weibo. Mostly on the mainland. He offered to mention my case. The shooting. Say all I did was my patriotic duty. That the boy brought it on himself."

"And what did he want in return?"

"He wanted the girls' names. He said one of them was carrying a laser pointer. Two others had gloves and a mask that stank of petrol. Evidence of bombmaking activities. I didn't reply, so he changed tactics. He said everyone in HQ knew my case had been decided and I would get a long jail sentence for the shooting. I was going to be made an example of to appease public opinion. All that BS."

"And you believed him."

"I did. He was in a position to know. And there have been other signs that something is going on behind the scenes. Anyway, Kwok said HQ would never dare scapegoat me if this went viral in China. If I was seen as a patriotic cop standing up to the cockroaches. Standing up for law and order."

"Like him."

"Yes. Like Kwok, God forbid."

"So you said no?"

Killian sighed again. "No, Father. I gave him the names."

The priest didn't respond.

"Mak Pak-lam. Candy Chiu Yim-fong. Edwina Lau Oi-lin." Killian recited the names mechanically.

"I see." Father Dec's voice was neutral. "What happened to them?"

"They were arrested at home the next day. Not Raptors. Just a couple of inspectors knocking on their doors at eleven o'clock. They're out on bail. But they'll get some kind of sentence. A few years. And it means no university. And most employers won't touch them."

"Did Kwok keep his promise?"

"No, Father. Of course he didn't. I was a fool to think he would. A desperate fool."

Now it was Father Dec's turn to sigh. "Coming here shows you are attempting to atone for what you did, Killian. It's not my part to say if those girls should have been arrested for breaking the law. I suppose technically you may not have committed a sin. Render unto Caesar and all that. But I can see you believe you betrayed your best self. I am going to ask you to say five Hail Marys every night for the next week as contrition."

"That's all?"

"Yes, Killian. That's all. You must settle with your own conscience on this. And then you must put it out of your mind. That's the beauty of the confessional. The miracle of it really. It allows us to confront our failings and expiate them. Move on, if you prefer more current phrasing."

Killian could hear him shift on the bench and the scrape of the curtain being drawn back.

"There are others outside waiting, Killian. Go on upstairs and I'll meet you there when I'm finished."

Then came the familiar words:

"Et ego te absolvo a peccatis tuis, in nomine Patris, et Filii, et Spiritus Sancti."

"Amen," said Killian, repeating it as much in hope as out of faith. "Amen."

* * *

Killian climbed up the stairs at the back to the second floor. The wooden plaque on the door hadn't changed: St. Joe's Youth Group. He thought they would have changed it to something more modern. From inside came the sound of a guitar, a breathy voice singing softly, barely audible.

Someone was coming up behind him. He turned, and a head bobbed into view on the stairwell, steel curls like a helmet. Father Dec saw Killian and grinned.

"There he is. Big as life," Father Dec said.

"You can't say, 'speak of the devil' about a priest, I suppose," Killian replied with a smile.

"We're all sinners, dear boy. Saints and sinners."

"Sounds like you're stealing from Springsteen again."

"It was the only way I could be sure you lot were listening to my sermons," the priest said, embracing Killian warmly. "Welcome back, Killian," he murmured. "Welcome home."

"Thank you, Father Dec," Killian replied.

A couple appeared behind the priest. The man was in his mid-fifties, trim, wearing a beautiful dove-grey suit and a dark-blue bow tie. The woman was the same age, petite, in a yellow cheongsam, with delicate, almost doll-like features, and only a tiny amount of mascara highlighting her large, limpid eyes.

Father Dec turned to Killian. "This is one of the most loyal members of our congregation. He started coming here about the same time I arrived in Hong Kong, didn't you, Raymond?"

The man examined Killian. His assessing eyes were cold, but then he smiled and his face transformed, charisma billowing.

"Yes indeed, Father. When I was twenty-five. Thirty years ago," the man said. He stepped forward, almost too close, and extended his hand. "I'm Raymond Suen."

He bent his head slightly, keeping his eyes locked with Killian's.

"I know who you are, Professor. I think the whole of Hong Kong does after you helped negotiate the end of the siege at St. Andrew's Poly," Killian said.

Raymond smiled, clearly used to hearing this. "I was just the go-between."

"Killian has also been coming here for years. Since he was a wee lad."

"I was baptized here. You should know, you did the baptizing."

"Guilty as charged. You didn't like the cold water either, and made us all aware. A voice you use on the parade ground now, I'll wager," Father Dec said with a chuckle, turning to Suen. "Killian is one of the youngest superintendents in the Force."

"I believe I know who you are too, Superintendent. I'm sorry for the . . . troubles you've had," Suen said.

"It comes with the territory. There are good days. And some very bad days," Killian replied.

"Indeed. And we've had far too many bad days in the last year. Let's hope we get the chance to make a fresh start," Suen said.

Father Dec smiled and nodded toward Suen. "I know one person who could make a fresh start. If the electors use their brains in choosing the next chief executive."

"Now, Father. Please. Let's not get ahead of ourselves," Suen said, glancing at his watch. "We must be going."

He leaned closer to shake Killian's hand, putting his left hand on Killian's shoulder. "It was a pleasure, Superintendent. We must meet again. I'd like to hear your perspective on the protests."

Killian knew that would never happen.

"The pleasure was all mine." When the couple had gone, Killian turned to the priest. "You really think he's going to be appointed CE?"

"Who knows what Beijing will do? But I'm told he's being considered very seriously. And if they have any desire to try and end this mad cycle of violence, he's their man."

"He's on the side of the angels?"

"There's no one else," Father Dec said with quiet conviction. "This city has been burning for years now. He's the only one who could forge some sort of compromise. Let us all go back to our old lives."

There would be no going back to the old days, Killian thought, but he didn't say so.

"You're not just saying that because he's a Catholic?"

"It would be a good thing to have a man of faith in that position, wouldn't it?"

"Good for the Church or good for Hong Kong?"

"Same old Killian, eh? Always the skeptic. Why not for both?"

Father Dec clapped Killian on the back and pulled open the door to the annex, waving him through. Inside, a boy playing the guitar on the couch jumped up, startled. Killian had forgotten he was in uniform.

"It's alright, Thomas. He's not here to arrest you," Father Dec said with a laugh.

The boy blushed and hung his head. He looked about twelve or thirteen, with long blond hair and fine features.

"Killian was one of us, you know. One of our stalwarts," Father Dec said.

"That I was," Killian said.

No response from the boy. Killian and the priest walked through to the small study at the back and sat down.

"It's been a while, lad. I thought you'd forgotten us," Father Dec said with a smile.

Killian smiled back. "I know, Father. I've been . . . busy."

"Of course you have." The priest reached across the desk to pat Killian's hand. "And we've spoken of that already. But under the seal of the confessional, so no one will ever know. Except God."

"And you."

"Yes. God's humble conduit here on earth," Father Dec said with a twinkle in his eye.

God's servant maybe, Killian thought. *But humble? Never.*

"Tell me, how is your mother? As pagan as ever?"

Killian laughed. "Resolutely."

"Well, the way she cooks, that's a form of worshiping God all on its own. How about Jun? We haven't seen her in a while either."

"She graduated last year. She's working for Greenpeace," Killian said.

"Always the firebrand, your sister. Is she involved in the protests at all?"

"Yes. But she doesn't talk about it. Not to me, anyway."

"I imagine not."

"In fact, she isn't talking to me at all right now."

"Not at all?"

Killian shook his head. "No, and I've no idea what she's getting up to at the demos. It's alarming, frankly. If she happens to come and see you could you . . ."

Father Dec was shaking his head.

"No chance of that I'm afraid. She hasn't been here for years."

"I thought so," Killian said, then smiled. "On the plus side, she has a rich boyfriend. Goldman Sachs. She doesn't seem to see a contradiction."

"We contain multitudes," the priest said with a matching smile.

"Saints and sinners."

"Yes indeed, my dear. Saints and sinners, all of us."

THIRTEEN

JUN

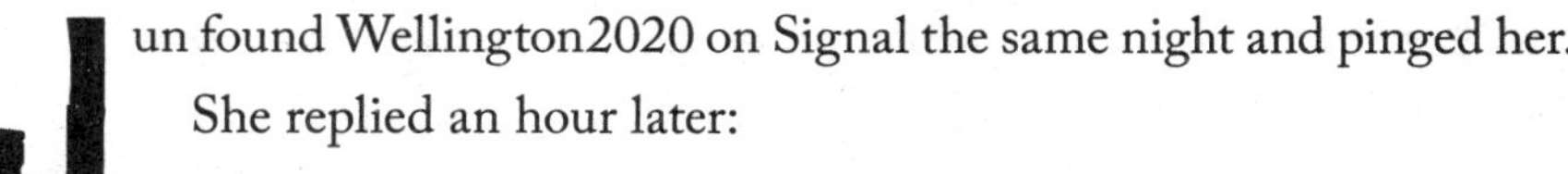

Jun found Wellington2020 on Signal the same night and pinged her. She replied an hour later:

1600 Exit B Tsim Sha Tsui MTR Thursday

There was a demo scheduled and the street was already crowded with protesters, onlookers, and irritated shopkeepers. Jun spotted her in the crowd marching down Nathan Road. She was already masked and helmeted, leading a crew of about fifteen other protesters, all similarly dressed, but Jun knew her immediately from her height and her lithe movement.

When she saw Jun, she peeled off, gesturing for her to follow and walking down a side street.

It was a typical Tsim Sha Tsui alley, narrow and packed with restaurants and shops, neon signs overhead. They turned a corner and found a group of protesters squatting on the pavement at the intersection, shielded by a wall of open umbrellas. She said something too low for Jun to hear and the umbrellas parted, then slid closed again behind them.

Four large jerry cans were lined up on the ground, with what looked like a glorified bicycle pump attached to the top of the first can.

It was a three-woman team, assembling petrol bombs. One worked the pump, another filled the bottles from the hose, then passed them to the third woman squatting on the road who stuffed a rag into the bottle top and slotted it into a plastic beer crate. All were wearing gas masks and pink rubber gloves.

"She's here to help," Wellington2020 said, then turned and ducked out.

The squatting woman stood gratefully, peeled off her gloves and handed them to Jun.

Jun spent three weeks on the assembly line. They rotated the volunteers of course. But Jun put in for the maximum time. It was a test she wasn't going to fail.

Halfway through the second week she fainted and had to go to the emergency tent. The medical student on duty advised her to take a break. She stopped for a day.

Then, at the end of the third week, gasoline got inside her right glove. She was exhausted and didn't notice anything until she finished her shift and peeled off the gloves. Her palm and wrist were a fiery scarlet.

By the time she got to the medical station, small weeping pustules had broken out on the inflamed area and the urge to scratch was almost unbearable. The same medical student wrapped the wound in a sterile bandage. But she said Jun had to get more treatment.

"Proper burn salve. Antibiotics. Pain medication. CNS check. But you can't go to the hospital. They're arresting anyone with wounds like these. But there are sympathetic pharmacists," the medic said. She handed Jun a name and address, told her to memorize it, then shred the paper.

When she got home, Jun dropped her keys twice trying to open the apartment door. The pharmacist had given her Tramadol for the pain and she could hardly stand up straight.

The door swung open before she could insert the key.

Kelvin. He stared at her, then recoiled, taking a step back and covering his nose with his forearm. Jun didn't blame him. Her clothes and hair were saturated with petrol fumes, the oily black smoke from the bombs, CS gas. Sweat.

"Thanks." She dropped keys on the table, then her pack on the floor, walked as slowly as an arthritic old lady toward the bathroom, peeling off her clothes.

"What the hell, Jun? Your work called me today to ask where you were. They said you haven't been there for a week."

She waved her left hand over her shoulder.

"Got to shower first."

He was still talking when the door swung shut. She turned the shower on, steam billowing up.

Pounding on the door. Kelvin was saying something.

"Just let me shower first, okay?"

He muttered something. Steps walked away.

Her phone pinged.

> 1500 tomorrow Sunday,
> Signal conference call

FOURTEEN
KILLIAN

By the time Killian got back to the ops room from the landfill, it was almost 8:00 P.M. He had taken over from Blue at the landfill at 3:00 and sent her home.

Then the bulldozer they borrowed from EPD had broken down. And he found out three of the constables were off sick with the flu. The EPD officer, a rat-faced man in his thirties named Yip, had tried to stop work at 7:00, even though they'd brought in lighting. More cajoling. More forms. A threat. The usual.

Blue was there alone, hunched over the computer.

"Damn it, Blue, I thought I sent you home?" Killian said.

"I've been home. I came back to finish some paperwork on another case."

"Your place is close?"

"Tin Tiu Estate. Two hundred yards."

"Too close."

"I know. It's too easy to never leave the station. By the way, I got an email from Chan at forensics. He said the other items were a washout."

"What other items?"

"Sorry. The other items we found around the arm. There was a wristwatch, some old photos in an album, some vinyl records. But no connection to the arm, unfortunately. He sounded so excited at first. Not like him at all, so I was hopeful. But . . ."

She shrugged.

"Poon is working on matching the arm and the torso though, right?"

"Yes. Should be ready soon."

Killian sat at his desk and logged into his police email. His stomach rumbled.

"I've got a couple of emails to take care of. Do you want to get some noodles after that?" he asked.

"Thanks, boss. But I can't. I've got to be back in ten minutes to put my boy to bed."

"You really are a superwoman, Blue. Your husband's looking after him?"

"My mother. Divorced. He's an accountant. Couldn't take the hours. Mine, I mean."

"No comment. But I'm glad you've got your boy."

"Me too, boss. Me too."

Killian looked at the screen. Four emails from Kwok. He deleted them unopened. One from Senior Superintendent Tse. Half an hour ago.

A few phrases jumped out: Superintendent Kwok . . . formal complaint . . . not sharing vital TSG information with the Red Team under his command . . . serious breach . . .

Killian felt a flush of anger and clenched his jaw, hitting reply.

Dear Senior Superintendent Tse:

Thank you for your note. As members of my team have repeatedly informed Superintendent Kwok, the communication from TSG was oral, left in a voicemail and merely stated that they found no reason to connect any of the individuals identified by face recognition to this investigation. At no time was any information withheld.

"Boss?"

Blue was at the door.

"Hmm?"

Killian was scrolling through the rest of his emails.

"You should go home too. You had a long day," she said.

Home, he thought. *Right.*

"I know. I'm leaving soon."

"If you want," she said tentatively, "you could come back to my place. I'm going to make something for myself anyway. It wouldn't be much, but . . ."

"It's nice of you to offer. But I've got work to do. Go home to your boy. What's his name?" Killian asked.

"Cheers."

"Cheers? Like . . ." Killian mimed raising a glass.

"Yes. My ex-husband's idea. He said it would always remind us of good times."

"What a nice thought. Thank you for the offer but I've got paperwork to finish here. Please give Cheers a hug from me. Goodnight."

"Goodnight, boss."

Forty minutes later, exiting the highway out of Tin Shui Wai, Killian gunned the Land Cruiser up the narrow uphill road that led to the coast. This was his favorite part of the drive—alternating scrubland and semi-abandoned light industrial projects, farms and junkyards, most of the lots hidden behind high steel gates and miles of corrugated iron fencing. It had a postapocalyptic, *Mad Max* feel that was unlike anywhere else in Hong Kong. He thought maybe that was why he liked it. It was the sense of escaping into another time and place, escaping into an alternate universe, escaping his failures. His sins.

A right on the coast road and up to the crest of another small rise, and there was Shenzhen on his left, rank upon rank of towers gleaming across the bay, reflections glittering on the water. This strange, neglected corner of Hong Kong wouldn't last long. Mainland developers had already started building their future bedroom communities for China's richest city.

On the passenger seat next to him, Killian's phone pinged once, then twice again. He pulled the car over and picked up his phone.

We need to talk

Zen.

Killian stared at the screen, considering his reply, then sniffed and realized he had stopped the car opposite the pig farm. All the lights were on and he could hear high-pitched squeals and grunts. And smell the cloying reek of pig shit. The farmer must be doing some late-night slaughtering. Killian buzzed the window shut, then typed:

When?

Now

He sighed. Even at the best of times, Zen was high maintenance. And he hated to speak on the phone, so it must be something earthshaking. On a night when all Killian wanted was to shower and fall into bed.

He pressed the call button on the app, then the speaker, and placed the phone on the dashboard.

Zen picked up after six rings.

"An actual voice call. To what do I owe this honor? There's something new on my landfill body?" Killian said.

"Your what body?"

"The murder case I asked you about? The body at the garbage dump?"

"Oh, yeah. I forgot. No. It's about your sister."

"Jun? Is she okay?"

"For now. But that could change any minute."

"All this because she attended a few protests?"

"Hell no. She's mixed up with the real radicals."

"And you want me to do what? Warn her to stop?"

"She has no idea how close she is to being arrested. And she needs to avoid that. I've seen things on the security cams from the detention centers that . . ."

He interrupted himself to take a sip of something. Killian could hear liquid gurgling as Zen topped up his drink.

"I've got a soft spot for her because I've known her since she was in pigtails," Zen said. "So tell her to stop going to the protests for a while. Get her to understand that this is a city under a microscope. There are already five, maybe six hundred thousand cameras. In another year there'll be a million. And our bandwidth to process all that footage will be much, much bigger by then too. We're buying a Sugon Dawning 8000, for God's sake."

"What's a Sugon Dawning, when it's at home?"

Zen wasn't amused.

"It's a supercomputer. Sugon is the Chinese equivalent of Cray. You must have heard of them?" Zen said.

"Vaguely," Killian replied.

"Jesus, Killian. What century do you live in? We have the whole city under surveillance. Every person who is considered a threat is tagged orange or red. A little rectangle appears above their heads when they show up on our screens. Red is for arrest immediately."

"So what color are we?" Killian asked. "Pink? Purple?"

"We're blue, of course. And it's not funny. Jun is flashing orange. That means the computer tracks her constantly. And if she meets any other oranges, the computer logs it for review. If she meets another flashing orange, it sends out an alert for an immediate supervisor-level review. And that almost always means an arrest order."

"With no charges?"

"You really don't get it, do you? No. No charges. And no comfy Hong Kong prisons either. One wrong move and she'll be on the no-hope express to a labor camp in Gansu or some other mainland shithole. And maybe they'll send you too. Just to be on the safe side."

"I'm a policeman, for God's sake," Killian protested.

"That's exactly why you're in danger. You're already in deep shit with the forty-seventh floor. That's why you're stuck out there in Bim Bam Bong or whatever, isn't it?"

"Tsim Bei Tsui," Killian corrected. "And I didn't get myself sent out here. You make it sound deliberate."

"Whatever. You're in deep trouble, right? And now on top of that, you've caught this case and you're treating it like a normal investigation. It's not. The top brass are watching it like hawks for some reason," Zen said.

"Let them watch. They can't make it disappear."

"Of course they can. This is the new Hong Kong, Kill. Nobody here wants to believe it, but Hong Kong is already just another part of China. You and most of the population are sleepwalking into the abyss. Wake up."

"It's not that bad, Zen," Killian said.

"Don't be naïve, bro. It's much worse than you can imagine. And it's going to get even worse in a hurry. But by the time that happens, I'll be living somewhere else, believe me."

"You're going to leave Hong Kong?"

"I'll move back to Los Angeles. Or the Bay Area. You should leave too. You're not even Chinese, for God's sake. You have the luxury—the privilege—of being able to go whenever you want. And you should take your sister with you too."

"This is our home. We're not leaving."

"It's not the same place, Killian. Get that into your thick head. And neither is the Force."

"There are a few outliers. Bad apples. But the majority are good people. It'll just take some time to adjust to . . ." Killian began.

"Bad apples, Killian. I knew you were stubborn, but this is straight up denial."

Killian didn't reply and he heard Zen sigh.

"Fine. Have it your way. When it all goes to hell, don't say I didn't try to warn you. Especially about Jun."

Zen clicked off. The sound of squealing pigs rose to a crescendo behind Killian.

He typed a message into his phone.

Jun, we need to talk. v important.

He hesitated, then shrugged and typed:

Please. for the sake of the family.

Killian sighed. Having to resort to a guilt trip was never a good sign.

He lifted his foot off the brake, and the car purred forward, leaving the indignant screeching of the doomed animals behind.

FIFTEEN

The phone buzzed on the nightstand, waking Killian. He reached out and picked it up. 3:04 A.M.

"Blue? Is everything okay?" he asked.

"Yes. Just something strange. At the station," Blue replied.

"What kind of strange?"

"Looks like PTU and Raptors are gearing up in the parking lot. I can see Kwok from my living room. Even from the fourteenth floor, his shiny head sticks out like a lighthouse beacon."

"Called out to a protest, maybe?" Killian suggested.

"No. The streets are quiet. And from the looks of the gear, they're going in light. No shields. No CS guns. Berets instead of helmets. Truncheons. Jugs of pepper spray. Tasers. About twenty in all. Rolling now."

"Okay, Blue. Thank you. I'll check it out."

"Do you need me to go down there?"

"No. No. Go back to sleep."

"Right, boss. Call if you need anything."

Killian walked over to the radio. It wasn't one of the huge bulky beasts of olden times. It was a sleek digital thing. The only new piece of equipment in the post.

"Tin Shui Wai dispatch. This is Tsim Bei Tsui station. Over," he said.

"Roger, Tsim Bei Tsui. I hear you loud and clear."

"This is Superintendent Tong. Please patch me through to Superintendent Kwok. He's out on an op."

"Yes, sir."

There was a pause. Static. The faint sound of sirens from the public estate. Was that Kwok? Must be.

Most of Tin Shui Wai was private housing. That was part of the deal the developer signed with the government when they'd been given the swampy land to reclaim. Some 70 percent of the apartments, over 50,000 units, were theirs to sell. But the rest, the blocks closest to his station, near the canal and the swamp gas, these were the fifteen low-cost public housing blocks they were obliged to build under the terms of their contract.

It was the poorest part of town, of course. And also the yellowest, the most virulently anti-police.

The radio crackled.

"Raptor one."

"Give me Superintendent Kwok. This is Superintendent Tong," Killian said.

"He's out in the field," came the brusque response.

"What's the operation? Over?"

"Apprehension of suspect. Over."

"Suspect in what case? Over?"

"The landfill case. Over."

"What suspect? What is the name?"

"Suspect Ngai, Tsinyi. His brother Ngai, Tsinyong also a suspect but not in Hong Kong at present."

That had to be the landscapers Zen mentioned. Kwok must have gotten the names from TSG.

"Give me the location of the arrests. Over."

"Tin Chak Estate. Chak Fong House. Flat number 2711."

He repeated the address to confirm, then signed out.

At the door, Killian hesitated, then went back inside. No policeman had been killed yet, though one plainclothes officer had been cornered under a flyover and beaten so badly he was still in the hospital.

Better safe than sorry.

The Glock was in the weapons safe. He took it out, strapped it on his belt in the small of his back, then lifted his loose shirt to cover it. He picked up the smallest can of pepper spray and hooked that on his belt too. Killian wasn't entirely sure he'd be able to fire the pistol if the time came. At least he'd have another option.

It had started to drizzle by the time he got to the estate, the blue and red police lights reflecting off the slick tarmac, five thirty-story blocks looming over the central plaza, more behind.

The two white police vans were parked in front of one tower block, a line of PTU men in a semicircle in front of the main doors. They'd suited up in the vans, helmets and mirrored visors, truncheons. But only light, round, hard plastic shields, not the heavy, full-body protectors.

He pulled around the corner, found a dark side alley and locked the car manually so no one would hear the ping.

A small crowd had gathered in the plaza, keeping their distance, more people joining them by the minute, almost all young, mostly men. Boys.

Many of the windows in the block were lit up and open, residents leaning out, despite the hour, a rising chorus of abuse raining down.

"Fuck your mother, police pigs."

"Leave our boys alone. Party dogs."

Nothing new. But the small number of PTU constables made it dangerous. Especially as Kwok was probably too proud to call for reinforcements. Or retreat.

Killian pushed to the front of the crowd, walked to the line of police. Their all-black uniforms and helmets marked them as Raptors, Kwok's men, a law unto themselves. Killian wondered if Kwok had told anyone about their encounter the previous day. Almost certainly not.

He flashed his ID card.

"Where's Kwok?" he asked.

No answer. Killian walked to the sergeant.

"Where is Superintendent Kwok, Sergeant?" he asked again.

No answer.

Killian took out his phone, reached forward, and in a quick motion flipped up the visor, taking the sergeant's picture. A flush of anger crossed the sergeant's face, and he raised his truncheon.

"Let me through, Sergeant. And if any of you so much as touch me, I'll have you and your entire squad charged with attacking an officer."

The sergeant glared but lowered the truncheon.

"Superintendent Kwok said to let no one through," the sergeant said.

"I'm filming this now and it will go into your records. Let me through."

Killian lifted his phone, hit record. The sergeant flipped down his visor, turned his head, and stepped out of the way.

Killian jogged toward the main doors. Glass was everywhere. No one would have buzzed them in. They'd had to use the ram. A crash came from behind him in the plaza. He turned. Someone had thrown a folding chair out of their window, narrowly missing the police line. Another object flashed out of the darkness, glinting dully. A cooking pot. It hit one constable's helmet with an almost comical clang. The sergeant barked something, and the line jogged back ten steps, out of range for the moment.

They had immobilized the elevators. Standard. Killian pulled out his key ring, inserted the fireman's key into the lock, and called the elevator down.

Twenty-seventh floor.

A corridor full of Raptors in their black berets. Heads turned as the elevator pinged.

Killian held up his ID card.

"Superintendent Tong. Where's the OIC?"

One of the men pointed to the end of the corridor.

Smashed door hanging off its hinges. Broken furniture. A middle-aged woman huddled in the corner, clutching two young kids to her, eyes wild. Into the bedroom. A fat man in his late forties, hands cuffed behind him, lay on the bed, chest bare. Pajama bottoms stretched over a round white belly.

Kwok was there, henchmen on either side. As Killian entered, Kwok snapped his right hand downward, the extendable twenty-one-inch baton popping out with a metallic thunk.

They were intent on their prisoner, not noticing him.

"Where's your brother, Ngai? Very convenient that he's traveling, isn't it?"

Kwok poked the man in the stomach, a hard prod, the steel tip of the baton sinking in, the flesh of his belly rippling. A groan. There was blood on the man's teeth and chin.

"A word, Superintendent Kwok," Killian said.

Kwok whirled.

"What the hell?"

Killian held up his hand. "Not here. Unless you want the whole building to hear."

Kwok took a few deep breaths, nodded to the open bathroom door. They stepped in. It was so small they had to stand inches from each other. Kwok stank. That same vinegary, sour mash smell he'd exuded at the station. His eyes were red with rage, small burst capillaries on his nose shining.

"What do you think you're doing?" Kwok growled.

He was still holding the extended baton in his right hand. Killian twisted a little, then dipped his hand under his shirt so it was resting on the pepper spray canister.

"Tell me this has nothing to do with my investigation, Kwok."

"He's a suspect. A suspect you missed."

"This is one of the landscapers?"

Kwok looked surprised, then laughed. "Of course you lied about not having the report."

"I didn't lie. TSG said they weren't to be considered suspects."

“That’s our job as investigators to decide. Not theirs.”

“They have no connection to the body.”

“No connection except they were at the dump. Twice. That’s enough in my book for an interrogation.”

“Is it enough to do a home invasion on the man at 4:00 A.M. and terrorize his family?”

“Go fuck yourself, Tong. You missed this and you know it.”

“I missed nothing. There isn’t a shred of evidence connecting him to the body. He’s at the dump regularly. It’s part of his work. You didn’t think to check that?”

“He’s political. A protest leader. I suppose TSG told you that too?”

“So what?”

Kwok stared at him, incredulous.

“So what? So everything. Don’t be naïve.” He shook his head, turned to go. “Leave me to finish this, Tong. Go home.”

Kwok swung the door open. More Raptors were in the room.

The man on the bed was invisible behind them, panting audibly, each indrawn breath a wheeze. Children were screaming outside in the living room.

“The superintendent is just leaving, boys. Please escort him out.”

Kwok stepped toward the bed. Four men, all tall, their bulk exaggerated by their padded chest protectors, stepped forward, blocking Killian’s view.

“Come on, you fat fuck,” Killian heard Kwok say. “Don’t waste any more of my time.”

One of the Raptors gestured with his truncheon to the front door.

“This way.” A pause. “Sir.”

The noise of a slap from behind them, an *oof* of expelled air. Killian, fists clenched, took a step forward. The four Raptors stepped forward at the same time so they were inches apart. The man facing him raised his canister of pepper spray. He was grinning behind his mask.

Killian spun on his heel and walked toward the door, the four men crowding close behind him, chests pressing against his back, propelling him out into the corridor, the apartment door slamming behind them.

Two of them were standing in front of the elevator, blocking it. He took the stairs.

Halfway down, the general roar outside solidified into a chant:

"Pigs go home. Pigs go home."

The sound of more objects hitting the tarmac. Killian stopped, looked out of the stairwell window. Something white flashed past. A microwave? It hit the ground with a crunch. The PTU line had retreated another ten meters to where the vans were parked. One van was already roaring away, but the other was still facing the crowd, a last officer climbing aboard.

Then the night was lit by fire, flames tumbling lazily through the air: gasoline bomb. It smashed onto the grill covering a van's windshield. The driver slammed the vehicle into reverse, fire rolling down over the hood.

The vehicle jerked to a halt, and a constable carrying a fire extinguisher popped out of the back doors. He sprayed foam over the front of the van in two quick, practiced sweeps, extinguishing the flames, then ran round, climbed back inside.

Killian ran the rest of the way down, two and three steps at a time. By the time he came out of the building, the police line was in full retreat, following the reversing vans. Masked protesters in hoodies were picking up garbage cans and throwing them at the constables.

The ten PTU constables waited until the protesters got within a couple of meters, then lumbered forward in a truncheon charge, pepper spraying the crowd until they retreated. But the protesters soon surged forward again, an overlapping wall of open umbrellas protecting those at the front like a formation of Roman legionaries. Another Molotov cocktail came sailing out of the crowd, smashing on the ground just in front of the police line. A bloom of flames and oily black smoke. The policemen retreated again and the crowd surged forward, howling with triumph.

Killian turned away. Time to leave.

As he made his way back to the alley where he'd parked, Killian heard the whump of rotors. Kwok had finally called in for help from the Government Flying Service.

The Land Cruiser sat in the shadows, untouched. Killian climbed in and sat there for a moment, bone-weary, watching.

The plaza had filled. Far too many people for the single PTU squad, which had disappeared around a corner. They wouldn't come back unless they had reinforcements.

Minutes later, the protesters returned, triumphant, chanting.

"*Gwongfuk Heonggong! Sidoi gakmeng!*"

"Liberate Hong Kong! Revolution now!"

The crowd in the plaza took up the chant, then the residents leaning out of the windows, the sound bouncing off the buildings, the whole enclosed space shaking, the words meshing together into a primal roar.

Despite himself, Killian felt his pulse quicken. He shivered. It was heady. Intoxicating.

Futile.

The chant faded. Some of the people in the plaza were pointing upward, shouting obscenities. Killian leaned forward, looked up through the windshield. The helicopter was hovering over the roof of Chakfu House. Not one of the ordinary surveillance choppers, a huge Super Puma. Big enough that the whole squad and their prisoner could be evacuated at the same time.

A mass of protesters raced for the building entrance. Too late. With the elevators blocked, even the fittest would take ten minutes to climb the twenty-seven stories.

The big machine was flaring onto the roof, red navigation lights blinking, a bright spotlight shining down. It settled, passed out of Killian's view, just the distant thrum of the rotors remaining. No point in staying. This was over. For tonight.

Killian started the Land Cruiser and drove away, the shouting and chanting fading into the night behind him.

SIXTEEN

JUN

It was 2:00 P.M. by the time Jun woke. Kelvin was gone. He'd left a note, scrawled on a sheet of A4 paper:

We need to talk.

Jun picked up the pen lying next to the note.

No need. I'm moving out.

When she opened Signal just before 3:00, there were five others already on the call. All the screens were blank except for one, a figure wearing a Guy Fawkes mask, her feed identified as Wellington2020. The others also had English names under the blank video feeds: Marbol, July, Eddison, Bingbing, and Marco.

Wellington2020 didn't bother to introduce Jun, just launched straight into her first question.

"You are Tong Bojun, also known as Siobhan Riordan."

"My name is Tong Bojun."

"But your father was Sean Riordan, correct? A policeman?"

She had no trouble with the name. Jun wondered if she'd studied in the United Kingdom.

"Yes."

"And your brother is Superintendent Killian Riordan?"

"Yes."

"You told me you had no connections with the police."

"My father has been dead for twenty years. And I don't talk to my brother."

"Why?"

"Because he's still a policeman. Because he won't leave the Force."

"You should talk to him. You have to know your enemy." A reedy voice like a teenage boy. Eddison.

"Maybe."

"When was the last time you talked to him?" Eddison continued.

"We spoke a few days ago. For the first time in months. My mother insisted we have dinner as a family."

"What did he want?"

"He wanted me to stop going to protests. Said that I was in danger."

"What did you do?" Another voice. A young woman. July.

"Nothing. I left."

Silence. Jun filled it. "There are tens of thousands of divided families in Hong Kong these days. Hundreds of thousands. Just because my brother is stubborn doesn't mean I'm a spy, for God's sake."

More silence. Jun was getting angry. "What do I have to do to prove it to you?"

"How did you find out about us?" Back to Wellington2020, the voice raspy behind the mask.

"I told you. I saw you in the play. Then at a demo."

"And who did you think I represented?"

"A frontline group. Not the wishy-washy Democrats. Or the politicians, the compromisers and grandstanders. Someone who would take real action. Something that will wake up the rest of the world."

"So you want to take part in such an action?"

"Yes." Exasperated.

"You'd be willing to risk your life?"

Jun reached down to her pack and pulled out an envelope. She held it up to the camera: Last will and testament, Tong Bojun.

"Does that answer your question?"

"Every one of us carries one of those."

"Exactly."

"You're really willing to risk your own life?" Wellington2020 again.

"If it would accomplish something. Yes."

Wellington2020 nodded. "Wait a minute."

A sudden silence. They had cut Jun off from the feed and were talking among themselves.

Finally, Wellington2020 nodded to Jun and her connection clicked back on.

"We'll contact you if we need you."

The screen went dark.

SEVENTEEN
KILLIAN

The next morning at 8:15, Killian was waiting outside Tse's office door. He'd tried what he could after getting back to the Tsim Bei Tsui station the night before, with little to show for it. The duty officer at Tin Shui Wai denied Ngai was in the holding cells and flatly refused to contact SS Tse at 5:00 A.M. It had been a reach anyway. Kwok would probably have taken Ngai to the Raptor base at PTU HQ in Fanling. Or the notorious San Uk Ling Detention Center next door.

At 8:30, Tse appeared out of the elevator. He looked even more exhausted than ever. Maybe the duty officer had contacted him after all.

Killian stepped forward. But Tse held up a hand before he could speak.

"If this is about Kwok, don't bother."

He reached into his pocket and produced a bunch of keys, inserted one in the lock of his office door, swung it open.

"I told you before, you two are on separate tracks. Let Kwok conduct his interrogation. That's exactly why we have the Red Team."

Killian had anticipated this. "Yes, sir. I know. It's not about that."

Surprised, Tse turned back. "What is it then?"

"If he's being interrogated in my case, I have a right to question the suspect myself. If Superintendent Kwok is on the right track, I'll be denied what might be valuable information."

"You'll see the transcripts. If you need to follow up after that, we'll consider it then," Tse said. "Now, go away and do some real work instead of bothering me."

Tse closed his door.

Back to Tsim Bei Tsui station. Two hours of exhausted sleep.

When the alarm sounded, Killian cobbled together a makeshift meal, shoveling the instant noodles and a fried egg into his mouth automatically. His thoughts drifted to Senior Superintendent Weng. Could he reach out to him for help trying to track down Ngai?

He shook his head. A ridiculous thought. The calculus would take Weng a nanosecond. Huge political downside. No visible advantage to his career. End of discussion.

He chased the last strand of noodle and speared it with his chopsticks, then got up to rinse the bowl.

Why was he wasting time thinking about this? He should let it go, ignore the whispering of his conscience. Leave Kwok to do whatever he had planned. Serve his time out in his Tsim Bei Tsui exile without ruffling any feathers, then slip back into his old life.

And yet. And yet . . .

The same images kept forcing their way back into his thoughts. Ngai's face distorted with pain after Kwok had poked him in his belly, the cowering children, the Raptors stomping around the apartment like Imperial Storm Troopers.

Was it just his injured pride at being shoved around by Kwok's goons? Surely he was grown-up enough to get over that? What was it then?

Killian didn't spend a lot of time examining his life. He didn't see the point. Forward momentum had worked until now. He knew there was an urge inside him, maybe a hollowness, that he filled with work.

Regardless of what was going on around him—politically, with the family, even when he was having relationship problems—this had been his constant, his polestar. Work. Career. A steady rise. Not flashy. Just very, very competent. Reliable. Known to never rock the boat.

Until he'd shot Shek.

He flipped the switch on the kettle. Coffee was mandatory at a time like this. Good for maudlin thoughts. And self-pity.

Eddie Tsang could help, of course. Uncle Eddie, Killian had called him as a child. Maybe the old days still meant something. Maybe. Maybe not. Killian wasn't sure he wanted to find out.

Eddie Tsang and his relentless quest for the Force's top job. He'd been at Da's funeral. The next time Killian had seen him was at his graduation parade from the Police Training School, when Eddie had walked over from the podium, the crowd of new inspectors and their families instinctively parting for him.

"Congratulations, Killian. Your father would have been proud."

The firm handshake. The left hand on the shoulder.

"Thank you, sir."

Eddie Tsang was already a chief superintendent at that point and clearly destined for great things.

"I'll be keeping my eye on you, never fear."

And maybe he had. But the only thing Killian recalled in the last decade was a get-well card when he was in Queen Mary Hospital five months ago.

With best wishes for a speedy recovery, Uncle Eddie.

Killian had heard nothing since, which was fine with him. Tsang's all-consuming obsession with becoming commissioner made him a dangerous man to know. Anyone who came between him and his goal could get steamrollered. Son of a mentor or not.

Still, if he wrapped up this case soon Eddie might give a nudge to someone behind the scenes. That was a hope, anyway.

Killian glanced at his watch.

Almost time. Ops room, then to his shift at the landfill.

His phone buzzed. Ringing. Not a message. Nobody under forty actually called. It had to be Mother. He'd called her the previous day after Jun had ignored his messages.

"Yes, Ma?"

"What are you doing? You sound exhausted."

He'd only said two words. How could she tell? Another Mother superpower.

"It's been a long few days. I need to go for a run or something."

She snorted. Mother didn't believe in exercise. "It's May already. You'll give yourself heatstroke."

"Was there something you wanted?"

"Your sister called me."

"Finally."

"She doesn't want to talk to you."

"Mother . . ."

"I'm not getting involved in your fights. You know that. I never have."

Killian sighed. This had always been her line. Sort it out yourselves.

"You have to get involved in this one."

"No."

"Do you want Jun to go to prison? For ten years. Maybe twenty?"

"Of course not. You're being melodramatic."

"You know me. Am I ever melodramatic?"

Silence.

"I'm serious about this. Jun is involved with some very, very dangerous people. I have to talk to her."

"This is from your colleagues, from the police?"

"Yes. Rock solid."

More silence. Killian knew better than to interrupt.

"Alright. I'll tell her."

"Thank you. And please hurry. This is urgent."

"I'm not a child, Gong. I said I would do it and I will."

"Good. Thank you."

She didn't say anything.

"Ma? Are you there? I have to go and . . ."

She had hung up. Her usual sign-off. Ma. She would do it. Call Jun. Killian could be sure of that. She had her own code. Like Da. And Jun.

Jun. Hers wasn't just a code. It was practically a religion. She and the other protesters would never compromise, even knowing they could never win. Knowing the horrendous consequences. For themselves. For their families. For the whole city. So stupid.

Killian took a sip of the coffee. Cold. Time to go.

His phone buzzed as he was starting the Land Cruiser. It was an old reminder, on daily repeat: JUN?????

There was nothing more he could do for her. He didn't even know where she was.

He started to put the phone back in his pocket, hesitated, staring at the screen, grimaced at his own indecisiveness.

He couldn't just leave it. He had to know what had happened to Ngai.

Zen would know. Or be able to find out.

Killian opened the Gmail app on the phone and typed in Ngai's name, then wrote:

I need to find this man ASAP, please. EMERGENCY

Saved it to drafts.

Then he typed a single word on Telegram and sent it to Zen:

FCUK

That was a brand, wasn't it?

* * *

When Killian left Tin Shui Wai station for his shift at the landfill he was relieved to get out. Even shoveling garbage was better than being stuck in the ops room and its empty whiteboards and oppressive atmosphere of defeat.

He reached the landfill site by 3:20. They had made visible progress, covering almost a third of the remaining ground, the bulldozer in almost constant use.

Killian took one of the shovels from a constable on the next shift change.

Killian swung the shovel down, the blade slicing into the orange soil, and dumped it on the smaller wire-mesh screen. Then back in again.

The rhythm was the simple. Dump. Scan. Tip. Repeat. It was monotonous and exhausting, the face shield steaming up rapidly, his entire body sleek with sweat after ten minutes.

Where was Ngai? He'd heard nothing back from Zen. Kwok must have him buried somewhere. What BS story had Kwok come up with to convince them to let him keep the man squirreled away? In theory, he could only be held for forty-eight hours without being brought before a magistrate. In theory.

The only communication from HQ had been an email message from SS Weng saying he was expecting an update briefing, ASAP. Also a reiteration: If Killian couldn't show concrete progress by the end of the week, the investigation was to be shut down.

With only a few days before the deadline and no leads so far, that was impossible unless there was an unexpected breakthrough in the case. And Weng knew it.

Killian swung the shovel down, but had to stop to wave away a cloud of flies so thick they were obscuring his vision. Flies. The night they'd found the body, the storm had kept them away. Then, when they'd first begun clearing the site, the birds were the main problem. But as they'd dug down into the compacted garbage, it was the flies. Swarms of them. Armies. Like a biblical plague, fat and greasy, so stupefied with eating they flew into his face shield, tumbling to the dirt.

He thrust down, twisted the shovel to free it from the gluey soil, then heaved the earth against the sieve, which was propped up on his right, one of a line of five.

Bend. Scoop. Heave. Back muscles on fire.

Bend. Scoop. Heave. His whole body was soaking with sweat, rivulets running down his back and legs.

"Time!"

The sergeant called out, then blew a blast on his whistle. The men in front of Killian jammed their shovels in the dirt and turned to walk back to the vans. Killian waited, then handed his shovel to the constable taking over. The constable said something inaudible, muffled by the respirator.

"What?" Killian asked.

But the constable had turned his back to him and plunged the shovel into the earth. Killian trudged out of the pit, careful to pull off the respirator only when he was well clear. In the Land Cruiser, he turned the air-conditioning on full blast, letting the cold air wash over him. He was done for the day.

A long drink of water. Then his phone.

A Telegram alert. A reply from Zen:

> FCUK yourself

Killian opened Gmail.

> your guy is back in tsw
> but proceed with EXTREME caution
> your friend K has convinced higher-ups this whole Venus de Milo thing is a setup by the cockroaches to blame the force
> DO NOT CONTACT ME AGAIN. TOO RISKY FOR US BOTH

Venus de Milo. The armless torso. Always a little too clever for his own good was Zen.

But a conspiracy? Kwok was telling HQ the protesters had murdered someone, then cut up the body and dumped it in the landfill, all so it would then be found and the blame put on the police? It was ridiculous. But it also played into the needs of the higher-ups. And it even made a kind of twisted sense. There were endless rumors that protesters had died in police custody, their bodies spirited away.

It didn't matter. Killian now knew where Ngai was.

He climbed into the Land Cruiser, started it, and dropped it into gear.

EIGHTEEN

The holding cells were in a separate block, a two-story annex at right angles to the main building, connected by a long, windowless corridor. At the steel door, he buzzed, held up his ID, and the door clicked open. The duty sergeant was behind a raised desk, the barred steel gate leading to the cells behind him. He was plump, forties, a mole on his chin sprouting a few long hairs. He was typing on a computer keyboard, a frown of concentration creasing his brow. The aroma of fried noodles hung in the air.

"Sorry to interrupt your breakfast, Sergeant," Killian said.

"What, sir?"

"Nothing. Relax. I'm here to see a prisoner. Ngai Tsinyi."

"Superintendent Kwok ordered no access to Ngai, sir."

"And I'm ordering you to give me access."

"I can't, sir."

"Why not?"

"Can you wait for Superintendent Kwok, sir? He'll be back in a few minutes."

"Now, Sergeant. That's an order."

The sergeant licked his lips nervously, shrugged his shoulders.

"Sir, I'm just doing what Superintendent Kwok told me. I . . ."

"Get me SS Tse on the line, would you? You can explain to him why you are refusing a direct order."

The sergeant blanched.

"Yes, sir. Cell seven." He pressed a button and the access door swung open.

"Thank you, Sergeant."

Cells lined each side of the corridor. Each one had a steel shelf built into the wall that served as a bed. And an aluminum toilet. No seat. A single flush button. The first few were empty. Then a grizzled-haired man, snoring, mouth open, the alcohol rising off him.

A big supply room, the door open, caught Killian's eye. He glanced in. Mops. Buckets. A watering can. Shelves of disinfectant. They spent a lot of time cleaning up. On the other side of the room, overalls hung on wall pegs, alongside shackles and leg restraints, a stack of cots, two stretchers. The rear shelves held linens, blankets, pillows, towels, stacks of khaki shorts and shirts with Hong Kong Correctional Services stenciled on them in large black letters.

Cell seven. Ngai was lying face down on the bare shelf, one leg dangling off the side. No mattress or blanket. His head was tilted at what looked like a painful angle, his right cheek bulging out, eye squeezed shut, mouth open and a pool of white liquid dripping from the edge of the shelf. Huge bags under his eyes. No visible injuries, but his skin was an unhealthy, doughy yellow.

Killian stepped forward. No sign of Ngai's chest moving. Was he dead?

"Ngai! Ngai!" Killian called out.

Nothing. But Ngai's eyes flickered under the closed lids.

"Mr. Ngai. Wake up, please." Killian kept his tone calm but firm.

Ngai's eyelids flickered again, then his left eye opened. The whites were heavily bloodshot, his gaze unfocused.

Ten seconds, twenty. Finally, the eye rolled up toward Killian.

"Mr. Ngai, are you alright? My name is Superintendent Tong and I . . ."

A convulsion ran through Ngai as though he'd been given an electric shock, his legs trembling.

"No more! No more!" Ngai screamed suddenly.

"It's okay, Mr. Ngai. Please calm down," Killian said, raising his hands to show they were empty.

But Ngai wasn't listening, cowering, hands up in front of his face, pushing himself backward on the shelf.

"No more! No more. Please, no more!" Ngai screeched, so shrill that Killian had to fight the impulse to cover his ears.

A door slammed at the end of the corridor. Killian turned his head. Before he could say anything else, a hand clamped down on his shoulder, spinning him around.

"What are you doing here?" Kwok's voice barked at him. Four of his goons loomed behind him.

"What have you done to this man, Kwok?" Killian demanded.

"Routine interrogation," Kwok said.

He signaled to his men, who took a pace forward.

"Now leave."

"If you've tortured him," Killian said, even as he heard how weak the words sounded, "there'll be an inquiry."

Kwok laughed, baring his teeth. "An inquiry. Really? Who do you think ordered this, Tong? Maybe you should ask your uncle, eh?"

The goons snickered behind him.

"What is that supposed to mean?" Killian asked, narrowing his eyes.

Kwok ignored him, gesturing to his men. "Get him out of here. Nicely, though. Understood?"

"Yes, sir!" one of the men replied sharply.

Before Killian could move, they swarmed around him, a well-oiled team. Two darted behind him, one on each side. The men at Killian's back pinned his arms to his sides. He was lifted by his elbows, a foot off the ground.

The group trotted down the corridor. The leading man hit the intercom button, shouting into the mic. The door swung open, and they surged through it, the steel entry door popping open in front of them.

Killian managed to free his left arm as they were going through the door. He drove his elbow back as hard as he could. It banged harmlessly against a chest protector. One of the men behind him trapped the arm again with the ease of long practice.

They set him down in the corridor, then backed away, still facing him. Killian staggered, fell to one knee, then recovered. The last man turned back, sneering.

"Serves you right," the man muttered.

The steel door slammed shut with a crash.

* * *

Killian stormed out of the annex that housed the cells, his fists clenched, jaw tight. He couldn't let this go, not now. Not after what he'd just seen.

He headed straight for Tse's office. The door was ajar when he arrived, and Tse was hunched over his desk, typing on his keyboard. Killian didn't bother knocking.

Tse looked up briefly, his face stony. "Get out of my office, Superintendent. That's an order."

"A prisoner is being tortured in your cells, sir," Killian said, keeping his voice even with an effort.

Tse shook his head, still typing, refusing to look at him. "No one is being tortured. We have cameras, constantly supervised."

"I know what they're doing. Or going to do. I saw the evidence. There was a . . ."

But Tse, finally stopped typing and turned and slapped his hand against the desktop.

"That's enough!"

A vein was pulsing in his forehead. Tse made a visible effort to calm himself.

"Now listen to me, Tong. Kwok says he's close to a breakthrough. You, on the other hand, are still farting around in the garbage dump."

He pushed himself up from his desk and leaned forward.

"Superintendent Tong, I gave you a direct order. Return to your duties immediately. Is that clear?"

Killian turned without another word and walked out of Tse's office.

* * *

Back in the patrol car, parked in the station car park, Killian sat staring out of the windshield, trying to calm down. He was supposed to be at the landfill, another shift of digging and sweating. But he couldn't bring himself to go. Not yet.

Clearly, it wasn't just Kwok he was up against. If Tse knew, Weng knew. And if Kwok was to be believed, maybe Uncle Eddie too. They all knew. It was the only explanation for why Kwok felt untouchable, why he could do whatever he wanted—including torture—and get away with it.

But why? That question burned in Killian's mind. At some level, it made sense for Kwok to have the backing of the higher-ups. They all wanted to curry favor with the chief executive, with Beijing. Uncovering a conspiracy to frame the police would be a propaganda coup, proof that they were winning the fight against chaos and disorder.

But even so, it was obvious that Kwok was manufacturing a scapegoat, fabricating an entire case against Ngai. And the higher-ups knew it. They were complicit.

What was so important that it could justify going to these lengths?

Whatever it was, if he risked continuing to fight it would mean the end of whatever career he had left. Maybe worse.

Let it go, Killian thought. Then the face of one of the four girls he had betrayed appeared, peering at him owlishly because, as he later realized, her glasses had been broken in the scuffling while they were arrested.

He owed it to them. He owed it to himself to make up for that.

Just as important, he owed it to Hong Kong to make sure Kwok wasn't left a free hand to bully and intimidate at will.

And Kwok wasn't just a bully. He was brutal. Killian had seen it with his own eyes. And he encouraged that brutality among the Raptors. Everyone knew it. The rumors weren't new. Stories of torture, strip searches, verbal harassment, even rape in detention centers. The abuse didn't stop with arrests; it escalated behind closed doors.

That wasn't the Force Killian had joined. That wasn't justice. It was cruelty. It was lawlessness. It was the kind of thing gangsters did—or mainland police.

He took a breath and picked up his phone. There was one more play.

Zen could hack into the station's system and retrieve the video from the cell. If that footage went viral, the world would see the truth, and they'd have no choice but to release Ngai.

Killian began typing furiously.

The reply came in under a minute.

WTF? I said never direct
messaging on this app.

Emergency. Do it, please.

No way.

A man's life is at stake.

No chance.

Make it look like it was hacked.

Killian hesitated, then typed a follow-up.

Blame one of the foreign powers
they say are behind the protests.

The reply came instantly.

No key words asshole

Killian began typing another response, but Zen's next message popped up before he could finish.

NO WAY. they'll trace it back to us both

Killian replied immediately.

I don't care. You said you
were leaving anyway. Do it.

There was a pause. Zen changed the subject. Deflection.

Forget about that. J is in danger.

Killian's thumbs flew across the keyboard.

I will handle J. Just do this.
Last time. Promise.

There was no reply for almost a minute. Killian stared at the screen, his pulse racing. Had Zen gone offline? Finally, a new message appeared:

Closing this account.

Killian's typed furiously.

Don't you dare, Zen.

No reply. Killian typed again.

Don't dare ghost me. Do it or . . .

He hesitated. Or what?

The image of Ngai's face twisted in terror flashed through his mind.

Or I'll out you to your bosses.

He hit send and leaned back in his seat, his heart pounding.

Five minutes passed. No reply. Killian typed again.

Not bluffing.

* * *

At the landfill, Killian picked up his respirator and gloves from the passenger seat, got out of the car, and walked straight over to the line of constables who were shoveling dirt into the sieves. He tapped one man on the shoulder and leaned over.

"I'll take over," Killian shouted in his ear.

"What?" The constable's face was barely visible behind the misted-up face shield.

"I'll take over. You can take your break," Killian repeated.

"Be my guest. Waste of time anyway."

The constable hadn't seen that Killian was an officer. Or didn't care.

NINETEEN

An hour later, Killian was trudging back to his car. His arms were trembling so much he could barely hold the shovel.

He propped the shovel against the car and pulled off his right glove, turning his palm up. Blisters on his first three fingers oozed blood. He reached into his pocket gingerly and pulled out his phone.

A message from Jun. Mother must have gotten through to her. Finally.

I'll talk but it had better be life and death.

Life and death. Close to it if Zen was right.

She picked up immediately. No hello.

"What do you want?" she asked.

"What do I want? I want to find out why my sister is refusing to talk to me," Killian said.

"Is that all?"

"No. But it would be a start."

"You know why."

"Shek?"

"Among other things, yes. And his name is Shek Ga Keong."

"I know what his name is. It was an accident, Jun."

Weasel words, he thought. He should tell her that it was supposed to be a warning shot. Over his head. That his elbow had been bumped, possibly maliciously. That he was deeply sorry for the boy. Had apologized to his family. But he just couldn't get the words to come out. And Jun was talking.

"An accident, Killian, seriously? You were there waving a gun around. How was that an accident?"

"It was someone in the crowd who . . ."

She cut him off.

"Enough. I don't want to hear your excuses."

He opened his mouth again to tell her he had gone to beg forgiveness. That the boy's mother had forgiven him, so why couldn't she? But the words wouldn't come out. Perhaps it was because he knew there was no point, she had made up her mind.

"I'm sorry, Jun. I really am. But I didn't call to talk about that. I wanted to tell you're in danger."

"From the police?" She snorted. "That's what you made all this fuss about?"

"No. There's a lot you don't know. I . . ."

She cut him off again.

"Please, Killian. That old line? We know things you don't. Spare me, please."

"It's not like that. I can explain, Jun. Give me five minutes. You owe me that much."

"I don't owe you anything," she said, her voice full of contempt. "You should have resigned after the shooting."

"Oh, for God's sake, Jun!"

He barked at her, checked himself, then continued, his voice soft.

"Please. Just listen to me. For Mother's sake if not mine."

Jun didn't reply and Killian began talking, explaining what Zen had said, the surveillance, her precarious status, the danger that she could be arrested and sent to China.

When he was finished, she was silent for a moment. Then she spoke, "None of this is new. Of course we know we're being followed."

"You don't understand. This is about you personally. They have you listed as dangerous. And they're tracking you wherever you go. Tracking who you meet with. They could arrest you any day. Or hour."

A long silence. Then she sighed.

"Killian, this time you listen to me. You work for a brutal paramilitary machine that is getting more violent and more paranoid every day. Save yourself. Get out, while you still can."

"Oh, Jun," Killian said.

Another long silence. Killian tried again.

"You're in denial about the danger you're in, Jun. You could go to jail for years. Decades."

"I know what I'm doing," Jun said.

"*Zeng dai zi wa*," Killian said.

"A frog in a well?"

"Yes. You can only see a tiny part of the sky, but you're convinced you know everything."

"Oh, please. If anyone is a frog, it's you. Sitting in the pot, boiled to death because it can't bring itself to jump out."

"Just promise me you'll drop whatever you're planning," Killian said.

"I won't promise anything. You may not want children, Killian, but I do. And I don't want them to come home, dressed in their red pioneer scarves, parroting party propaganda at me."

"So, burn down the city to save it?" Killian asked.

"Help the city save itself before it's too late. We have taken a stand. And we're sticking to it. You should try it sometime," Jun said. "Goodbye, Superintendent."

Killian sat in the car after she hung up, overwhelmed by a feeling of helplessness. Jun and her fellow protesters were convinced that protests and civil resistance were the only way to defeat the government's efforts to cleave to Beijing's will. They didn't seem to care that it would destroy the city too.

Chaos and bloodshed were coming. Soon. It was just a question of when it would happen and how many people had to die in the process. That, above all else, was a reason to stay in the Force: To try and keep whatever violence broke out to a minimum. And to try to keep Jun from making herself one of the victims.

Killian shook his head and reached for the car keys. But before he could start the motor, he heard shouts.

A group of the diggers had dropped their shovels and were clustered together in a circle, looking down.

One of the figures—probably Lin from his height—was waving him over.

Killian climbed out of the car and pulled on the respirator, slick and reeking of his own sweat. Two constables moved aside. It was a lump about the size of a football. Wrapped in black plastic.

The same plastic trash bags the torso had been wrapped in. Dozens of flies buzzed around it.

Killian looked at Lin, who mimed removing the respirator.

Killian stepped closer until he was right over it, could see the fat flies crawling over the plastic, trying to find a way in. The stink hit him the moment he raised the respirator. It was unmistakable. The reek of decay. Like rotting meat sprinkled with perfume. But there was also a smell of charred flesh.

He took a step back, pulled the respirator back down, his gorge rising.

Lin was looking at him expectantly, and Killian nodded, gesturing to the foldable picnic table they'd set up next to the vans. Lin reached forward, hands in heavy rubber gloves, gingerly picked up the object, a cloud of flies rising up, hovering around him as he walked slowly over to the table, holding it as far out in front of him as possible.

The second crew had stopped work, and all twelve of them were gathered around the table, those not wearing respirators standing a meter or more back.

Lin waved his hands to get rid of the flies, swatting several that tumbled sluggishly through the air.

Killian reached down and pulled at the plastic. But this wasn't loose like the plastic around the torso had been. It was tight, possibly taped. He made a snipping motion with his fingers to one of the constables. There was no point in speaking through the respirator.

The constable returned with a pair of scissors from the van's first aid kit, seven inches long and hooked at the end, designed to cut the clothes off accident victims. Killian found a fold and snipped it loose, revealing another layer underneath. He folded it back, cut away around it so a flap of plastic came loose, then snipped again. A third layer. He repeated the process, cut the third layer, then leaned forward and used the tips of the scissors to lift the last section up.

An eye.

Or what was left of it, buried deep in the socket, charred flesh all around, no lid, clogged with soot. But still recognizably an eye. A human eye.

Killian put down the scissors and stepped back, pulled off the respirator.

"Call forensics," he said, then cleared his throat, coughing. "And get the cooler. And the ice packs."

* * *

An hour later, Chan was there again, the same unflappable demeanor as before. He hadn't even opened the cooler, just listened impassively as Killian recounted what they'd found.

"First priority, once you've confirmed it's a human head, is to get a DNA sample. See if it matches the torso."

Chan nodded. "Of course, sir."

Killian watched as the white forensics van came and went, carrying away the head in a white-and-red cooler. After using up the remaining daylight, the crews began to pack up. Killian sat in his car, the air-conditioning on full blast. His right hand was swaddled in bandages. He wouldn't be digging for a few days. Stupid. He looked across at the van where the off-shift constables were sheltering from the heat. Five of them huddled together, watching something on a phone.

Killian's phone dinged. A Telegram message.

Video online

He pumped his fist.

Thank you thank you, your
skills are off the chart

fuck off

Killian sat there, thumbs poised over the keyboard. There was nothing to say. He had blackmailed the man. For a good cause, yes. But it was still blackmail.

His phone pinged again.

Never contact me again

Killian googled, "Tin Shui Wai police cell."

The headline came right up on the *Hong Kong Free Press* site: ALLEGED WATERBOARDING OF PRISONER BY POLICE "RAPTORS"

He clicked the link. Color video. Timestamp: 10:12 A.M. Today. They had started a few minutes after throwing him out of the cells. No actual board, so they'd improvised. A stretcher from the supply cupboard. Ngai's legs were tied to the carrying handles on one end, arms above his head tied to the other. The stretcher was propped at an angle, the top resting on the lap of one of the Raptors sitting in a plastic chair. Ngai's head was completely covered in a bright red towel knotted under the back of his neck, the seated Raptor held the knot tight with both hands.

As the video started, Ngai was immobile, Kwok standing over him holding a metal bucket.

Then Kwok shouted something, only a few words coming through: "body," "dump," "murder."

Ngai shook his head back and forth, his shouting muffled by the towel.

Kwok shrugged and began to pour water out of the bucket, the water soaking the towel dark red.

Ngai began to writhe, throwing himself back and forth so violently that the Raptor seated behind him had to clamp his forearms around Ngai's head to immobilize it. His legs thrashed upward, his chest bucked, nearly tipping the stretcher over. Another Raptor pressed down on his knees.

More water. A pause. More thrashing, though weaker. Another pause. Kwok said something. No response. More water. Thrashing again, very weak.

It seemed to continue forever. But it was less than a minute.

At last, Kwok put down the bucket and spoke again, his words inaudible except for the last four: "ready to confess now?"

No answer. They removed the towel. Ngai's face was the color of brick, his eyes bulging. He tried to speak, leaned sideways, gagged, then vomited a thin stream of water.

He tried to speak again, gagged once more, then finally choked something out. Kwok smiled with satisfaction. The video ended.

Killian stared at the screen, his stomach churning.

They'd claim it was doctored. Fake news. The usual BS. But they'd have to let Ngai go. And Kwok was clearly recognizable. That shining pate.

Serves him right, the evil bastard.

A rap at the window startled Killian. He looked up. Blue was standing outside, gesturing for him to lower the window. Killian complied.

"Are you looking at the video, boss? From the holding cells?" Blue asked.

"You've seen it?" Killian asked.

Blue nodded somberly. "This will . . . I don't know. People will go crazy."

"So they should. It's a disgrace," Killian said.

"Yes. But this is bad. Very bad." Blue's tone was heavy.

Killian frowned. "Why?"

"You don't know Tin Shui Wai, boss. We have to get back to the station."

"Now?" Killian asked, confused.

"Yes. Before it gets blocked off."

"Seriously?"

"Yes, boss. A lot of young people. No jobs. Angry. And he's local. From the housing estate. This will be like petrol on a fire."

A jolt of unease ran through Killian.

What had he done?

TWENTY

There were small groups of people gathered across the street from the station when Killian and Blue pulled into the side street leading to the entrance gates. But traffic was still flowing on both sides of the four-lane road.

"This is only the start. People are just getting off work," Blue said. "And other protesters will rally from all over Hong Kong."

The Land Cruiser pulled through the big steel gates of the station. The exercise field was empty. But four, dark-blue PTU buses were lined up next to each other in the parking lot, and knots of constables were milling around, smoking and talking.

"Not geared up yet," said Blue.

"And not STS either. I wonder where that shit Kwok is. It's not like him to miss an opportunity to crack skulls."

Killian parked, then headed over to the holding cell wing, telling Blue he'd meet her in the ops room.

"What are you going to do?" Blue asked.

"See if Ngai is still there."

"And if Kwok's still there?"

"I'll play it by ear."

There was a different sergeant behind the reception desk. He shook his head when Killian asked about Ngai.

"He's gone, sir. About an hour ago."

"Gone? Gone where? Did the STS take him?"

"I don't know where. But it wasn't STS, sir. It was an ambulance crew. A superintendent was with them."

In the ops room, Killian sat, staring down at his phone. What the hell? He opened Telegram, typed: DKNY

Killian turned to log onto his email. But the phone buzzed. Incoming message.

Zen hadn't closed the account.

No more I told you

I said I was sorry. Just tell me what happened to Ngai

you've got to be joking. you threatened to rat me out

I wouldn't have done it.

The line hung there, lame even to Killian's own eyes.

Zen was typing.

Liar

A pause. Killian hesitated. What else could he say? Zen was typing again.

Only talking coz Jun is a nice kid:
u better deal with your sis asap

why? what's happening?

ask her

ask her what?

No answer. One tick. Sent. Unread.

are you there?

Nothing. Killian put the phone down.

He couldn't blame Zen. Blackmail was a nasty thing. But it had worked. He'd query Jun again in the evening. Not that it would make any difference.

Killian swiveled around in the chair and pulled a new file from the top of the pile on his desk. It was the digitized list of license plates from the landfill's registry book. At last.

He had sent Blue back home to her son, again, against her strong protests. Before going she had suggested they ask Chan to go back and do a luminol test for blood traces on the items forensics had recovered around the body.

"Every object on the list?" Killian had replied, looking skeptical. "That's over four hundred, if I remember correctly. Why?"

"The list is useless right now," Blue said. "No connections to the body. If we get a hit for blood we can do a DNA test for a match. Then we'd have a lead."

Killian nodded.

"That's smart. Forensics is going to scream about having to dig them all out again from evidence. But it's definitely worth a try. Good thinking."

"Thanks, boss."

She smiled, looking pleased. That was when he'd sent her home.

He flipped open the list of car plates.

April 2

1147. AR24567; Mun Fatt Bakery; Ford Econo Van, 2011

1149. TT62213; Green Cross Milk Co.; Hyundai Grand Starex, 2014

1150. GR40023; Lim Goh Mok; BMW 728i, 2018
1151. DB66887; Chor Kok Ting; Bentley Flying Spur, 2018
1153. BG44342; Ma On Pik; Mercedes Benz 500e, 2018

All these people driving to the landfill in their luxury cars. Even for Hong Kong, it was odd. What in God's name were they getting rid of? Dead pets? Dead Spouses?

He turned to the next page.

A knock at the door of the ops room.

"Come in," Killian called out.

A constable entered.

"Superintendent Tong?" she said.

"Yes?"

"SS Tse would like to see you in his office."

★ ★ ★

On the third floor, Killian tapped on the office door. No answer. He rapped loudly.

"Yes, yes. Come in."

Tse was standing at the window looking down at the road and smoking. As station commander, he had a corner office on the third floor of the station, giving him a view of the Tin Yiu Road and the Tin Yiu Public Housing Estate towers on one side, the Lockwood Estate towers on the other. He had the window open and was blowing the smoke out, the clamor of traffic, horns, scattered shouting washing into the room.

Tse didn't turn around.

"Tong, is it?"

"Yes, sir."

"Smoke detector, if you were wondering why the window is open."

"I see, sir."

Tse gestured down to the street where car horns were sounding.

"It's starting."

"What, sir?"

"The demo. They're stopping traffic."

Killian walked over to stand beside him and looked through the wire mesh-covered windows. Black-clad demonstrators had dragged garbage bins into the middle of the westbound lanes and laid them out end to end, forming a makeshift barrier. Some were digging up bricks from the pavement, others already pulling on the steel poles that held up the pedestrian fences, hauling back and forth to break them out of the ground.

Traffic was backed up, cars and buses honking. As they watched, more demonstrators poured over the center divider, some pulling wheeled metal garbage containers with them and upending them in the street. They moved in teams with the ease of long practice.

"Thugs. They're thugs," Tse sounded defeated. "And right in front of my station. I never thought in a thousand years that we'd see this in Hong Kong. Thank God I hit thirty years in two months. I'm going to Taipei the day my pension kicks in. Never coming back."

He stubbed out the cigarette in an ashtray balanced on the edge of the windowsill, then turned to face Killian. Tse had looked exhausted the last time they met, but now he looked half dead, eyes bloodshot, skin hanging off his face like an ill-made mask. He turned to walk back to his desk and staggered, almost falling. Killian grabbed his arm by the elbow, but Tse shook him off and dropped heavily into his seat.

"Between those *lamchau* crazies and goons like Kwok, we're all trapped on an airplane in a nosedive."

Lamchau. The new catchword of the most radical demonstrators, the Cantonese version of that *Hunger Games* phrase: "If we burn, you burn with us." To Killian, it conjured up an image of two combatants locked together as they plunged off a cliff.

He frowned, puzzled.

"You thought I was a big fan of Superintendent Kwok and his methods?"

It seemed better to say nothing. Tse continued.

"He's scum. The kind of sadist the psych tests are supposed to weed out. The bane of every police department."

"Kwok isn't here, sir?" Killian asked.

"No, Superintendent. You'll be happy to hear that he's been put in deep freeze for the moment thanks to that disgusting video." He shook his head. "But I'm sure he'll be back. Thank the Lord I'll be gone by then. Retirement has never looked better. That this sort of thing would go on in my station. It's enough to make you . . ."

He trailed off, shaking his head again, obviously in distress. Killian felt a strong urge to point out that he'd told Tse exactly what was going on in his station and been rebuffed. But he repressed the impulse, wondering instead if he should suggest Tse get himself checked out by a doctor. But then Tse looked up and seemed to remember why he had asked Killian to his office.

"You'll be on duty here tonight, Tong. My two deputies are out. One sick with gout of all the damned things. The other's in Thailand on a beach. Lucky bastard. So that leaves you to help me deal with this nonsense."

He waved his hand over his shoulder toward the windows. A chant started up, indistinct at first, then clearer as more voices took it up.

"Free Ngai Tsinyi! Free Ngai Tsinyi!"

"Is Ngai still here?" Killian asked.

Tse shook his head. "No. He's at the Queen Mary Hospital. They sent a chopper to take him out. He's a mess. Mentally as well as physically."

Killian didn't say anything. A loud banging of metal on metal had started outside in time with the chants.

"Maybe if we told them Ngai wasn't here?"

"What? Then they'd just magically go away? I don't think so. And anyway, we're under strict orders to leave them alone as long as there's no violence."

"So what are my orders, sir?" Killian asked.

"Coordinate with the officer in charge of the PTU boys. You've had some experience with demonstrations."

"Yes, sir."

"The routine station duties are taken care of. Just make sure they're ready to deploy if things kick off."

"Without the Raptors here, I think we can safely leave them alone until they get bored and go home to bed," Killian said.

"Let's hope you're right. The MTR is shut down and protesters have closed the road from town, so we're on our own."

"There's always the Government Flying Service," Killian said, thinking of the night Ngai had been arrested.

Tse gave a weak smile.

"Let's pray it doesn't come to that. Now, off you go, Tong. Do your duty." He flapped his wrist toward the door.

"Yes, sir."

* * *

When Killian opened the rear door of the station, the six PTU platoons were lined up in rows on the exercise field doing calisthenics. Each man's gear was in a pile at his side, stacked on the inside of the full-body shield. An officer wearing a chief inspector's three pips was leading them. Situation under control.

He returned to his desk in the ops room, still stinking of stale cigarettes and BO. What had happened to Blue's automatic air freshener?

All four desks and two side tables were covered in stacks of binders and files—so much for the paperless office. Forensics reports. Autopsy report and follow-ups. Interviews of the EPD officers. Follow-up interviews of the scavengers. The guards at the gate. Reports from the missing persons office. Printouts from Transport Department Vehicle Registration. Endless paper. No result.

There was little new on the whiteboard either. A printout of the word "HEAD" had been tacked up under Lines of Inquiry.

The rest of the board was all dead ends. They won't have to worry about putting the case in deep freeze. The thing was in the morgue already.

Killian's mobile trilled, and he swung back to his desk.

"Tong."

"Superintendent, this is Doctor Poon."

"Doctor. I was just thinking of you. How's my head? I mean, the head I sent you."

"I can confirm that the head is a match to the arm and the torso."

"You're sure? So quickly?"

"Ninety-nine point five seven three percent sure. It's a new technique that uses two types of variations in DNA: short tandem repeats and single nucleotide polymorphisms."

"If you say so, Doctor. Anything else?"

"The head is badly disfigured. A mess, to use an unscientific phrase. The murderer cut off the nose. Ears. Lips. Ripped out the teeth with pliers. And then burned what was left with a blowtorch."

"A blowtorch?"

"Yes. To start with. There are patches where the burning is intense. But he must have realized how inefficient that was. So he doused the head with petrol and set it on fire. The different depths of burns are quite clear."

"That's all?" Killian couldn't hide the disappointment in his voice.

"You'll have my full report tomorrow. But the short answer is, yes. That was the purpose of the whole exercise, of course. Disguising the victim's identity."

"What about reconstruction? Can't they do marvels these days?"

"Just so. But marvels are expensive, Superintendent. I have already inquired, of course. Senior Superintendent Weng was most emphatic that he had no intention of spending—wasting, as he put it—a few hundred thousand dollars that could be better put to use on overtime for the PTU."

"Two hundred thousand? That's how much it would be?"

"Possibly more. Thirty thousand pounds is the minimum. We would have to send it to Scotland. The University of Dundee. They have one of the best facial reconstruction labs in the world. Richard III. They found his skeleton in a car park and reconstructed his likeness. You must remember that?"

Killian had a vague memory of a prominent, broken nose. A black beret.

"Yes. I think so."

"Marvelous work. They even did a Neanderthal. Of course, it's different with a real person. But in our case, they would have most of the face, which eliminates much of the uncertainty."

"But it's not going to happen."

"No. And, sadly, it probably never will."

Poon cleared his throat with finality. The conversation was over.

"Goodbye, Superintendent."

"Goodbye, Doctor."

Almost the last hope of solving the case, Killian thought. Killed by Weng and the bean counters. The government had added hundreds of millions of dollars to the Force's budget to cope with the costs incurred by the demonstrations. But it was never enough.

Maybe, after this weekend and the mysterious announcement, Killian could approach Weng himself. Weng had promised that the suspension of the investigation would be temporary. Or had he?

The Axe's grim features appeared in Killian's head.

No. There was no point in deluding himself. Once the deadline was over, this case would be done. Buried for good. For reasons he still didn't come close to understanding, Weng and probably others higher up were determined to close this down.

A crash from outside reverberated through the building. Mostly the low murmur of the crowd was oddly innocuous, like a distant cocktail party. Then an outburst of chanting would come.

Killian had instructed the station staff sergeant to contact him if it took a turn for the worse.

Killian swung back to his desk just as another crash from above reverberated through the room, quickly followed by a low boom from outside. Was that a petrol bomb?

Another boom. Molotov cocktails, definitely.

Killian stood. He'd better get up to the roof and see what was going on.

TWENTY-ONE

JUN

Jun heard nothing for three days. Then Thursday morning her phone buzzed. A long message.

> Go to 222 Chamlong Street in Sai Ying Pun. Go through the hallway to the back door and turn left, then continue until you get to number 36 Gongbo Lane. Press button number three and say Ah Long sent you. He will buzz you in. Again, go through to the back and turn left. Climb two sets of stairs until you see the seal carver's stall on your right. Across the way is Lamlin Park. 1500 today.

There were no cameras in the alleys, Jun noticed as she walked. Nor on the stairs.

The park consisted of a lone tree, a kids' climbing frame with a swing, and a bench, forty-story apartment blocks rearing up on all sides. There was a camera mounted above the park gate, but the lens had been sprayed over with black paint.

A figure was on the bench, hunched over a phone. She looked up as Jun approached. No mask. No smile. A somber nod.

It was the first time Jun had seen her features uncovered. The tight black curls were cropped close to her skull, the cheekbones wide, topped by those intense eyes.

"What should I call you?" Jun sat down next to her.

"King."

"King like King George?"

A joke. She didn't smile, just shook her head.

"This king." She traced the character on her palm. Jun nodded.

"Got it." She gestured to King's face. "I didn't know you were one of us."

A puzzled look.

"Us?"

"A halfie."

Jun was smiling. But King didn't get it, shook her head.

"A what?"

"A halfie. Eurasian."

Her brow cleared. "Oh, I see. But I'm not a halfie. A quarter, if that's a thing. My mother is half."

"African?"

"African American. He was an American sailor. Vietnam. My grandma was a bar girl."

"That's . . ." Jun stopped. King, seeming to think she was embarrassed, shrugged.

"It was a long, long time ago. He probably never knew. The old story."

Jun nodded.

"She never tried to find him? Your mother?"

"No. She couldn't see the point. She's born and bred in Hong Kong. Her English isn't even that good. She couldn't see herself walking around New York or Los Angeles, asking for someone who didn't even know she existed. What about you?"

"What about me?"

"You never wanted to go back to Britain? You don't have relatives there?"

"Nope. Hong Kong born and bred and proud of it."

"Not even for university?"

"Science U. Environmental Sciences. You?"

"HKU. Chemistry."

Steps on the stairs. A couple, whispering to each other. King waited until they passed, then turned back to Jun.

"What about politics?" King asked.

"Politics?"

"How did you get to the point where you want to join us? Most people are happy to stay on the sidelines."

Jun hesitated. Still a vestigial sense of shame.

"I was arrested. It was the first protest I had been to for a long time and I was careless. Things had changed in the last few years."

"Yes, they have. Was it bad?"

Matter-of-fact.

"They took us to the New Territories in a bus. Only women. One was just wearing panties and a shirt. Her skirt had been ripped off in the arrest. They must have known she was a bystander. Who would go to a protest in a skirt and heels?"

"Sai Uk Ling?"

Jun shook her head. "No. This was a small detention facility. Somewhere they could do what they wanted and not be noticed.

"When we arrived, they herded us into a room. Except the woman with no skirt. They dragged her away. She started screaming and kicking. Her shirt was ripped open. They threw her on the ground, grabbed her feet and dragged her out. I could hear her head banging on the floor."

"Did you see her again?"

"No. There was silence for a while. And then this thumping started from above us."

"They raped her?"

"I think so. No. I'm sure they did, yes."

Jun shivered and looked away. A mother and child had come into the park while she was talking. The child was on the swing, high, clear giggles trilling through the air.

"It was horrible. Sitting there listening . . ."

King didn't respond or try and comfort her. Finally, she said:

"And then?"

"And then they came in again. We were huddled together in a corner. One of them, a fat sergeant, pointed to one of the women, told her to come with him. I stopped her from getting up, told him my brother was a superintendent, that we had memorized their faces and ranks, that I would make sure they were dismissed, prosecuted, that their families would know what they did . . ."

"That was brave."

Jun shrugged. "I had no choice. That's when I realized, if you don't resist, there are no limits to what they can do. That's why I want to join you."

She nodded again.

"When was this?"

"Late last year. Before Christmas."

"And you didn't tell your brother?"

"No."

"Because you knew he wouldn't do anything?"

"No. The opposite. I knew if I told him he would have turned the place upside down to find the men responsible. And would have probably lost his job too. Or worse."

Silence.

"I never told my mother either. Or my friends. It was weird. I felt ashamed. As though I had done something wrong, not them."

"That's normal." King cleared her throat. "Something has come up. That's why I asked to meet you."

Jun waited.

"We have people in government who are sympathetic. They're saying there'll be a big announcement from the Liaison Office on Saturday about the new National Security Law."

The government had been trying to pass the Security Law for almost two decades but had been stymied by mass protests each time. The passage of the law would allow the government to arrest anyone it wanted and keep them imprisoned indefinitely under the pretext of national security.

"What about it?"

"It looks as though they're going to circumvent LegCo. Pass the law in Beijing."

Jun stared at her, shocked. It had never occurred to Jun or most people in Hong Kong that Beijing would—or could—simply bypass LegCo and pass the law unilaterally.

"Can they do that?"

"If we allow them to. That's why we must do something now. Something that will catch the world's attention. Only outside pressure will make them pull back."

"What are you thinking?"

"We'll brief you tomorrow. We have a flat someone has lent us. In Wan Chai. We're meeting there. If you're definitely interested . . . ?"

It was so low-key. As though she was asking if Jun wanted to join them for a mahjong game.

"Just tell me when and where. I'll be there."

"Good. And you should probably bring some clothes. A toothbrush. That kind of thing."

Jun looked at her, puzzled.

"In case we need to hole up somewhere. Afterward."

Afterward.

TWENTY-TWO
KILLIAN

There were about thirty officers on the flat roof of the police station when he got there. Most were gathered at the front, looking down at the crowd. The others were on the right-hand side overlooking Tin Ho Road, the side street that led to the station's main gates. The other two sides of the station were inaccessible: The exercise yard backed onto a four-story warehouse while on the east side a fence ran along a storm drain four meters deep.

Two constables with video cameras were filming the crowd. The rest were a mixed group of officers and rank-and-file policemen, some armed with stubby Federal tear gas launchers, others shining flashlights down into the crowd. Killian pushed his way to the front and peered over the side, then pulled back, momentarily blinded. Protesters were shining lights back up at them. He noticed small spots of green and red light dancing on the edge of the wall and on the chests of the men around him.

"Lasers, sir," one of the officers said.

Killian extended a hand. "Tong."

"Sim. PTU," the officer replied. Sim was the chief inspector Killian had seen leading calisthenics earlier.

"Are they dangerous?" Killian asked.

"Mostly a nuisance, but they can ruin your night vision," Sim replied.

Killian peered over the wall, more cautiously this time, shielding his eyes with a hand. There were a dozen small fires burning, throwing up oily black smoke. Scores of bobbing lights came from handheld flashlights.

The front section of the crowd was lit up in stark white glare by the station's floodlights. At the rear, three TV vans were parked under an underpass that ran north, another on the far eastern side, each van playing their spotlights over the back of the crowd. The chanting was continuous, and in one section of the crowd, protesters had started drumming.

A rock concert from hell.

It occurred to Killian that he had caused this. Why? Out of compassion? Or was it wounded pride?

No matter. It was his responsibility now.

He leaned over and looked directly down. The front protesters—their mosh pit—were bunched up directly under the two-meter high barriers. As Killian watched, two were boosted up from below and scrambled to climb over. Both slipped back down.

Medieval. They would need boiling oil soon. Something had to be done.

He beckoned over a sergeant.

"Where's SS Tse? Is he up here?" Killian asked.

"What?" the sergeant shouted back, the noise of the crowd drowning out the question.

Killian leaned forward, shouting in the man's ear. "Is Tse here?"

"No sign of him, sir. I tried radioing, but there's no response," the sergeant answered.

Killian had tried his own shoulder radio twice, also with no response. He had assumed Tse was on the roof and couldn't hear.

"What about headquarters? Have you been in touch?" Killian asked.

"With regional HQ in Yuen Long. They say field commander SS Tse has control," the sergeant replied.

"Not much control here," Killian muttered to himself.

He coughed, the acrid smoke from the fires catching at the back of his throat.

What were they burning in those drums? Not garbage. Petrol? Where was it coming from?

"I'm going to find SS Tse," Killian said.

He turned to the PTU officer and gestured to the roof access doorway. They stepped inside where the roar of the crowd was much lower.

"You'd better get a couple of platoons into the front lobby in case they manage to breach the barriers," Killian said.

"Yes, sir. I'll go. What about stationing snipers up here?" Sim asked.

Killian shook his head.

"No. Absolutely not. Nonlethal stuff only. The station sergeant has already brought up CS gas and Pepper pot guns."

"Are you sure, sir? If they storm the station, it could be very ugly," Sim said.

Killian made a chopping motion, shaking his head.

"No. Nonlethal only, understand?" Killian reiterated.

"Nonlethal only, yes, sir," Sim confirmed.

"Good. And get on the radio to PTU in Fanling and alert them that we may need backup."

"Yes, sir," Sim said.

Sim saluted and Killian turned and hurried toward the stairs.

Where the hell was Tse?

* * *

Tse's door was shut. Killian rapped on it with his knuckles. No response. He hammered on the door with a fist, then turned the knob and stepped in. No sign of Tse. There was a sickly, burned stink in the air. The only light came from Tse's desk lamp and the reflected light from the chaos outside, shadows dancing on the walls.

A radio squawked. The sound was coming from behind the desk. Killian strode over. A polished black shoe. A pants leg. An outflung arm. The hand was palm down. The smell of burned meat.

Killian gagged. The blackened remains of a cigarette were wedged between the first two fingers, burned down to a stub, the flesh around it charred.

He took another step forward. Tse was lying on his back, the chair upturned next to him, face ashen. His mouth was open, eyes half-closed, whites showing.

Killian bent down and put a finger to Tse's neck. Nothing. He pressed harder. A flutter. The faintest of pulses.

Killian stood and keyed his shoulder radio.

"Dispatch, this is Superintendent Tong. Get a medical evac helicopter here immediately. SS Tse is critically ill. Do you copy?"

"Yes, sir. Medical evac immediately for SS Tse," came the reply.

"And get a couple of constables to his office with a stretcher so we can move him. Tell the chopper to land in the exercise yard," Killian added.

* * *

The noise from the crowd was noticeably lower when Killian went back to the roof after seeing Tse off in the evac helicopter. The chants had stopped. Killian keyed his microphone.

"Get me Chief Inspector Sim."

"Yes, sir."

Killian jogged to the side and looked over. The front rows of protesters had raised their umbrellas and were sheltering behind them. The line extended perhaps six rows back. But there was also a corridor of raised umbrellas running back toward the overpass, the whole line swaying from side to side. What the hell were they up to? Killian's radio crackled.

"Sim here, sir."

"Where are you, Chief Inspector?"

"I have two platoons deployed in the lobby. Do you want us to proceed outside? We can deploy under the shields in the area behind the barriers. Clear the cockroaches with CS and Pepper pots."

"Not yet. Wait for my order."

"Yes, sir." He sounded disappointed.

Killian looked around for the sergeant, spotted him, and waved him over.

He pointed at the underpass.

"What the hell is going on over there? Did you get a spotlight?"

"No. We're using these." The sergeant handed Killian a pair of binoculars. Night vision. He should have thought of that. But they weren't much help. Just a sea of green umbrellas. White static. Undulating movement.

Killian swept the binoculars along the corridor of umbrellas leading to the barriers. They were passing something. Petrol bombs probably. The smell took Killian back to that evening at the flat when Jun had arrived fresh from a protest, stinking of petrol. Only a few days ago, but it felt like a hundred years had passed. *Jun*, he thought, *what are you planning?* Nothing good, that was for sure.

A string of detonations from below—probably firecrackers—brought him back to the present with a jolt.

"Sergeant, get the hoses lined up and start spraying the nearest protesters. The ones in front of the barriers."

He focused the binoculars on the mass of umbrellas under the bridge. Another pause. Then the crowd parted for a moment and Killian saw a group of three men bent over what looked like an oil drum.

They were pumping something into a hose.

The umbrellas swarmed back around the three figures, blocking Killian's view.

Killian leaned over the parapet again. More movement at the front of the crowd.

"Sim. Come in, Sim."

"Yes, sir?"

"I want you to go ahead and deploy outside the front doors now."

"Yes, sir."

The section of the crowd opposite the station entrance was heaving. A yellow helmet appeared above the umbrellas, a figure being lifted by four men. Something was tied around his waist.

"*Yat, yee, sam*!"

The protesters heaved and the man flew up and over the barrier. A huge cheer. He tucked into a ball, rolling as he landed, a long tail of hose trailing behind him.

He stood up and began to fiddle with the knot of the belted hose.

"Sergeant. Start CS into the crowd now, maximum fire in front of the barrier."

"Sir!"

Four men with Federal CS guns ran to the parapet and pointed their barrels downward.

Killian keyed his mic. "Roof to Sim! Respond immediately."

"Sim here, sir. We're opening the doors now."

"No. Abort, abort! Do you copy? Abort!"

"Sir. We're almost . . ."

"Abort immediately and pull back to the rear of the station. Explosion is imminent. Do you copy?"

"Yes, sir. Aborting."

Killian leaned over again. The man had untied the hose and was laying the nozzle on the ground in front of the steel gates that covered the glass doors. They were not sealed. The petrol would flood underneath and into the station.

"Shall I shoot him, sir?"

The sergeant was standing next to Killian, leaning over, an SG 561 on his shoulder, squat but lethal. An assault rifle. High-velocity bullets. A killing weapon. In theory for emergencies only. But when there were guns around, they tended to get fired.

Killian leaned over again. The white CS smoke was billowing around the protester.

"Any rubber bullets?" Killian called, his voice cracking. "Does anyone have rubber bullets left?"

"None left, sir. And the angle is too steep."

"I'll do it," Killian said. He put out his hand, and the sergeant handed him the rifle. Killian put it to his shoulder, squinted down the barrel. The red laser poked through the smoke, dancing on the man's neck as he bent forward again.

Killian adjusted his aim, breath coming short and hard.

The red dot was dancing madly around, swinging from side to side and up and down, over the man's back, legs, skittering over the grass, the wall of the station.

The vision of Shek Ga Keong splayed on the tarmac bloomed in his mind. Killian closed his eyes and willed it away, then opened his eyes and resighted, took a breath and squeezed the trigger.

Bullets tore up clods of earth from the flower beds. The man straightened and looked up, flipped his middle finger at them, then bent down again.

He didn't believe they would shoot him.

Killian, panting, bent again, sighted the laser beam just over the man's head. His heart was hammering in his chest. The beam wavered. He took a deep breath, held it, and squeezed.

Another rattle of automatic fire and bullets tore into the wall above the main doors of the station.

The man barely flinched. He was bent double, almost completely covered by smoke. The hose behind him, which had been lying flaccid on the ground, bulged, then snapped up, rigid, tumescent.

Killian aimed. Center mass. The red laser dot danced on the man's bent back.

No.

Killian moved the barrel a fraction lower and fired twice.

Now the protester responded, leaping away as though scalded, dropping the hose to the ground. The punctured hose pumped out spurts of gasoline as the protester scrambled up the fence, desperate to get away.

The protesters on the other side saw what had happened. Screams, dropped umbrellas, a chaos of struggling bodies, all trying to get away.

Killian looked back at the hose, which lay flat and spent on the trampled earth, just a few last dribbles of liquid heaving out in diminishing spurts. Like a cut artery. The heart fading. Failing.

TWENTY-THREE

Eddie Tsang was in his element, leaning back in his leather chair, the panorama of the harbor spread out behind him, the silver spike of the 108-story International Commerce Center in Kowloon over his right shoulder, Lion Rock looming beyond.

There were three offices facing the harbor on the forty-seventh floor of Police Headquarters, two of them the prized corner suites. The commissioner had one, of course. It faced the eastern harbor entrance: better feng shui. The deputy commissioner for operations—Eddie Tsang—occupied the western suite. The DC management was sandwiched between them, a consolation prize. Short of a spectacular blunder or scandal, Eddie Tsang would eventually move over to the eastern office. That was how the system worked.

Killian couldn't keep his eyes open, feeling the grit behind his lids. He'd changed into a fresh uniform. But the smell of petrol and burning rubber was still in his nostrils and the skin on his hands and arms felt itchy, infested, the blisters from shoveling throbbing under the bandage.

Tsang flicked a speck of dust off the top of the desk, a long chunk of polished oak that was bare except for a closed MacBook, the brushed aluminum shining in the sunlight. He leaned forward, smiled, and pointed at Killian.

"Killian, you look like hammered shit."

Tsang was proud of his command of American slang. Before everything had shifted to China, he'd spent three months at the FBI Academy at Quantico. He'd come back larding every other sentence with expletives.

"Thank you, sir. It was a long night," Killian replied.

"And now a long day on top of it. Did you get any sleep at all?"

"Not yet. I have a few things to take care of and then I'll . . ."

There was a peremptory rap on the door behind him, and the door swung open before Tsang could say anything. Oscar Ping Yee Man, the commissioner of police, walked in. Both men jumped to their feet.

"Sit, sit. Please sit down," Ping said.

The commissioner strolled over to the window and stood next to Tsang. They could have been brothers. The same slicked-back wave of black hair, not a strand of white anywhere, copying their masters in Beijing. The same stocky physical bulk. The same genial, easy air that covered a cold, steel will. The will to power. That and years of command made for a formidable presence. Frightening when needed. They could both break careers with a few words. Had done.

"I just dropped in to say, well done, Tong," Ping said.

Killian leaned forward over the desk, hand extended, forgetting about the bandage. The commissioner looked down, frowned, then brought his hands up in a gesture of polite refusal.

"Sorry, sir. That's from the dig. Just blisters."

Ping waved his hand in dismissal.

"Of course, Superintendent. Honorable wounds. Sit down, please."

Killian sat and Ping leaned forward, his expression turning serious.

"I hear that it was touch and go at one point last night."

"The men behaved very well, sir," Killian replied. "Especially PTU Chief Inspector Sim."

"We're all riot control experts these days, unfortunately. Very nasty business with the barrel of petrol."

"Yes, sir. As I said, the men handled it very well."

"I've seen the report. Your role won't be forgotten, however modest you try to be about it."

He held up a hand to stop Killian from speaking.

"And we'll find whoever was behind it, rest assured."

"Can I ask if there's any news of SS Tse, sir?"

"Recovering after an emergency triple bypass," the commissioner said. "At Queen Mary. In good hands."

Killian opened his mouth to speak, but Tsang raised his hand, palm out, and gave a tiny shake of his head. No more questions. On cue, Ping took two steps forward, still beaming at Killian.

"Keep up the good work, Tong. How are you physically, the blisters apart? The other injuries not troubling you?"

"No, sir. Thank you. I'm fine," Killian replied.

"Excellent. We'll get you back to regular duties soon, won't we, Tsang?"

Eddie nodded emphatically.

"Yes, sir. As soon as this murder case gets sorted out."

"The torso?"

"Yes, sir."

"Very nasty. Barbaric." He turned to Killian. "Where do we stand on that, Superintendent?"

"We've got one good lead, Commissioner," Killian said.

Ping frowned. "A lead? I thought it had dead-ended and we were closing the case."

"The head, sir. Recovered at the landfill. We'd like to do a reconstruction. What the victim looked like. But Doctor Poon says . . ."

Again, Eddie Tsang held up his hand to stop Killian.

"We don't need to bore the commissioner with the minutiae of the investigation, Superintendent. Let's focus on bringing him results, not problems, eh?"

The commissioner took a step forward, patted Killian's shoulder and looked him directly in the eye. "The chief executive has been briefed about this case and she's anxious about it possibly becoming a political football. Tidy it up and we can all move on."

"Yes, sir. But how would that . . ." But Ping was already halfway to the door, and Killian let his question trail off.

The commissioner turned at the door and gave Killian a half salute.

"Change is coming, Superintendent. And we'll need officers like yourself more than ever. Promising officers who can adapt to the times. The future will be very bright for them. Very bright."

"I would look forward to that, sir," Killian said.

"Excellent," Ping said. He dipped his chin to Tsang, then pulled the door shut behind him.

Eddie Tsang and Killian sat down in silence for a moment. They heard the commissioner's door close at the other end of the corridor.

"So, Uncle Eddie, what's going on?" Killian asked.

Tsang smiled again, not his normal high-wattage charmer, but a grin of genuine amusement. "I can't remember the last time you called me that, Killian. You must want something."

"I want to know why this case is so sensitive that the CE has to be briefed about it," Killian said.

"It's just a sign of the times, Killian. Everything is political," Tsang replied.

"Even the CAPO inquiry? And the shooting tribunal?" Killian pressed.

"Especially those, Killian." Tsang smiled. "We look after our own. You know that."

As long as I'm still one of yours, Killian thought.

"And Ngai. What's going to happen to him?" Killian asked.

"He'll be sent home when he's better," Tsang answered.

"And Kwok?" Killian continued.

Tsang flapped his hand in dismissal. "I'll worry about Kwok, Killian."

"He won't be charged?" Killian asked.

"No," Tsang replied flatly.

"What about the video?"

Tsang shook his head. "It'll be forgotten in a week. Eclipsed."

"Eclipsed by what, sir?" Killian asked.

Tsang looked at him. "No harm in telling you, I suppose. Our friends up north have lost patience. They're going to override LegCo and pass the National Security Law themselves. At the National People's Congress in Beijing."

Killian sat up in his chair.

"This is the big announcement on Saturday we've been told about?"

Tsang nodded.

"But they can't do that. It's not legal under the Basic Law," Killian said.

"They can do anything they want, Killian. Don't be naïve," Tsang replied.

This was the third time in as many days he had been accused of being naïve.

"Maybe so, sir. But plenty of people in Hong Kong think that way. The protests when this comes out are going to make everything else this year look like a tea party."

Tsang nodded gravely. "Yes. We're going to have to bring a couple thousand officers off their regular duties to serve as reserve PTU units for riot duty."

"Full time?" Killian asked.

"For the first week. Then we'll reassess. But we'll be very, very understaffed."

"Why don't they just have the People's Liberation Army march out of their barracks and be done with it?"

Tsang looked shocked. "That can never happen in Hong Kong. You know that, Killian. It would look like the PLA was an occupying army."

"And instead we get to do the dirty work for them. We get to become the occupying army."

Tsang held up a hand. The smile was gone. "Don't get carried away, Killian. We'll just do our jobs, won't we?"

"Yes, of course, sir. All I'm saying is that the Force is caught between two fires, and we always seem to be the ones who take the blame."

"It's our duty, Killian," Tsang said. "Now, getting back to your murder. Forget about the reconstruction of the head. I want you to go back there tomorrow and put the case into deep freeze until everything blows over. Is that clear?"

Killian's throat was dry, and he cleared it loudly several times.

"Superintendent?" Tsang said with an edge to his voice. "Any problems with that?"

A pause. Killian cleared his throat again, the taste of grit in his mouth. "The murderer is still out there. We have a duty to find him before he kills again," Killian said.

"You have no evidence of that. And we have a more urgent duty to Hong Kong, to the present," Tsang responded.

"The two don't exclude each other, sir," Killian said.

Tsang frowned again, unaccustomed to being contradicted.

"Listen to me, Superintendent. Our city is in crisis. That's the reality. And if you can't acknowledge that, if you can't follow a direct order then you should consider resigning. Do you wish to resign?"

Killian shook his head. "Of course I don't want to resign, sir. The Force is in my blood. You know that."

"Then act like it. We're at war. And in war you follow orders."

Killian nodded again, wordless.

Tsang stood and walked over to the window, gazing out at the harbor.

"The good news is, Killian, when you've done this, you can leave Tsim Bei Tsui behind. You'll report back here for reassignment as soon as the protests die down. As the commissioner said, the future is very bright for officers who can change with the times." He turned, his grin back in place. "I'm very happy I was the one who told you. You must be relieved that your exile is finally over, Killian."

"Yes, sir. I am," Killian managed, his voice still croaky. "Thank you, sir."

"Good. But first let's get the murder settled. You can come back to it when all this has blown over if you still feel there are leads that weren't followed up. Okay?"

"Yes, sir."

"Go home and get some rest, Killian. You've earned it."

Killian stood.

"And don't forget wise old Uncle Eddie's advice. Get this case put to bed, then focus on the future."

"Yes, sir. I will," Killian said.

Outside in the reception lobby for the executive offices, Killian stabbed at the elevator button. This was an express, for the use of the denizens of the forty-seventh floor only. It seemed to be moving very slowly today.

The air-conditioning up here was arctic. He shivered, then felt a wave of exhaustion wash over him and closed his eyes, swayed forward, and put his hand on the cold steel of the elevator doors for support.

This should be a moment of triumph. Or at least deliverance. Why did it feel so hollow?

He looked up and saw that the constable behind the marble reception desk was watching him with concern.

"I'm fine. Just tired."

She nodded and looked down again. The elevator pinged.

* * *

Killian emerged into the main lobby of the HQ building, navigating through crowds of civilian office workers and uniformed police officers returning from a late lunch.

Two flags hung on the wall behind the reception desk, manned by two staff sergeants. On the right-hand side was the scarlet-and-yellow banner of the People's Republic, while on the left, several feet lower and two-thirds the size, was the Bauhinia flower of the Hong Kong Special Autonomous Region. Between them was a huge police crest, the post-1997 handover version which featured a bland skyline. No more British merchants selling opium as on the crest of the Royal Hong Kong Police.

"Superintendent Tong!"

Killian turned and scanned the crowd behind him. A middle-aged man in a pinstripe suit and a yellow bow tie was hurrying toward him, his right hand raised in salutation. For a moment, he thought it was the coroner, Poon. Then he recalled his encounter at Saint Joe's when Father Dec had introduced them so effusively. Raymond Suen, the man of the hour after mediating the Poly siege. More importantly, Hong Kong's next chief executive, if the priest was to be believed.

"Professor Suen. How are you?" Killian asked.

Suen grasped his hand, ignoring the bandage, and pumped it, his left hand on Killian's forearm.

"What a coincidence. I was just talking to the deputy commissioner earlier this morning and he mentioned your name," Suen said, still holding onto Killian's arm.

"DC Tsang?"

Suen nodded, dropping Killian's hand, but stepping closer. The unforgiving eyes Killian recalled were now warm, and a smile hovered on Suen's lips.

"Indeed. He told me you were involved in a very sensitive murder case."

Killian nodded. So much for the total ban on publicity.

"I'm sure you'll resolve it with your usual efficiency. And discretion," Suen said.

"We're a long way from solving anything at the moment, Professor. But thank you."

"It's good to know people like yourself are handling issues like this."

"I'm just doing my job, Professor." *What does he want?* Killian thought, tiredly.

Suen leaned in close. The smile was gone, the eyes blank. "There's a storm coming, and Hong Kong will look very different when it's over."

Killian frowned, puzzled. "I'm not sure what you mean, Professor."

"These are troubled times, Killian. Those who have sown the wind will reap the whirlwind, I fear. Not you, of course, Superintendent. I have every confidence you will do your duty."

Killian, stupid from exhaustion, nodded. "Yes, Professor."

Suen stepped back and held out a hand to his side, palm up. A much younger man hovering over his shoulder pressed a business card into Suen's open palm.

Smiling once again, Suen held the card in front of him with both hands and Killian took it, bowing his head slightly.

"Please don't hesitate to contact me if I can help, Superintendent."

"I can't imagine any reason for me to bother you, Professor. But thank you all the same," Killian said, slipping the card into his top pocket.

"You never know, Superintendent," Suen said, still smiling. "I can step in as a neutral intermediary in tricky situations, as you know. In any case, perhaps we'll see each other at mass one Sunday."

"Perhaps we will. Goodbye, Professor."

Suen was already turning to walk away and raised a hand in farewell, striding into the crowd in the direction of the front entrance, his young aide trailing a few steps behind.

TWENTY-FOUR

There was no one in the apartment when Killian got there. Mother would be at mahjong. Or the races. Was it Wednesday? He could hardly remember. Yes, it was Wednesday so race day.

And no Jun, of course. Always Jun. Had Mother called as she promised? He would ask her in the morning.

He put his boots in the shoe cupboard by the door and thought about heading to the kitchen to see if there was something to eat. He'd had only a bowl of instant noodles at the station that morning, shoveled into his mouth while he was writing the report on the night's demonstration.

Instead, he sat down on the living room couch, stared dully at the blank television screen, still tasting grit in his mouth and smelling petrol. He had showered and changed his uniform so it must be his imagination. Or just exhaustion.

Killian swung his feet up and lay back into the soft cushions.

Just for a moment, he thought. *Just for a moment.*

He closed his eyes.

* * *

When Killian woke, the room was dark. A blanket had been thrown over him, a pillow tucked under his head.

The flat was still except for the low hum of the dehumidifier. So was the street outside. Even Hong Kong had to sleep sometime. The room was almost totally black except for the glow from an appliance in the kitchen. Mother must have come back and decided to leave him there, switched off the lights, drawn the curtains.

What had awakened him?

A sound from the door. Someone was turning the handle. They had used a key to open it.

A swoosh came as the door sighed closed, then the click of the latch engaging. Swish of material. Muffled wheels on carpet. The change as they hit the parquet.

"Jun?" he called.

A gasp answered him.

"Who's there?" Jun called after a pause. "Gaw? Is that you?"

"Yes. Sorry. I must have fallen asleep."

"God. I thought . . ." Jun trailed off.

That the Ministry of State Security had come to get you? Killian thought but didn't say. He didn't want to start a fight.

"Here. Let me turn on the light," he offered.

"No. Don't. Mama will see it under the door. She's a light sleeper."

"I know. 'Mothers don't really sleep. They just rest their eyes,' right?"

"Yes. 'Because I have so much to do . . .'"

"'For my children.'" They said it—whispered it—together.

Both stifled a giggle.

"What time is it anyway?" Killian asked.

"3:00 A.M., I think. Or 3:30."

Killian wanted to ask where she had come from at this hour, but he stifled the impulse.

"What are you doing?"

"Dropping off my bag. I'll only be a minute."

"Come on, Jun. Sit down with me for a minute," Killian said. "I'm not going to arrest you, I promise."

No laugh came. But then he heard her pulling back the chair. The whisper of the felt coasters on the wood. Killian remembered attaching them. The downstairs neighbor, a fervent anti-Communist who hung a Taiwanese flag out of his window every year on October 10, had complained about the noise the chairs made. Killian smiled in the darkness. Mother loathed him. She was no fan of the party, but just let an outsider criticize "those mainlanders," then you'd better watch out.

"What?" Jun asked.

"What, what?"

"You're thinking of something. I can tell."

"I was thinking about the chairs and that guy downstairs. Do you remember when he came up to complain?"

"Of course. And Ma reacted by banging the chairs on the floor for the next week," Jun replied.

They laughed together.

"And then you bought the coasters for the chair legs. Always the peacemaker, eh, Gaw?"

"I hope so."

He heard a thunk, something heavy hitting the floor.

"What was that?" Killian asked.

"Just my backpack."

"What have you got in there, Jun? It sounds like rocks."

"Just stuff. Laptop. I came to drop it off."

A silence settled for a while, companionable. It made him ache for the old days when they would have been happy to sit like this, reading. Thinking.

But he couldn't afford to leave the silence unfilled. Killian had to grasp the opportunity before Jun slipped away. It felt urgent, a last chance.

"Why?" he asked.

"Why what?"

She sounded far away. What had she been thinking about?

"Why do you continue to go to the demonstrations when you know you can never win?"

"We can still win," Jun said.

"No, you can't. Beijing is passing the National Security Law on Saturday. That will be the end of the protests, believe me. These people don't play by Western rules, Jun."

"Which is exactly why we're out on the street, Killian."

Using his English name felt deliberate, as though Jun was trying to distance herself from him.

"That doesn't matter anymore. I know you think the police are the source of all evil. But it won't be us doing the rounding up. It'll be the Ministry of State Security."

"I know," Jun said.

"Yes. You didn't sound surprised."

"There have been rumors of this for a while."

"Of course, there have. You forced Beijing's hand. You must have known they couldn't—wouldn't—sit by and watch another year of riots."

"Protests," Jun corrected.

"Of increasingly violent protests. And now you've gotten them to react."

"You're saying it's our fault?"

"No. I'm trying to understand why you go on doing it when you know it's futile. When you knew all along it could come to this."

She was silent for a while. The refrigerator compressor started up with a small clunking noise. A distant siren sounded from the street.

"Someone once wrote that protest rarely achieves its stated aims. So-called success isn't the point," Jun said quietly.

Killian shook his head even though she couldn't see him in the dark. "If achieving your aims, the five demands or whatever, isn't the goal, then what is?"

"Protest that endures." Jun wasn't quite declaiming, but Killian knew she was reciting from memory. "It is moved by a hope far more modest than that of public success: Namely, the hope of preserving qualities in one's own heart and spirit that would be destroyed by acquiescence."

That's it? Killian wanted to shout. *That's your justification for all these years of chaos?* But almost against his will, the words resonated in his head. There was power there.

"Is that enough?" Killian asked. "Enough to justify the injuries, the chaos? Enough to die for?"

"Yes."

No hesitation. Again, Killian wanted to stand, grip her by the shoulders, and shake sense into her. Didn't she realize that it was going to ruin others' lives, whatever it was she was planning? How could she be so selfish? Didn't she care about him? About Mother?

He tried to marshal his thoughts, knowing this was his last chance to keep her from going out the door and disappearing again. The words and phrases formed and fell apart. But nothing felt right.

"Can I ask you a question?" Jun broke into his thoughts.

"What?"

"You asked me a question. Can I ask you one?"

"Of course," Killian said. "What is it?"

"It's the same question you asked me. Why? Why do you stay in the police? You know the Force is turning into a machine for crushing protest. And now it will be worse. Far worse. You'll be doing the dirty work for China, tracking down dissidents, handing them over to the MSS thugs for torture, or worse. Like that poor man Ngai. You know that and still you don't resign. Why?"

Now it was Killian's turn to be silent. She was right. But she was wrong too. It was complicated. Much more complicated than that simple yes or no.

"Wouldn't you rather I stayed? That there were good people on the inside?"

"No. It's too late for that."

Again, no hesitation. *The certainty of youth*, Killian thought.

"I'm not going to resign. There's still a lot I can do. But I'll know when the time is right. Trust me."

She didn't reply. Her phone flashed momentarily, lighting her up. She was dressed in black, of course. A backpack was on one side, a wheeled carry-on bag on the other, the handle extended.

"I've got to go. Tell Mama I love her," Jun said. She stood up. Killian stood too.

"That sounds final."

"Don't be melodramatic, Killian."

"So that's it? You're willing to let us burn with you?"

"What do you mean?" Jun asked sharply.

"I mean that you'll torch our lives too. Have you thought of that? When you get sent to some camp in Qinghai for thirty years."

"Oh. That."

Jun sounded almost relieved.

"You're so stubborn, Jun," Killian said.

"It must run in the family, Killian." She used his English name again. The third time. It felt like an insult. "I know you. You're just as likely to end up in Qinghai as I am. You won't resign from the Force. Ever. But you will do what's right. I know that too. And one day you'll refuse an order to arrest someone. Or beat a confession out of them. And then they'll send you away too."

Killian heard her slide the deadbolt open, then turn the door handle.

He had nothing to say that would keep her.

"Goodbye, Gaw. I love you," Jun said.

"Jun . . ."

The door closed and he was alone.

* * *

When Killian woke again, the flat was empty, Ma's bedroom door open. He lay there for a while, brooding about his talk with Jun.

What had he done, letting her go out into the night, headed God knew where? Not that he could have prevented her, short of physical restraint. How though? Handcuffs? And then what? Lock her in the flat? It was absurd.

But maybe there was still something he could do.

He would message Zen, tell him to find Jun as soon as he could. Beg, grovel on his knees, whatever was needed. She had made it clear last night that she was on course for disaster, and he—reluctant to intervene in her life, distracted by his own problems—had left it far, far too long. He had to act now or risk losing her forever.

Then he would go back to Tin Shui Wai. As ordered. And then, yes, he would bury the case like a good boy. Like Tsang had asked. And he would take whatever new job they offered him.

Killian swung out of bed and stumbled into the bathroom, flipping on the radio as he lathered up. Some morning DJ was blathering happy platitudes. Traffic updates followed.

He scraped for a while, staring at his face, the bloodshot, exhausted eyes, then looked away. A holiday would help. A holiday from policing. From this police force. From just wearing the uniform. Wearing the hatred. A long break.

He was in the shower, radio on. RTHK. Weather. Twenty-seven degrees. Unseasonably cool. Rain was expected later in the day. Then the news. More speculation about the announcement at the liaison office. An item about a wild boar riding the MTR and swimming in the fountain pool in front of HSBC headquarters in Central.

He began shampooing his hair, then froze.

". . . police shooting incident on November 31 of last year."

Killian pulled the shower curtain back to hear better. A woman was speaking in Cantonese.

"We offer our thanks to the Lord Buddha for his intervention. And to the medical team who cared for him. Our prayers have been answered. Now we only ask that you leave us alone."

A translator came on, speaking over her in English. Then the DJ was back, reading, his tone slightly bored.

"Doctors at Queen Mary Hospital say that Mr. Shek has many challenges ahead of him, including a lengthy rehabilitation program after being in a coma for such a long period. But they added that he seems to have suffered no long-term mental or physical damage from the shooting itself, which is extremely rare in victims of gunshots to the head.

"A police representative contacted by RTHK said that, while Shek's emergence from his coma was good news, charges against the fifteen-year-old hadn't been ruled out.

"While it is of course extremely regrettable that the young man suffered this injury, a lengthy investigation showed that the blame for the shooting lies entirely with him and his fellow rioters who attempted . . ."

Killian climbed out of the shower and switched off the radio, then stayed there, head bowed, bracing himself against the mirror, shampoo suds dripping down his face and neck, his soul aflutter.

"Thank you," he said. "Thank you, thank you, thank you."

Was this what was meant by a state of grace?

He lifted his head, catching his eyes in the mirror again.

He grinned at himself, joy bubbling up.

Not the face of a killer after all.

Would Jun now forgive him? She had to, didn't she? He vowed to himself that the next time they met he would tell her about his visit to the boy's family. Surely, if even the boy's mother could forgive him, his own sister would?

Surely.

* * *

Killian was closing the front door of the flat when he felt his phone buzzing.

It was Chan at forensics.

"Mr. Chan, how are you? Rested I trust?" Killian asked.

"It's about the luminol test you ordered," Chan said.

"Sorry. Which test?"

"The test of the objects found near the body. The 452 objects, sir," Chan said. He wasn't happy.

"Right, sorry. Of course. Did you get any hits?" He picked up his back-pack, slung it over his shoulder.

"We did have one positive result. Confirmed blood traces on a necklace," Chan said.

"I don't recall a necklace," Killian said.

"The blood DNA was a match."

"It matched the victim's blood?"

"Yes, sir."

Killian restrained the impulse to punch the air. "That's fantastic, Chan. Good work."

"Thank you, sir." Chan could have been reading the weather.

"Is there anything else?" Killian asked.

"No, sir. Except, I . . ." He trailed off.

"What is it, Chan?"

Silence.

"Chan? Are you there?"

"Yes, sir. I was just wondering, if this luminol test does not produce a new lead, will you close the investigation?"

"We never close a murder investigation until it's solved, you know that Chan."

"Yes, sir. But this one is different. Political, like SS Weng said at the meeting. I thought you might do things differently."

Killian felt a spike of irritation.

"Absolutely not, Chan. You know that."

"Yes, sir. I thought you'd say that. But can I say, sir, if I was conducting this investigation . . ."

"Which you are not."

"Which I am not, sir. But if I was, I would look more closely at the other items recovered from the site."

"What are you talking about, Chan?" It came out more sharply than he meant. "Didn't you just tell me you reviewed all 452 items found around the body and the only item of interest is this necklace?"

"Yes, sir."

"So, there's no other result I need to worry about among those items?"

"Yes, sir."

A sigh from Chan. He sounded almost exasperated.

"Is there anything else you want to tell me?"

"No, sir. There's nothing else I can tell you. Goodbye sir."

"Chan I still don't . . ."

But he had already hung up. Killian shook his head, irritated. What on earth had gotten into the man? He must be even more exhausted than usual.

It didn't matter. They had a concrete lead. Finally.

TWENTY-FIVE

Killian stood in front of the whiteboards, the other three sitting on their office chairs in a semicircle behind him. He shook his head in disgust, then turned.

"We've got to take a fresh look," he said.

Riding the MTR to Tian Shui Wai from Central, Killian had pondered what to do. He'd promised Eddie Tsang to shut down the case. But that was before he'd known about Chan's new lead. He'd compromise, he decided: They'd take one last crack at solving the murder, then put everything into the deep freeze as ordered if nothing turned up. All well before Saturday's announcement. No one could object to that, surely.

"To be fair, boss, we've had some other things to think about," Lin said.

"Things in Tin Shui Wai are relatively quiet now though, aren't they?" Killian asked.

Lin nodded. "Almost back to normal."

When Killian had arrived at the station, a crew of constables was out in the forecourt, daubing blue paint on the façade and a crane-equipped truck was replacing two of the blue-and-white barriers. Otherwise, it was as though the madness of two nights ago had never happened. Shoppers strolled by on their way to the wet market two streets down or the Tin Yiu Shopping Mall next door. The Public Works Department still hadn't repaired the pavement. But the bricks had been cleared from the streets, and the graffiti—a priority—was all painted over.

"Once they knew Ngai wasn't at the station, a lot of the crowd left," Killian said. "And even the frontliners didn't try and rally people the next day. Not after they nearly blew themselves and half the protesters up with that petrol drum. Which is just as well. We have a hard deadline from SS Weng," Killian waved at the whiteboards behind him, "Midnight tonight. As of Saturday, the case is closed."

Groans echoed around the room.

"And that's exactly why we have to start all over again, reviewing everything from scratch," Killian said.

More groans followed. Killian held up his hands to silence them.

"I did get some news that may help, though," he added.

Killian opened a file on the desk in front of him and pulled out a photo mounted on an A4 sheet of paper.

"Who recognizes that?" Killian asked.

"I do, boss," Blue said. "A Christian necklace. It was one of the items I sent for the luminol test."

"Tell me, Chief Inspector, were you raised in a religious family? Buddhist? Christian?" Killian asked.

"No, sir," Blue replied, shaking her head. She looked puzzled. "My mother was raised in China and still thinks Mao was right about everything, including religion. Opiate of the masses. Superstition."

"How about you, Lin?" Killian asked.

"It looks a bit like the beads my mother sometimes uses when she's chanting sutras. Helps her count the number she's done," Lin said.

"That's exactly right, Lin. It's a rosary. Catholic prayer beads."

"That's why it has the cross," Blue said, looking mortified. "Sorry, boss. I didn't recognize it. Thought it was just a bead necklace with a cross on it."

"Many people probably wouldn't. Most of the Christians in Hong Kong are Protestant. They don't believe in using rosaries."

"I should have known it was something religious from the cross," Blue muttered.

"It was your idea to do the luminol test and now we know the blood is a match to the victim. We have a solid connection," Killian said.

"Fantastic, sir," Yeong said. "It's about time we got a break in this case." He frowned. "But what exactly does it mean for the investigation?"

"It means we go over all our evidence again, specifically the car registrations, looking for anything, however tiny, that could connect to this rosary. Flag anything Christian. Red flag anything Catholic."

"How do I tell the difference?" Yeong asked.

"Saint names probably mean Catholic. But don't worry about it. Let's see what we get and we can sort it out afterward."

Killian glanced at his watch.

"We'd better get started," he said. "We have less than thirteen hours left."

* * *

Killian sat at his desk, a plastic ruler in hand, going over the list of license plates, line by line. The second coffee of the morning steamed on his desk.

The others were there too, heads down, each reviewing their sheets in silence. The private and commercial vehicles had been separated—Blue and Lin working on the private list while Yeong and Killian handled the commercial vehicles. Killian knew he had to stay extra vigilant. Yeong had improved, but he was still too lazy to be a consistently good investigator.

Killian finished one page and flipped it over to the next.

His phone buzzed. It was the landline.

"Tong," he answered.

"Superintendent, it's Doctor Poon," came the familiar voice.

"Doctor, what can I do for you?"

"I have some good news, I believe," Poon said.

"I'd like some good news. For a change."

"I had a message overnight from Dundee. They expect to have a finished model of the head by 9:30 A.M. their time today. About 4:30 this afternoon here. I will forward the results to you by email as soon as I have them."

Killian was silent for a moment, dumbstruck.

"But you said there was no money for a reconstruction, Doctor."

Poon laughed—a creaky sound, clearly enjoying Killian's astonishment. "Circumstances changed, Superintendent. I sent it off soon after we talked."

"What circumstances? Did you win a triple trio at Sha Tin?"

"Certainly not," Poon replied primly. "I never bet. I have a discretionary fund for exceptional cases. I chose to exercise it."

Killian doubted that. The amount was too large for any civil service discretionary fund. He guessed that the mercurial Poon had probably paid for it himself. Poon could afford it—his grandfather had founded the Victoria Bus and Tramway, now a ten-billion-dollar conglomerate. If Poon chose to put a little of his fortune toward public service, Killian wasn't going to argue.

"That is fantastic news. Absolutely fantastic. Thank you, Doctor."

"Thank the discretionary fund," Poon said.

"Thank you, discretionary fund. And you say that the results . . ." Killian began, but Poon had already hung up.

Elated but tamping it down, Killian turned back to the printouts.

He'd already reviewed the last entry of the day for April 2, logged at 4:59, when they closed the gates. Civil service hours. The staff would have been battling to get through the door at the stroke of five.

He flipped the page over.

April 3
0946. RT34092; Joy Luck Mansions; Toyota Hiace, 2015
0947. YW050493; Lai On Building Contractor; Toyota Hilux, 2010
0948. CD090807; Dah Sing Bank, Queens Road East, Central; Kia Sorento, 2017
0949. HT33209; Oxford English School; Honda City, 2014

0949. TT62213; Green Cross Milk Co.; Hyundai Grand Starex, 2014
0954. HR3002; Mok Man Cleaning Services; SsangYong Musso Grand, 2018
0957. GG44355; YMCA; Ford Transit 250, 2017
0958. WY777234; Gum Fatt Hair Salons; Suzuki Alto, 2018
0959. RT99394; Body Works Gym; Volkswagen Transporter, 2018
1000. DF33567; St. Joseph's High School, Kwun Tong; Nissan Titan, 2016

Killian shook his head, then picked up his pen and noted the St. Joseph's entry on his pad. He had caught another Catholic high school—St. Francis's in Yuen Long—on his second read through. This was the kind of police work that everyone hated—plodding, repetitive, exhausting—but was the core of the job.

He put the pen down and massaged his eyes.

A shrill bleating broke the silence. His mobile phone buzzed—5858, an HQ number. Killian ignored it.

At 12:05, Killian turned his chair to face the center of the room.

"Okay. Time's up," he announced.

All three of his team swiveled around in their chairs to face him, sitting in a circle.

"Is everyone finished?" Killian asked.

A row of nodding heads answered him.

"Good. Let's hear what you've got. Lin, how about you?" Killian said.

"Nothing much new, sir. Only a couple of repeat visits that we missed before. We've already called all the rest. That's it for the private cars, sir," Lin replied.

"Okay. Chief Inspector Choi?" Killian said.

Blue looked down at her notebook.

"I've got the same two repeats, sir. I also went back and matched some of the most expensive vehicles to the period for which we have tape, looking for possible Triad connections. Or drugs. Or both. Didn't get much. Three possibly worth a follow-up. Early twenties in a Ferrari, another in an Aston Martin, the third a Maybach," Blue said.

"Not just rich daddies?" Yeong asked.

"Probably. But worth checking," Blue responded.

"Okay. Let's check them anyway. Inspector Yeong, what about you?" Killian asked.

Yeong picked up his notebook.

"I found four churches. Three Protestant. One Baptist. One Pentecostal. Something called the Korean Church of the Holy Spirit. And the Church of Jesus Christ of Latter-day Saints, whatever that is," Yeong said.

"Mormons. That matches what I've got too. Go on," Killian said.

"One Catholic church, I think. You said saint something means Catholic, right?" Yeong asked.

"Sometimes," Killian replied.

"Okay, then that's Saint Paul's from Tsing Yi. And one other," Yeong added.

Killian realized he had missed Saint Paul's.

"What's the last one?"

"It's not a school or a church. Green Cross Milk," Yeong said.

Something clicked at the back of Killian's head. Of course. The Cistercian monastery where they made milk and bread and sold it to the public. Killian had missed the connection, and Yeong had seen it. He'd misjudged the man. Not so lazy after all.

"The monks have a place on Fu Tei Mountain. A farm. They make the milk there. Or they used to. Most of it is processed in a factory in Castle Peak now. But there's still some production at the monastery itself," Yeong explained. "The same van showed up twice in two days."

"That's excellent work, Inspector Yeong," Killian said.

Yeong beamed. "Thank you, sir. There's also a place for teaching priests there. Much bigger. All on the same piece of land. It's possible they have access to the Green Cross vehicles."

"The seminary," Killian said.

"Yes, sir." Yeong looked down at his notes. "Our Lady of Lourdes seminary."

Killian shook his head. It was only the vaguest of possibilities. But it was all they had.

"Congratulations again, Yeong. Now let's swap papers and do one last run-through. Then we go out and ask questions," Killian said.

Back at his desk, Killian glanced at the list of non-Catholic churches and put them aside. They'd go back once they had checked the Catholics. He'd have to check the Mormons. All he knew about them was that they liked a big cathedral and choirs. Maybe they used rosaries too.

But a seminary. There'd be plenty of rosaries there. Unless there'd been a memo he'd missed.

Father Dec would know.

Killian looked it up on Wikipedia.

> Our Lady of Lourdes is a Catholic seminary located near the village of Mo Yan Jai in the northern New Territories, Hong Kong. It was founded as a nunnery in 1902 by the French order Les Petites Soeurs du Sacré-Coeur on fifty acres of land donated by Pierre Le Cartouche, a wealthy French doctor.

He skimmed forward: Used as a hospital for Japanese troops during WWII . . . Cistercian monastery established in a remote part of the property in 1950 after the monastery outside Qingdao was destroyed by the Communist Party. The monastery is known in Hong Kong for its Green Cross milk, French Country Bakery, and triple-strength Abbot's Ale beer . . . new building added in 1964, Hong Kong's first seminary . . . opened by Bishop Finlay MacIntyre. Nunnery closed in 1996 when the last nun died. Converted to a home for retired priests. Student numbers at the seminary dropped steadily in the 1990s and 2000s.

The same old story. A sad story if one believed the church was God's direct representative on earth, as Father Dec did. Anything for Mother Church. Even if it meant getting involved in worldly affairs. Getting involved with men like Suen.

Killian thought of the moment in the HQ lobby when he'd met Suen. He had the politician's trick of stepping forward into someone's space, almost uncomfortably close, staring right into their eyes, hanging onto their words. Then the hand on the shoulder for just long enough to establish intimacy. Old tricks. But they worked.

There was no doubt Suen was charismatic. And shrewd. He had managed to appear independent while always saying what Beijing wanted to hear. And all that even though he was religious. Not just in name either, but an active Church member since his early twenties. Lay deacon. Regular reader of the homily. Fundraiser.

All that ostentatious public sanctity. It might be Killian's suspicious police mind at work, but his gut told him Suen was too good to be true. Especially since that last encounter at Police HQ. Reap the whirlwind. Those cold, blank eyes.

Father Dec would always want another Catholic chief executive, even though the last two had been disasters, one still in jail, the other in disgrace. Not that Father Dec could make any difference to the choice. That would be entirely on the old men in Beijing. The party elders. Boot-black hair, slack, toad faces, rheumy eyes. A conclave of geriatrics. They had much in common, the Church and the party. Obsessively secretive, run by old men, convinced they were keepers of the sole truth. And, of course, utterly ruthless.

Killian shook his head; not his problem and he shouldn't waste time thinking about it. He pushed back from the computer and got up to refill his coffee cup.

Idle thoughts and idle hands do the devil's work. Another of Da's favorites. Echoes on echoes.

TWENTY-SIX

JUN

King left the flat at 7:30 that morning. She didn't say where she was going.

There were no books. Or TV. People stayed on their phones all day, getting up only to plug them into the wall to recharge. Or eat lunch. Instant noodles. Egg.

An old-fashioned, blue plastic radio sat on the kitchen counter. It was just like the one they'd had for years in the Sheung Wan flat. Mama would listen to the government radio station while she was cooking. Radio Television Hong Kong. Supposedly modeled on the BBC. She said it helped with her English.

Just before 1:00 P.M., Jun switched it on and the smooth Oxbridge tones of the newsreader rolled out:

> The one o'clock news, read by Alan Jenkins.
>
> The Liaison Office of the People's Republic has confirmed there will be an important announcement regarding Hong Kong tomorrow at 3 P.M. The announcement will be made from the Liaison Headquarters in Sai Ying Pun. Police have issued a warning to the public of possible traffic delays due to public order incidents.
>
> "We appeal to members of the public to avoid the area between the hours of 1:00 and 3:00 P.M. tomorrow afternoon,"

said police spokesperson Sheung Li Mei. "There will be a heavy police presence and attempts to disrupt the announcement will be met with the strongest possible countermeasures."

While there has been no official word of the details of the announcement, it is widely believed that it will concern the likely enactment of a new Security Law for Hong Kong.

Under the agreement between Britain and China reached before the handover in 1997, Hong Kong's lawmaking body LegCo was supposed to pass a National Security Law for Hong Kong. The first time the government attempted to pass the law in 2003, hundreds of thousands took to the streets to protest, eventually leading to the resignation of the then-chief executive, Tong Chee Wah. Repeated attempts over the years to table the law have led to similar reactions.

It now appears that Beijing has lost its patience, and will sidestep the issue by passing the law at China's National People's Congress, currently meeting in the capital. The new law will fundamentally alter life in the city, removing the right to assemble, drastically curtailing free speech, and allowing mainland security forces free reign to operate.

While it is unclear whether the new law would breach the terms of the 1997 . . .

Jun reached over to switch it off. The silence echoed, the sprawled shapes of the others not moving, eyes still fixed on their phones. But they had been listening. And probably feeling the same way she did.

It made what they were doing seem more official. Legitimate. Even hearing it read out by the pompous Englishman. As though the rest of the world was listening. Watching. As though what they were going to do really might make a difference.

TWENTY-SEVEN
KILLIAN

Killian held out until 4:20 before checking his email to see if Poon had emailed.

Nothing.

He was alone in the ops room. He had sent Lin and Yeong to query the two Catholic schools about the landfill visits. Face-to-face was always better.

Blue was at home. Her boy—Cheers, his name was Cheers—came home from preschool at 3:00. Killian had explained about Poon and the reconstruction and she said she would be back at the station by 5:00.

This would be their last gasp before the announcement. Already, the mood in the city was tense with crowds of young men gathered at street corners, the usual precursor to a protest.

Did they have any idea of what was coming? How fast things would change? The old men in Beijing didn't fool around. Once the new Security Law was passed, known dissenters would be taken in, probably overnight. There'd be no more Lennon Wall. No more games of cat and mouse with the PTU squads. No more lawyers, bail hearings, appeals. All gone. This was going to be a new Hong Kong. Chinese Hong Kong. No. Beijing's Hong Kong. The party's Hong Kong.

Killian was no different from them. Trapped. Impotent. Caught up in changes far bigger than himself.

He thought of Jun. He was just as powerless, couldn't stop her from carrying out whatever pointless act of defiance she was involved in. His own sister.

He checked his phone. Again. He had messaged Zen asking—begging—him to find Jun.

Still nothing. He typed a message directly on Telegram.

Z: this is me groveling again. please please reply. very worried about J

He stood up and stared at the whiteboard, trying to distract himself. But his mind kept skittering back to Jun, her infuriating stubbornness, the unshakeable conviction that she was right. He should have done something, anything to stop her.

Killian reached down and picked up his coffee cup, cradling it, then, without thinking, hurled it against the wall. The cup splintered, a brown stain blooming.

He stood still, staring at the wall.

Killian shook his head and walked over to the sink to get a rag.

A faint ping. He turned back.

Email. He poked at the mouse, typed in his password. A new message from Poon. Five attachments and a link. A brief note:

Superintendent. We got our money's worth. Go get him!

He clicked on the first attachment. A sharp jolt of disappointment. It was a blurry photograph of the reconstructed head, sitting on a desk, turned to three-quarter profile. The eyes were glassy, the hair shiny, the skin matte. What was Poon thinking? This was like a bad waxwork, the features muddy. It could be anyone.

He clicked on the next attachment, drew in a breath in surprise. This was a computer CGI image, but startlingly lifelike, the eyes alive, the mouth parted as though he was about to speak, cheeks showing a tiny tinge of pink.

He leaned forward to look more closely. The bottom teeth were visible, slightly protruding, yellow, uneven. Had they been able to reconstruct that from the stumps the murderer had left? Whatever they'd done, Poon was right. This was a real person. A recognizable person.

He clicked the next attachment. The hair in the previous picture was cut short, almost a crew cut. Here it was much longer, receding at the top of the scalp, combed over, the sides covering the ears, shot through with streaks of grey. A vain middle-aged man's hair.

The next picture showed the face with a scraggly mustache. Then with a little chin beard, all white.

What else could they do? Killian clicked again and stared. The previous faces had been healthy-looking. This was the face of a sick man, ravaged by ill health. Or perhaps just abuse. The cheeks were sunken, the eyes bloodshot, broken veins crisscrossing the nose. Even the lips looked dry and chapped. It was the face of a defeated man, a man who'd given up.

There was also a link in the email that took him to a Dundee University server. He clicked and the first picture loaded. There was a row of pull-down menus at the top:

Age, Weight, Hair, Facial Hair, Health.

Killian opened the Age menu and found a sliding bar. He used the mouse to push it to the left. The face changed as he moved the bar, skin tightening, wrinkles disappearing. Even some hope seemed to appear in his eyes. He pushed back the other way and the face collapsed into age, everything sagging, a pout of disappointment forming, resentment in the eyes. It was eerie.

A click on the weight tab and the cheeks swelled out, rippling bulges of fat appearing under the chin. Even the ears seemed to grow plumper.

Enough. This was just fooling around. Killian forwarded the email to his personal account, then opened the attachment on his phone. On the small screen, the CGI effect was almost invisible. They looked like real photographs.

He called Lin.

"Boss?"

"Where are you?"

"Between one Saint and the next."

"Nothing so far?"

"Nothing at all. Routine. They said they were disposing of some sets from their . . ." the flipping of paper, ". . . Nativity play last year. Something to do with Christmas."

"Okay. You'll have to go back."

"Why?"

"I'm emailing you some pictures of the victim. You have work email on your phone?"

"Yes. Of course."

"Show them around. No copies for anyone. And strictly no forwarding. Keep it vague. See if anyone recognizes him."

"Yes, boss. Show the picture. Police interested in talking to him as part of their inquiries, that kind of thing?"

"Exactly."

"Got it."

"Good. Any result, report to me ASAP."

The door opened as Killian hung up. Blue. She raised her eyebrows, looking at the stained wall.

"What happened there?"

"Too much coffee." Killian waved a hand dismissively. "How's your boy?"

"He's fine, thanks. Did you get the reconstruction?"

"I did. Come and see."

Blue nodded appreciatively when she finished paging through the pictures.

"We should give it to all the papers, get TVB and Pearl to . . ."

"We can't. Orders from the forty-seventh floor."

"Why not?"

Killian stood, picked up his car keys from the desk. "Come on. I'll explain it to you in the car."

"Where are we going?"

"To show the pictures. At the seminary."

"But I thought we'd been ordered not to."

Killian shrugged. "They don't know about the reconstruction yet. Poon did it on his own initiative and didn't tell anyone else. If this is a dead end too, then everything goes into deep freeze, as ordered."

She nodded. "Ask forgiveness, not permission. I get it. That will work if we solve the case. But if nothing turns up and they find out we were still investigating . . ."

"There'll be hell to pay, yes. Probably. But while there's still a chance of solving this, we can't let things go. I can't, I mean."

She nodded again, but Killian frowned.

"You don't have to come with me, Blue. In fact, maybe it's better if you don't."

"And miss all the fun? No chance."

"You're sure?"

"Absolutely. I'll just blame it all on you, boss. Say you ordered me to come."

"Excellent idea. Meanwhile, let's chase down this last lead and then . . ."

"Deep freeze, as ordered."

"Right."

Blue got up.

"Okay, but I have to make a rest stop first, boss."

"Got it. Meet you at the car."

The door banged behind her and he was alone in the operations room, staring at the big whiteboard and its multiple dead ends. This was by far the best lead they'd had. But he felt like a dog chasing cars. What happened if he caught the car?

TWENTY-EIGHT

When they crested the hill and the valley came into view below them, Killian pulled the Land Cruiser to the side of the road and stopped. The lush green pastures stretched away and upward, cows dotting the fields, the higher slopes heavily forested and draped with wisps of mist.

The road ran straight through the middle of the valley, disappearing upward into the trees on the far side, perhaps six kilometers away. A cluster of buildings sat in the saddle, dominated by an ugly four-story glass-and-concrete structure. A big passenger coach was parked in front of the building along with twenty or so cars. Forty meters away was a church built from white stone, English Gothic, definitely colonial. A little farther down the road was a much older structure, built when the absence of electric fans or air-conditioning dictated design, high ceilings, wide verandas circling each of its three levels, the muted redbrick at home in the landscape.

At the far end of the valley where the road disappeared into the trees, there was another cluster of buildings. They were shielded by the forest and all single-story except for what looked like a barn. The spire of another church poked up above the treetops.

"I wouldn't mind contemplating the mysteries of the universe there for a while," Killian said, nodding toward the monastery.

Blue nodded.

"They've got all the necessities of life. Milk. Bread. They even make their own honey."

"Don't forget the beer. And the odd T-bone."

"You're a White man at heart, boss, however good your Cantonese is," Blue said, smiling.

"At stomach, maybe," Killian said.

He put the car into gear.

* * *

The dean of the seminary shook his head, the neon light reflecting off his shaved scalp. He was bent over Killian's phone, swiping through the photographs.

"Never seen him before. What is this about?" His tone was abrupt.

"We urgently need to speak to this man in regard to an ongoing investigation," Killian said.

"Not about a crime, surely. Not here?"

"He would be of material help in a murder inquiry, Father Leung. That's all we are permitted to disclose."

The priest shook his head again, his lips pursed with disapproval. He was younger than Killian had anticipated, in his late thirties, dressed in a checked shirt and jeans, looking more ready to attend a Cantopop concert than impart the mysteries of the Catechism.

"You're wasting your time, Superintendent, let me assure you. Apart from anything else, we have a very heavy flow through here. The seminarians themselves of course. Twenty or thirty boarders, some here for a term, some for a year or more. Plus visiting lecturers, priests from all over Asia on refresher courses, some from Rome itself. Then there's the lay staff. Cooks, cleaners, maintenance. Do you plan to show the picture to every one of them?"

"If we need to. What about the monastery?"

"What about it?"

"Do we need to make a special arrangement to talk to someone?"

The priest smirked.

"They don't take a vow of silence, Superintendent. The rule is they only speak if they have to. Or if they have something important to say."

"That sounds like a pretty good rule. We should probably enforce that at the Tin Shui Wai station too," Killian said.

Leung pursed his lips again. "The police could benefit from following their own rules, if you ask me. Or perhaps the Ten Commandments."

Killian felt his jaw clench again. He forced a smile. "Do you mean we should tear down our graven images? Or are you worried we'll be coveting one of your cows?"

A deeper frown.

"I'm talking about the brutal beatings of children, as you're perfectly well aware."

Was there a special penalty for punching a priest? Five hundred Hail Marys a day for life?

"What about the old nunnery?" Blue cut in. "What's that used for?"

"Overflow accommodation if our dormitories here are full. But mostly it houses retired clergy. It's peaceful here, as you can see."

The priest turned away, but Killian stepped into the man's line of sight and patted him on the shoulder. He recoiled as though he had been struck.

"Thanks for your help, Father. We'll see ourselves out."

No reply.

At the door, Killian turned.

"One last thing. Have you been posted here long, Father?"

"Seven months."

"In that case, is there someone we could talk to who's been here for longer? Has some institutional memory?" he asked.

"My secretary. Mrs. Chow. The office on the left."

Another shaking head. This time the neon lighting bounced off a black helmet of hair that looked as though it had been shellacked into place.

"No. He's not one of ours."

Mrs. Chow took off her reading glasses and handed the phone back.

"You're sure?"

Her sharp eyes rested on Killian for a moment, and she frowned with exasperation as though he'd asked a silly question.

"Yes. He's too old to be a student. And he's not one of the lecturers. I know the permanent ones of course. And I book all the temps in myself."

"Do you have photos of the lecturers?" Blue asked.

"We do. But you'll have to get permission from the archbishop's office if you want to see them."

Which, he'd bet a month's salary, they would never give.

"But you're sure he hasn't been teaching here?"

She nodded emphatically.

"Absolutely certain, as I said."

"How far back can you be confident of that?"

"Five years. At least."

There was no doubting her. It was her kingdom, and she knew every corner. And inhabitant.

"And the staff?"

"Even more certain if anything. We only have, let me see," she paused, contemplated the ceiling for a moment, then directed her gaze back at them. "Two men working here in his age bracket. They get too old for maintenance or the kitchen. Can't take the physical wear and tear. And the men don't like to do the cleaning. Leave that to the women. What's he supposed to have done anyway?"

Killian ran through his homily again. Important inquiry. Not permitted.

She raised a carefully penciled-in eyebrow.

"Is he homeless? He looks perfectly healthy in the first few photos, but much the worse for wear in the last."

"Something like that." Killian closed his notebook. "At the monastery, we just ask anyone for the head monk, do we?"

Blue also closed her notebook and replaced the pen in her top pocket.

Mrs. Chow laughed, a low, throaty chuckle.

"Your faces are a treat. They're not going to bite you. They're not saints. Just sinners like the rest of us, but trying to do something about it."

Saints and sinners.

Mrs. Chow chuckled again, genuinely amused. Hard not to share it. Killian smiled back.

"Thank you for your help, Mrs. Chow. What about the nunnery? Who should we ask for there?"

"Sister Evangeline. Her office is the first door on the right as you enter."

At the nunnery they found Sister Evangeline in her office and showed her the photo.

"No."

Another shaking head. The nun was a Filipina in her mid-forties wearing a voluminous white habit, her hair hidden under a wimple. Killian closed his notebook.

She handed him back his phone, shaking her head again. "Sorry."

He let out a sigh of disappointment.

"It's been at least three weeks," Sister Evangeline said.

"What?"

She shrugged.

"Maybe a month. I'd have to check."

"Sorry?" Blue this time, both of them not quite able to process. The nun looked at them, puzzled by their expressions.

"I said no, he's not been here for some weeks. But that's not unusual. He has family in China, I believe."

A beat, then Killian spoke.

"You're saying this man was here until a few weeks ago?"

She nodded. “Certainly. I’d have to check for the exact date.”

“He’s been living here?”

“Yes. Room 305. He retired early last year. From a parish in the Philippines, I believe. Again, I’d have to check the exact date.”

“What is his name?”

Blue’s voice had risen half an octave with excitement.

“Deacon Chiu. Chiu Lok Mun.”

“You’re sure?”

“Of course, though I’ve never seen him with a beard. Or mustache. And if truth be told, he’s more like the last photograph than the first.”

Blue and Killian exchanged a glance.

“You said his room number was 305.” Killian could hear the tension in his own voice. He cleared his throat.

Another nod. She was clearly taken aback by their excitement.

“Is he in some sort of trouble? He’s a quiet soul, rarely comes out of his room, even for meals.”

“The room hasn’t been given to anyone else?”

“Of course not. We’re not a boarding house. These rooms are their homes.”

“And all his belongings are still in there?”

“Yes.”

“We’d like to see the room, please.”

Blue took a step forward. But Sister Evangeline frowned, folded her arms.

“I don’t think that would be right. It’s his home, as I say. We’d need his permission before I could open it for you.”

“The chief inspector wasn’t asking, Sister. This is a murder investigation. The room is a potential crime scene. We don’t need permission.”

Her hand flew to her mouth. “Murder!”

“Yes. We’ll take a look from the outside while we’re waiting for the forensics team to arrive.” Blue pulled out her mobile.

“Let’s go up and have a look.”

She led them to a broad hallway lined with doors. They turned left, heading for a set of stairs. Ahead of them an ancient priest dressed in a white singlet and striped pajama bottoms, hunched back poking up, was heaving himself forward on a walker, stopping to catch his breath after each step.

"Afternoon, Father," the nun shouted as they passed. No response. Killian saw the man's body tense as he steeled himself for another step, arms like an egret's legs, bony yellow tubes, swollen joint in the middle.

"Do you sleep in the building?"

"No. This is only for priests."

She pushed open the door to the stairwell, marched through. Killian caught it as it swung back and held it for Blue.

"What happens if there's an emergency?"

"The other sisters and myself are just next door in the women's dormitory. And they each have mobile phones. The special ones for the elderly. With the big letters and the SOS button."

They began climbing the broad stairs, Sister Evangeline taking them two at a time, her skirts swinging.

"Did the deacon have one?"

"No. He was too young. Only in his late sixties, I think. But I'm sure he had a mobile phone. Everyone has one these days."

The door to 305 bore a small metal slot in the center, the white paint flaking off it. Inside was a white piece of cardboard with his name in neat handwriting. Deacon Chiu Lok Mun. The nun reached into the front of her habit and pulled out a large bunch of keys.

Killian held up a hand.

"Wait."

He reached into his coat pocket and pulled out a pair of surgical gloves, then took the keys from her. They were each marked with a room number. He sorted through until he found 305, turned the lock, then reached forward with a thumb and forefinger to turn the knob. The door swung open, creaking wearily. The smell of whisky and sweat. Stale cigarette smoke. Carbolic soap.

A long, narrow room, high window at one end with a view of the mountain slope, iron-frame single bed at the other, crucifix overhead. Wooden floorboards painted white. A chair sat next to the bed serving as a side table, a half-full glass of water and a paperback book folded open lying on the seat. A wash basin to the left of the bed, above it a white medicine cabinet, next to it a plywood clothes cupboard. The doors of the cupboard were wide open. There was one worn red-leather armchair next to the window, beside it a small table on which sat a green reading lamp. Also a half-full whisky bottle.

Killian squatted down, peered under the bed. A cardboard box labeled Famous Grouse. A picture of a preening bird. Whisky.

He reached around and flipped the heavy black Bakelite switch next to the door. The overhead neons flickered on. Four white shirts hung on the left side of the cupboard along with a black vest fitted with a priest's dog collar. The shelves on the right side held socks, underclothes, singlets, stacked trousers. A battered black suitcase stood on the floor of the cupboard. It was unzipped and empty, the top hanging open.

All very neat. No signs of a kidnapping.

Killian stood.

"The cleaners?"

"Twice a week."

"Even when there's no one occupying the room?"

"Yes, though they'd be much quicker about it. Just a quick mop and dust."

"We'll need to talk to all those who have cleaned this room since he left."

"Boss," Blue said. "Forensics say ETA is ninety minutes, earliest."

"Okay." He turned back to Sister Evangeline. "Is there a storage space? Somewhere the residents keep bulky things?"

"We have a basement. There is a locked storage area for each room. Cages."

"We'll need to see that."

"Deacon Chiu never used the storage locker for this room. He said he didn't need it."

"So everything he had with him was in that suitcase?" Killian pointed to the bag.

The nun nodded.

"Traveling light, even for a priest."

She didn't say anything.

"You're sure he didn't have anything in storage? Something for his memories. Letters. Photos. Diaries. That kind of thing."

The head shake again. "Maybe somewhere else. Not here."

"Okay. Thank you, Sister. You can leave it to us from here."

She stood there, clearly reluctant to go.

"We'll be careful," Killian said.

"It's not that. Is he dead? Deacon Chiu?"

"We can't discuss investigations. But something may have happened in the room. That's why we have to examine it."

She nodded, brows still furrowed. "He was such a quiet man. Forty years in the service of the Lord. Why would anyone want to hurt him?"

"That's what we're here to find out."

She nodded again, then turned. They watched her hurrying down the corridor, head bowed.

"She's right," Blue said. "Who would want to kill this sad old man, much less torture him to death?"

Killian fished in his pocket for his mobile.

"I've got to make some calls. If I'm not back when forensics get here, make sure they know I want every centimeter of the place gone over. Drains, under the floorboards. Down to the subatomic level. This is not going to be another damned dead end."

"Got it, boss."

TWENTY-NINE
JUN

King came back at 7:00 P.M. with dinner in white Styrofoam boxes. Roast goose and roast pork with crackling. Kailan in oyster sauce.

After they'd eaten and cleared up, they sat at the dining table, waiting.

Finally, King spoke.

"The operation is confirmed. Tomorrow. During the announcement."

On Jun's left, someone let out a loud sigh. The others were silent.

"I'll brief you on the timing and other details. But once I have done that, no one can leave. This is your last chance. Anyone?"

Jun felt the icy clutch of doubt on the back of her neck. But the others just shook their heads, faces grave, calm. So she did too.

King nodded.

"Good. The first thing we have to do is assign roles. The way we talked about."

She reached into her backpack and produced a familiar green cloth bag.

"We're playing Scrabble?" Jun smiled to make sure she knew it was a joke.

A shake of the head. No answering smile.

She passed the bag to Jun.

"You go first. Jun. Take two."

She put her hand in, mixed the tiles up from habit, then pulled out two.

"Z and J. Eighteen points. You didn't say, King. Do we want to win or lose this game?"

THIRTY
KILLIAN

Killian yawned. He should be in bed.

A flash of lightning followed immediately by the boom of thunder. Close. Rumbling turning into a series of rolling detonations. A spatter of rain against the glass in the observation room. Killian looked around for Gau. The dog was lying next to the desk. Killian sat, then reached down, scratched his head, flipped up the errant ear. It flopped over immediately. Gau opened an eye, looked up, then closed it again.

The wind whistled in the rafters, and the sound of the rain became a steady roar. More thunder. Gau didn't move.

No fear at all. It was almost unnatural.

Killian looked at his laptop. The email from Chan in forensics was on the screen. Killian had hit reply, then stopped. There was nothing to say.

They'd finished at the nunnery twenty minutes before. Nothing. Not a spot of blood. No sign even that it had been cleaned up. Most of the fingerprints matched those on the whisky bottles, so almost certainly Chiu's, the remainder probably the cleaners. Nothing in the pipes. Nothing under the floor but dust. And, excepting the clothes, some toiletries, a few paperbacks, and the whisky, nothing in the room in the way of personal possessions. It might as well be a hotel room.

Another dead end.

Killian walked over to the phone and checked the screen, knowing it was ridiculous. Compulsive.

Still nothing from Zen. Had he left Hong Kong ahead of the announcement?

Nor from Jun. Of course. He felt his stomach knot with fear for her.

He sighed and put the phone down, then walked over to the sideboard, opened the door, and pulled out the whisky bottle. Still three-quarters full. The Macallan had been a present from someone long ago. He rarely touched the stuff. But today he needed it. Killian poured out three fingers, peaty, astringent fumes in his nostrils, took a long swallow.

Famous Grouse. Cheap whisky for a heavy drinker. A whole case under the bed. Did Chiu pass out every night? Had he woken to find a dark figure in his room, a hand at his throat?

Or had he been blissfully asleep, the heavy blow to the side of the head turning slumber into unconsciousness, slung over the murderer's shoulder like an animal carried to slaughter, waking to find himself trussed, naked, doomed.

Killian put his feet up, took a gulp of the whisky. The glow spreading in his stomach. The Irish solution.

The wind shifted to a higher pitch, the whistling reaching a scream, windows rattling in accompaniment, the rain hammering on the glass, high and hard, snare drum, a deeper pounding on the roof.

Almost 1:00 A.M. Well past Weng's midnight deadline and he hadn't even noticed. Too much had happened. Still, that was before. They had the murderer in their sights now. He had to have the extra time to do the needful police work. To catch this man and stop him from killing again.

Time he didn't have.

They desperately needed the records from the seminary so they could review where Chiu had been posted, who his superiors had been, who he had interacted with. Anything and everything that might help them discover why he had been killed.

Killian had called the archbishop's office earlier, but was stonewalled at every step.

Archbishop Chang was always happy to cooperate with police, his secretary said. But his schedule was full until next Wednesday, at the earliest. Ditto with requests for records. The priest responsible for diocese records was away for the weekend. Call back Monday.

Normally, Killian would have threatened to haul the secretary in for questioning at HQ. And with charges for impeding a police inquiry. Even the possibility of a leak to the media that the Catholic Church was blocking a murder investigation, seemingly to protect one of their own.

But news that they had discovered the victim would be percolating upward. By tomorrow it would reach Eddie Tsang. So, none of that was an option. He only had one arrow left to fire.

Killian put the whisky down next to the phone. Looked at it, scrolled down the contacts list.

O'Halloran, Declan.

He hesitated, then put the phone down.

It was very late for a priest. Late for anyone with a job.

But he'd almost certainly be awake. The man hardly slept. Always had the phone by his side. The most tech-savvy of any older person Killian knew. He'd had a mobile in the late nineties, when Killian was in his early teens. A Nokia. Always on it. Who would he have been talking to? Parishioners? Fellow priests? A memory of him striding back and forth, wearing shorts, sandals with socks, barking into the phone. Killian and the other boys waiting patiently on the beach. One of the Saint Joe's summer camps? On a beach?

Killian swirled the whisky around in the glass. Why was he hesitating? Because of the risk.

To get the information on Chiu, Father Dec would have to go public, use his contacts in the Church. And out of it. That was the nature of the man. He had spent a lifetime trading information. And eventually the ripples would spread all the way to the forty-seventh floor. To Eddie. And the commissioner.

He juggled the phone from hand to hand, then put it down.

Ever since he'd shot Shek, Killian had been trying to convince himself that all he wanted, all he needed, was to be readmitted to the Force. But now, with solid leads and the real possibility of finding the murderer, he realized that wasn't true anymore, if it ever had been.

He would make the call. And then he would do whatever it took to catch this torturer. This murderer. He was going to finish this investigation, no matter what Eddie Tsang said.

Eddie and the commissioner had spoken of the new Force, adapted to Hong Kong's new future. But if the new Force was ready to bury a horrific murder and leave the murderer free to kill again, all for the sake of politics, he wanted no part of it.

Feeling relief wash through him, Killian drained the last of the whisky, punched Father Dec's number.

"Killian. Are you alright? Your mother? Jun?"

Father Dec sounded wide-awake, alert. Voice charged with concern. Killian felt a flood of relief. What had he been worrying about? He explained, the priest only interrupting once to confirm the deacon's name. When Killian had finished there was no hesitation.

"Leave it with me."

"What will you do?"

"I'll get the files. I may be able to access them from my computer. If not, I'll go to the diocese office."

"And if they refuse?"

"They won't. And if they do, I have other options."

"Like what?"

"I can put pressure on them. You remember Raymond Suen, the man I introduced you to? He could ask the archbishop directly. He's . . ."

"No. Not Suen." Killian said it without thinking. If he'd had trouble trusting Father Dec, he certainly didn't trust Suen. That cold, assessing gaze behind the politician's warmth.

"Why so vehement, Killian? He's a good man, I told you, one of our oldest . . ."

"Sorry. But please keep this to yourself, Father."

"Of course, if that's what you wish, Killian."

"It's complicated. Apart from anything else, my bosses can't know."

"My dear boy, have I ever let you down?"

Had he?

"You've never heard of this man before, Deacon Chiu? I thought you knew every Catholic in Hong Kong, never mind the priests."

"There are near on a million Catholics in Hong Kong. And two hundred priests. But he's a deacon, which is a different thing. A lesser office. You know that. You were an altar boy."

"That was a very long time ago. Anyway, please let me know the minute you have something. The murderer is still out there."

"Of course, Killian. Of course. Now get some rest, would you? You sound utterly banjaxed."

Killian smiled. He hadn't heard that word in years. Father Dec showing his Derry roots.

"All right, Father, I will. Thanks again and apologies for calling so late."

"Any time, Killian. Any time at all. You know the church never sleeps."

Killian hung up and poured another whisky.

Mere mortals like him were burdened with original sin. And he needed his sleep—blissful, redemptive oblivion—even if the Church didn't.

THIRTY-ONE
JUN

Jun woke, her heart pounding, gasping. She jerked upright and banged her head on the board above.

"What?" A mumble from Eddison.

"Nothing. Sorry. Go back to sleep." She lay back, slowed her breathing, willing her heart to follow.

She had been trapped underwater. Drowning. But on fire. Drowning in flames.

Another juddering breath.

First grey light in the windows. Sound of trucks on the highway, heading for the container port, thumping over the joints in the road.

Her phone said it was 5:43. No more sleep tonight. When would they get up? King would be up early. Jun strained to hear if she was moving about already. Nothing but the refrigerator compressor. And breathing sleepers. Soft susurration.

She could still get up, leave without waking anyone. Just vanish.

No. That would be betrayal.

She was committed. She had promised. And that had to mean something. Or it all meant nothing.

The light was stronger now. She could see a sticker on the wooden bed board above her head:

I SAW THE ORCAS AT OCEAN PARK

It was Killian who put her to bed, read her stories. When she was small and couldn't sleep, she would climb up the ladder on the bunk bed and snuggle. Big, warm body. Soft, soothing voice.

Why couldn't Killian change? He called her stubborn. But he was worse. He probably didn't know why himself. Tribal loyalty. Some confused impulse to outdo their father. All the time and energy he had invested in his career. Who knew why he wouldn't budge?

And then, he kept asking her why. Why. Why. Why are you doing this? Acting as though she'd been brainwashed, as though she couldn't make up her own mind.

Why? Because it was right and proper and in defense of the things that are best about us.

Things worth fighting for. Worth dying for.

What was he fighting for except blind, stupid loyalty? And habit. And fear of the future. Fear of change.

So much waste. So much love wasted because of pride.

She felt a hot flush of rage course through her.

Stupid, stubborn idiot.

Then, as abruptly as it had come, her anger faded, nothing left except the bitter taste of regret.

No more thinking. It was time for action.

Jun swung her legs out and over the side of the bed, stood.

Bingbing was stirring in the upper bunk set against the far wall. She rolled over, opened her eyes. Puffy, traces of makeup smeared on her eyelids. Their faces were on the same level, inches apart and Jun could see that Bingbing was older than she had originally thought. In her forties.

What had brought her here? Did her family know? Her husband or boyfriend? Surely not.

"It's today, isn't it?" Her voice was croaky from sleep.

Jun nodded.

Bingbing sat up, yawned. "Is there anything to eat?"

"Eat?" Jun's stomach was a fist. Closed. Closed as though it would never open again.

"You know, breakfast?"

Jun forced a smile. "You love your food, don't you, Bingbing? A true Hong Konger."

Jun smiled, but there was a catch in her voice. Bingbing looked at her seriously.

"And so are you, Jun. You are a true Hong Kong patriot."

Jun nodded, then turned away.

THIRTY-TWO

KILLIAN

Early morning light filtered through the curtains. Killian heaved himself up, suppressing a burp. The sour taste of whisky at the back of his throat. That was why he didn't drink it. That and the pounding head.

Killian swung out of bed. Despite the hangover, the questions from the night before still chased themselves round and round in his head.

The total absence of personal things in the deacon's room just didn't make sense.

What about a picture of his parents? His mother. Or his ordination certificate from the archbishop when he was made a deacon, where was that? It said deacon on his door. The other doors they passed only had a name. They didn't say deacon. Or father. So he must have been proud of it.

Letters. People always kept letters. And diaries. If he was a solitary man there might be diaries. Where would Chiu have kept them then? Somewhere nearby. Somewhere hidden, assuming he wanted to keep it private. No one wanted their diaries read. Their innermost thoughts. Their sins.

He shook his head. Sister Evangeline might be able to help but she wouldn't be in until 10:00 A.M.

At 7:45, Killian stepped out of the station's front door and looked up at the sky. An azure vault, washed clean by the rain. The waters of the bay were a deeper blue, sparkling, the sunlight reflecting from Shenzhen's rampart of glass-clad skyscrapers.

An inquisitive whimper. Gau. Killian walked to the Land Cruiser, held the passenger door open.

"Why not? Come for a ride."

Gau leapt in.

When the valley came into view, it was glowing from the rain, the fields almost dazzling, the bright-green rice seedlings of life, the woods on the upper slopes a deeper, darker green. Killian discovered on the net that the monastery ran retreats. Ten days. No phones. No television. And no talking. Absolute silence. Ten days of self-examination and bad food. It sounded like hell. And probably wasn't cheap either.

On the center console, Killian's phone trilled insistently. A 5858 prefix: HQ. He mashed down the power button until the phone asked if he really wanted to shut down. He did.

He put the dead phone back down on the console, grinning at Gau. He should feel like a condemned criminal. At least like someone who was probably already unemployed. Instead, he felt like a boy cutting classes.

"Right. Let's go, eh, Mad Dog?"

Gau didn't look around but thumped his tail against the seat obligingly. They'd revisit the seminary first, then the nunnery.

The coach was still there in the seminary car park. Where did they go? Prayer meetings? Football matches? Bowling?

He let Gau out, and they walked to the front of the building together, scanning the walls. Motion sensor lights. But no cameras. None visible anyway. They walked around the whole building, stopping at the back for Gau to pee on a rose bush. No cameras in the rear of the building—not that they would have been much use anyway. Killian needed a view of the road and the passing vehicles.

A van had pulled into the slot next to the cruiser. A sign on the side said The French Bakery in Chinese and English, a picture of a monk pushing a tray of loaves into an oven, a big smile on his meaty, flushed face. The driver, mid-twenties, sallow, with a bored expression, wearing greasy blue overalls, the Green Cross logo on his breast pocket, was leaning against the side, smoking a cigarette and staring at the hills.

"You work for the bakery?" Killian asked.

"No," the man said, not turning. He flicked away the cigarette. "What's it to you?"

"Turn to face me, please."

The man turned, narrowing his eyes at the sight of the uniform.

"Police, as you can see."

A grunt. The man looked away.

"So who do you work for then?" Killian continued.

"Work in the seminary. Maintenance."

"What's with the advertisement for the bakery then?"

"Some smartarse's idea. Free advertising. The others have Green Cross Milk. Or the beer."

Killian felt his pulse quicken. The Green Cross Milk truck had been on the list. Twice.

"All the other maintenance vehicles?"

"Yeah. Pointless. We're here in the valley 99 percent of the time. Not going to persuade anyone here to buy any bread when they get it for free, are they?"

"So you do maintenance for all three places? The seminary, the monastery, and the nunnery?"

"Yeah. Even though we're paid by Green Cross. They shouldn't lend us out. It's exploitation. We should unionize."

The man looked over Killian's shoulder. Another man in overalls, older, walked to the truck, ignoring Killian. He beckoned, and the two of them got in the van without a word.

Killian made a note.

"Inspector."

Mrs. Chow approached, head down, hair like a black, shiny prow of a ship steaming toward Killian at ramming speed. She pulled to a halt, panting slightly.

"I saw you from the window. Could you tell me why you're here?" she asked.

"It's superintendent."

"Very well. Could you tell me what you're doing here, Superintendent?"

"Routine inquiries, ma'am. Do you have any security cameras?"

"Security cameras? Certainly not. Whatever for?"

"For security? Unless you believe in donating to criminals as well as the poor? Letting your televisions walk out the door?"

She sniffed.

"We have night watchmen. And there's never been a robbery here. Is that a police dog?" She pointed a red lacquered nail at Gau.

"He's helping the police with our inquiries. But don't mention it, please."

"What? Why?"

"He's undercover. Disguised as a pet."

She sniffed again. "Make sure you notify us next time you are on Church property," she paused. "Superintendent."

* * *

Killian was still smiling when he parked at the nunnery. Another maintenance van was there, a smiling monk lifting a tankard and the logo for Abbot's Ale on the side. A man in familiar blue dungarees was unloading bricks from the open rear doors into a wheelbarrow.

Killian patted Gau on the head, buzzed down the passenger side window a crack. "You better stay in the car this time."

As Killian walked toward the front doors of the nunnery, he saw that part of the low retaining wall had been knocked down, shards of brick and redbrick dust covering the rose bushes.

"What happened?" Killian asked the bent back of the maintenance man, who continued to unload bricks from the van, a wisp of cigarette smoke drifting above his head.

"Young idiot trying to show off is what happened. Three-point turn straight into the wall."

Killian laughed. "The exuberance of youth."

"The stupidity of youth," the man growled.

"They usually go together."

No answer. Killian shrugged and walked on toward the nunnery.

* * *

The office was empty, the hall silent. Looking for Sister Evangeline, he climbed up to the third floor. The name slot on 305 was empty, the door locked.

"Hello? Anyone here? Sister Evangeline?"

Echoes in the corridor. No heads poking out of doors. 305 was the last room on the corridor, hence the hillside view. He knocked at 306. The card in the slot read: Paul Sung. No answer.

Killian walked to the far end of the corridor, opposite from the way he'd come up, to the matching staircase, then down one flight. Another empty corridor. He crossed again, repeated the exercise. No Sister Evangeline.

When he got to the ground level there was a hunched figure at the far end. The ancient priest with the walker. Killian caught up, leaned in so his mouth was inches from the man's ear.

"Good morning, Father."

"There's no need to shout, officer. It's my limbs that don't function as I command them. Not my ears. Or my intellect." He swung the walker forward, thumped it down.

"Sorry, Father. I was wondering if you've seen Sister Evangeline."

"No, I have not." He took a shaky step forward.

"Are you Father Sung by any chance? Paul Sung?"

Another swing of the walker.

"No. You're too late for him." He pointed upward.

"I'm sorry."

"No need to be sorry. The Lord called and he went. Quite normal."

"Right. Thank you."

Step forward. Left leg this time. "Goodbye, young man."

"Goodbye, Father."

The office was still empty. He pulled out his phone.

9:16 A.M. Too early to try Father Dec? Yes. Give the man some time. He pocketed his phone, then walked back to the corridor.

A fire door opened into the basement. Killian pressed the light switch. Overhead fluorescents flicked on one by one, illuminating a double row of cages constructed from chicken wire and steel rods. The wire was triple-layered, and the rods concreted into the cement floor. Most of the cages nearest to him were empty. Six cages down, 107, held two wheeled bags that looked fairly new. The latch was welded into the frame and secured with a padlock. Solid.

Killian continued down to the far end, what would be the rear of the building up above. A sloping ramp led down from ground level, closed metal doors overhead.

On one side of the ramp, a row of bicycles collapsed onto each other. Rusty, cobwebbed, covered in dust. Women's bikes. A jumbled pile on the other side. Suitcases, big and small, some looking vintage 1950s. Cardboard boxes. Black garbage bags. No dust on any of it.

One box had split and spilled its contents onto the concrete. Letters. He picked up one. Addressed to Sem. Kevin Dingwall, Catholic Seminary, New Territories, Hong Kong. Queen's head on a red stamp: ER. Elizabeth Regina. Ten d. Was that shillings? Pennies? The date on the franking was August 12, 1966.

He put the letter back. Next to it was a single man's brogue. Huge, a little worn at the heel, but gleaming under the thin layer of dust. Lovingly polished. For years and years. A prized possession maybe, for someone who didn't have many.

Down another row of cages and he came to 305. Empty.

Next to it, 306 was closed with a large steel padlock. Double Phoenix.

Inside were two large black suitcases stacked on top of a steamer trunk. A set of golf clubs propped up against the wall. Were priests allowed to own their own clubs? In one corner a couple of dusty glass cases. He leaned in for a better look. One held a mounted, stuffed bird with a curving yellow-and-red beak in a glass case, the glass broken and taped together. The other was another animal, some sort of squirrel or stoat.

A dead end. Literally.

* * *

Killian stood on the edge of the meadow that rolled away from the nunnery, watching Gau trot back and forth, nose down, tail doing its slow back-and-forth wag. What could he be on the trail of? A civet cat? Maybe a pangolin, if there were any left that hadn't been sold for their meat on the mainland.

"Is that your animal in the field?"

Killian hadn't heard Sister Evangeline coming in her rubber-soled, sensible shoes.

"That's no animal, Sister. That's my dog. His name is Gau."

She laughed, a lovely gurgling chuckle that turned her back into a teenager for a brief moment.

"That's a very good name for a dog. A practical name."

"A bit literal I suppose if you know it means 'dog,' which you obviously do."

"I'd be a sorry sort of nun if I couldn't speak to my charges in their own language," she said in flawless Cantonese. "And speaking of my charges, I'm told you were snooping around this morning, all three floors and the basement too."

"I was looking for you," Killian said, still smiling. "And I only saw one of your residents. How did you know about the basement? You don't have cameras, do you?"

Another gurgling laugh. "Cameras? Like a museum? Or a bank? Heavens no. Just a bunch of old men with nothing better to do than peer out their doors and windows."

"Oh."

She cocked her head to one side. "What did you want to ask me about?"

"A few things. The basement for one—how does that work?"

"What do you mean?"

"I was told by one of your priests that Deacon Chiu's neighbor in 306 died."

"Father Sung. Yes. Some time ago."

"But I saw his storage unit is still in use."

"We keep their belongings for a year after they pass, in case any relatives turn up to claim them. Most don't have any immediate family. No children or wives, of course. And very often they've outlived their siblings or cousins. Taking holy orders does seem to bless them with longevity."

Unless someone wants to murder you, Killian thought.

"I also saw some things piled up next to the ramp," he said.

"Those are ready for transport to the rubbish dump. The drivers prefer to do four or five loads in one trip, so they let them accumulate there."

"It's sad. Seeing their keepsakes, their memories, dumped like that," Killian said.

She nodded in agreement.

"It is. I've asked them not to, but they don't listen. The church has a rehabilitation program to employ ex-prisoners. Mostly petty crimes. They can be a little . . . rough." She pulled out her phone and glanced at it. "Almost ten. I must be going, I'm afraid."

"One other thing, Sister. Could I have the keys to 305? I'd like to take one more look."

"Your people were there for half the day yesterday. Isn't that enough?"

"This is just for me. I like to get a feel for the place where the victim lived. A feel for the person. You can't get that from a forensics report."

"I don't think you'll get much of a feel for anything. These men don't come to us with much in the way of material possessions, being priests. But I've never seen anyone with so little as him. It's almost as though he rid himself of everything connecting him to his past."

"Yes, Sister, it is," Killian agreed.

* * *

Killian sat in the armchair in 305, his left leg jiggling, hand open on his thigh, the bunch of keys dangling from his finger jingling. Mother had always hated this habit. He stopped his leg bouncing. Silence. The caw of a crow over the meadow. Crickets. The building creaking. A slam of a door somewhere below.

He sniffed. Nothing but a vague unpleasant scent. Chemical. Likely cleaning fluid. Maybe left behind by forensics. The chair faced a patch of blank wall marred by a brown stain on the cream paint. Ancient.

The armchair was upholstered in red leather, cracked and rough under his fingers.

Killian ran his hands along the sides of the cushion, then stood and lifted it. Clean. Forensics.

The bed was stripped of sheets, the mattress rolled up, exposing the steel bedsprings. The paperbacks were gone. Forensics, and then the sisters after them probably. Mopping, wiping, polishing.

There was no trace of the man left. There hadn't been much to begin with.

* * *

Sister Evangeline was sitting in front of a computer, frowning.

"Bad news?" Killian asked.

"Accounts."

"Ah." Killian dropped the bunch of keys on the counter. "I'm sure you've already been asked, but was there anything that struck you about Deacon Chiu's personal effects when you cleaned the room?"

"You saw it all yesterday," she replied.

"Yes, but you knew the man. Something might have jogged a memory," Killian pressed.

She shook her head. "I'm afraid not. The books we took back to the common room library. Mysteries, I think. There was nothing much else, apart from clothes. And the whisky, of course. We put that in the common room too."

"And you don't recall whether he had more than one suitcase when he arrived?" Killian asked.

"You mean they could have taken some of his things away when he . . ."

"When he was kidnapped, yes," Killian finished.

She shuddered. "The thought of someone creeping around here late at night, a murderer. It's horrible. But no, I wasn't here when he arrived. I could ask one of the other sisters if they saw a second suitcase when they were cleaning his room."

"It's all right, thanks. It's gone anyway."

Her face brightened.

"He did once ask me about where he could get a computer repaired. A laptop. I told him to go into Yuen Long. But I never saw him with it."

"Could he have asked someone to store his things for him?" Killian asked.

She looked doubtful. "It would be unusual. As I said, every room has its own storage space in the basement, so there'd be no need," she said.

"Unless . . ."

She raised her eyebrows. "Unless what, Superintendent?"

"Unless he didn't want anyone to know where his things were," Killian said.

She nodded but was clearly puzzled.

Killian pointed at the keys he had dropped on the counter, a different set from the big bunch she'd used when first letting them in. A small keychain was attached. It depicted a smoking volcano and had "Bacolod City" written across the bottom.

"That's in the Philippines, isn't it?"

"Yes. On the island of Negros. Famous for their grilled chicken."

"Is that your hometown?"

"Oh, no, I'm a city girl. Manila. That was Deacon Chiu's. He told me once he lived there for many years, doing missionary work."

Killian picked up the keychain.

"That's pretty far south?"

"Yes. Sugar plantations. Very poor. The church runs most of the clinics. As well as the schools, of course."

He bounced the keys in his palm.

"A lot of keys for a man who had so little to lock up."

Sister Evangeline took them from his palm. "This is the front door. We lock it after midnight, though most of our residents have gone to bed long before that. This one is for his room, as you know. And this small one is the post box. The rest I don't know."

"May I?"

She handed the keys back. There were three extras on the ring. Two that looked as though they had been cut as copies. No identifying marks. And another: newer, brass, unusual looking, one of the teeth sticking out sideways.

"Can I borrow these one more time, Sister?"

She waved her hand. "Be my guest, though I don't see how another search of his room can help."

"I'm not going back to the room."

She was already bent over the computer and didn't respond.

* * *

Killian pressed the light switch in the basement. Overhead fluorescent lights flicked on.

He walked down the row of cages to 306. The big steel padlock gleamed in the light, looking impenetrable. The first key Killian tried slipped into the lock, then didn't turn. He pulled it out, slotted in its companion, took a deep breath, and turned.

Bingo.

He pulled a pair of latex gloves from his pocket, snapped them on, then swung open the door and stepped over to the suitcases. The first one opened without protest, releasing the smell of mothballs and fust. Old man smell.

Winter clothes. A black overcoat, leather boots, a couple of scarves, two pairs of gloves. The second suitcase was empty. Killian put it on the floor with its companion and squatted in front of the trunk.

Another padlock. He slotted in the second key and turned. The lock popped open and he uttered a grunt of satisfaction.

He took a breath, then lifted the lid. A fitted tray four-inches deep. Compartments. Packets of letters. Orange and green envelopes full of printed photographs, from when people actually printed their photos. Three photo albums.

Killian picked up one of the bundles of letters. The rubber band, stiff with age, broke as he pulled it off. The top envelope was addressed in a shaky hand: Deacon Chiu Lok Mun, St. Vincent Ferrer Church, Kanakalon, Negros Oriental, The Philippines. The franking was dated March 7, 2006 and the writer had scrawled "Hold for Pickup" across the bottom-left corner.

He pulled the single sheet out. The same spidery hand, now writing in Chinese.

My Dear Son: Your mother is very sick and asking for you. You have been gone for so many years, surely now that your parents need you, the church will allow you to come home?

Killian replaced the letter and flipped through the rest of the bundle.

Two or three each year until 2009, when the letters stopped. He put the bundle back. Had Chiu ever written back?

He picked up the nearest photo album. Fuji green. The pictures were mostly group shots in some junglelike location. Chiu in shirt sleeves with a group of children, teaching in a classroom, laughing with another priest, a tall, blond man with a red face and a patchy beard.

A plastic file yielded a Hong Kong birth certificate, a baptismal certificate from St. Thomas's Church, Ngau Tau Kok, and an elaborate ordination certificate from the seminary.

FRANCISCUS XAVIERIENSIS

MISERATIONE DIVINA ET SANCTAE SEDE APOSTOLICA GRATIA

PRINCEPS EPISCUPIS HONG KONGENSIS

UNIVERSIS ET SINGULIS PRAESENTES LITTERAS MANU NOSTRA

SUBSCRIPTAS ET SIGILLO PROPRIO

On and on it went, all in filigreed, scrolled calligraphy. And all Latin. But the name and date leapt out: *Nobis in Christo* CHIU LOK MUN *Anno Domini* 1994, *Quinto Kalendas Maii*. There was a scrawled signature and a stamp showing crossed keys and a triple crown. The papal coat of arms.

Killian put aside the documents, then lifted the tray and set it on the floor beside the trunk. Most of the space in the main section of the trunk was taken up by a military-style steel footlocker secured with a heavy padlock. Next to it was an old Sony camcorder. He picked up the video camera, found the power switch. A whirring and grinding and the side popped open, revealing a slot for a mini-cassette. The battery had been charged recently.

Why keep using this ancient camera? Why not transfer the videos to a hard drive?

Killian put the camera down and reached into his pocket for the key ring. The padlock was solid brass. Still shiny. No scratches. Made by Lemen.

The brass key slipped into the lock with a clink and he turned, the hasp popping open.

The locker was divided in half. One side held an assortment of DVDs and tapes, both VHS and mini-cassettes that would presumably fit into the video camera. There was also a plastic container holding rows of USB flash drives. There were dates scrawled on the covers of the DVDs and on the backs of the tapes. The first VHS tape, bottom-left corner, was labeled 12/1/1998.

The other side of the locker was divided like an index card file with tabs marking successive years. The first year was 1990, the last 2004. There were rows of envelopes stacked back-to-back, some years holding three or four, some none.

A dark, hollow foreboding settled in his chest.

He pulled out an envelope from the middle section of 2004. Three pictures inside. Polaroids. He slipped the top one out.

A boy's face looking back over his shoulder, mouth opened in a scream, eyes wide with fear, two big hands on his stick-like arms.

Killian dropped the photo as if it was on fire. It fell face down on the floor.

He'd never worked vice. Or the Child Protection and Sexual Violence unit.

He'd seen pornography, yes. Everyone looks at porn. Every man.

But this wasn't anything like pornography. It was acts of horror against a child.

He'd read about it. But seeing it like this, unprepared, the normal world felt as though it was coming loose from its moorings, a gateway opening to a place where men were slaves to their inner beast. Ready to rape and murder on a whim.

Killian bent and picked the photograph up, keeping it face down, put it back in the envelope.

No wonder they were Polaroids. You couldn't get pictures like this developed. Or digitize the old tapes.

He reached for one of the mini-cassettes, hesitated, stared at the neat rows, then finally took one out, slotted it into the camera.

The camera had a fold-out screen three inches across. The scene was fuzzy at first, glistening brown skin, water running.

Then the camera pulled back. A narrow brown back, mop of black hair, rhythmic movement, a wet slapping sound.

Killian gasped and slammed the screen shut.

The sound continued to play.

He jabbed the stop button, once, twice, a third time, banging it so hard he nearly dropped the camera.

The noises continued, a deep grunting now audible.

Killian threw the camera to the ground and the cassette door popped open, the tape flying out and skittering across the concrete floor.

The label on the side showed neat handwriting:

Edgardo, 2001–2004
Joshua, 2002–2005

THIRTY-THREE

The contents of the trunk's upper tray lay on the spare desk in the operations room, each item wrapped in an evidence bag. On one side was a record of Chiu Lok Mun's public life. On the other his meticulous record of the torture and sexual abuse of children.

Killian, Yeong, and Blue stared down at the bags. Twelve in all.

Letters. Certificates. Seven sets of photographs. Three albums.

Yeong's normal waxy features were flushed with anger. "Could it have been revenge? One of the victims? That would serve the pedo right."

"Not enough information," Killian said. "We don't even know if any of these were taken in Hong Kong. We'll have to go through the whole stash. Every tape. Every picture."

Yeong shook his head. "I'm going to need counseling after that."

"We'll have help," Killian said. "I've called the Child Protection unit. They're going to send two officers over this afternoon to help. They're experienced with this kind of thing."

"Do you think he was selling it?" Yeong asked.

"He didn't live like it," Killian replied. "But he must have had an accomplice who was doing the filming. They often work in pairs, from what I've read. Or groups. Exchanging material."

"If there was an accomplice," Blue said, "he must be a worried man."

"Let's hope so," Yeong said. "Let's hope he goes to bed shaking with fear every night."

"But he wouldn't necessarily know what happened to Chiu," Blue added. "At most he'd know he's disappeared. Maybe that's why the killer went to so much trouble to try and disguise the identity of the body."

"That probably means that if the other man exists, he isn't in Hong Kong, or he would have been targeted too," Killian replied. "But I think the killer expects him to come back. Hence the elaborate deception."

Blue shivered. "When I think of the poor children. From what you said, they weren't much older than my boy . . ."

Killian was typing a message on his phone. He spoke without raising his head. "As a parent, you can be excused from this phase of the investigation if you want."

He looked up. Blue was glaring at him. "Don't make any excuses for me. I want to catch the bastard as much as you do."

"Sorry. I thought anyone with children might . . ." Killian trailed off. Blue had turned and walked away, shoulders stiff.

He had never heard her swear before.

Killian looked down at the message:

Father D. Where are u? Need the info asap. Call me.

He pocketed the phone. "Alright. Let's get to work. Everyone pick one bag. When you're finished, pass it on. You know the drill. Record anything that could help with identification of place or person. Clues to who the other pair of hands is, if there is one. Whether any of this happened in Hong Kong."

There were nods of agreement.

Killian took a bag containing a sheaf of photos and the ordination certificate. He pulled out the certificate, staring at the yellowed paper.

He'd had the formal sanction of the Church. It was hard to believe someone hadn't known what was going on all those years. Very hard.

Killian's phone buzzed. Father Dec, at last?

No. It was a blanket message to all active-duty discipline officers to be available for call-up within ten minutes' notice. They were anticipating large protests because of the announcement from the Liaison Office.

Protests: Jun would be there surely.

He punched favorites and then her number. But the call went straight to voicemail. Not even her own voice—the automated version. He shook his head, feeling anger at her bubble up in his chest like acid reflux. How could she do this to him, to Mother?

Killian put the phone down on the desk next to the photo folders. What about an online search? He had been so preoccupied with the physical evidence that it hadn't occurred to him to do a Google search. Even if Chiu had been off the grid for years, there must be some trace.

He swiveled to the computer, typed in Chiu Lok Mun.

Nothing. Plenty of Chiu Lok Mans, the more usual spelling. But nothing at all for Chiu Lok Mun. No Facebook. Or Instagram. No social media at all. Nothing. Even for a man in his sixties, even for a priest or whatever he was, it must have required an effort to stay anonymous like this.

He typed in the Chinese characters for the name. This time hundreds of results. Twenty-two names. He scrolled down. Not one even close. Mostly kids in their teens and twenties.

What else?

Killian picked up his phone.

"Sister Evangeline? Superintendent Tong. Sorry to bother you."

"What is it, Superintendent? Have you found him yet? The murderer?"

"No, Sister. It'll take a bit longer. I was wondering whether you knew what Deacon Chiu's English name was?"

A pause as she thought. "I do not. Many of our guests use their English names. Their Christian names. But he didn't."

"Is there anywhere he might have written it down? A registration form when he . . ."

"Wait, please."

Killian heard her put the phone down, then the shuffle of her indoor cloth slippers. A minute later she was back. "He didn't write his full name when he first came to us, I'm afraid. Only the initial. Deacon S. Chiu Lok Mun. Strange. They usually list the English name last."

"S for . . . Sugar, Sister?"

"Solomon. Saul. Samuel. Something like that, Superintendent. They take a biblical name on ordination. It's almost always from the Old Testament. I don't know why."

S for Satan, Killian thought. That was biblical.

She cut the line. Killian turned back to the computer. A biblical name.

He googled "Biblical names beginning with S."

Biblicalnames.com had the list and their meanings.

Sampson. Sampson Chiu. Scores. Also Samson. Real estate agent. Head of Forex trading. Film director. Professor.

No deacon.

Saul? Ditto.

Killian continued down the list. Sharon? A woman's name, surely. Shem? Shiloh? Someone famous had named their child Shiloh.

Not Sheba. Or Shamir. Too Muslim-sounding. Simon. Shimeon. Solomon? Lots of Solomon Chius. But not his man.

What had he missed? Killian went back through the list.

Silas. He'd missed that. There was just one Silas Chiu. A famous hairdresser, apparently. Wasting time. He moved the mouse to close the page, then saw a link at the bottom of the list. Not a person. A newspaper story, the URL scmp.com.

He clicked. It was a short piece. Only a few paragraphs.

TRAGEDY STRIKES OUTING FOR ORPHANS

by Priscilla Forester

Published 12:00 A.M., July 14, 1996

A rare outing for boys from the St. Marks Orphanage in Lai Chi Kok was struck by tragedy yesterday when two of the party drowned.

"The boys were swimming a relay race, and, in the excitement, we didn't notice them missing until it was too late," said Father Helmut Kunst, who was leading the three-day adventure camp on Po Toi Island.

"They were lovely boys and would have had a bright future," said Silas Chiu, a seminarian who was helping Kunst supervise the expedition. "It's a terrible shame."

The bodies of the two boys, Mak Tzekok, 10, and Lau Taibak, 11, were not recovered. A Marine Police spokesman said the search for the bodies would continue today, adding that the strong tides in the area made prospects for recovery poor.

"Got you, you bastard," Killian said, slapping the desk.

"What did you find, boss?" Yeong asked.

"Come and see," Killian said and read it out.

"*Diu nei lou mo*," Yeong said. "'Lovely boys.' Makes you want to punch someone."

Blue nodded in agreement. Killian pointed to an ancient PC in the corner. "Does that computer have access to the government database?"

"That's why it's there," Blue replied. "Access is not allowed on laptops."

"Good. Let's look them up on the immigration database for ID cards."

The priest came up first.

"Kunst, Hans Helmut. Ordinary HK ID issued on March 22, 1988," Blue said.

She leaned forward to look at the photo on the screen more closely.

"He got permanent ID after fulfilling the seven-year residence requirement on April 2, 1995. Nothing after that."

"When did the mandatory switch to chip-enabled IDs start?" Killian asked.

"2003, I think," Blue answered.

"If he was here then, he would have had to get a new card. So he was gone by then. And hasn't come back."

"Not to live, anyway," Yeong added. "He can still come in and out, as long as it's no more than, what? Ninety days?"

"Let's try the two boys who died," Killian said.

"Mak was only ten. He wouldn't have had an ID. Not compulsory until he was eleven," Blue pointed out.

"Try Lau," Killian said.

"Lau Taibak, born June 23, 1985. ID issued June 30. He'd only had it for a week, poor thing," Blue said.

"His home address was the orphanage. Should we head over there?" Blue asked.

"We'd have to apply for a warrant to look at the records," Killian said. "That would take days. We've got hours."

"I know. So I was wondering about looking for siblings," Blue suggested.

Her fingers were poised over the keyboard. "How would you do that? Lau is one of the commonest names in the city. There must be hundreds of thousands."

"We could use the family name plus the generational name and then a wildcard. Lau Tai-whatever," Blue said.

"Okay. Try it," Killian said.

Her hands flew over the keys. "One hundred twenty-two results."

"Can you filter?"

"Of course," came the reply.

"Filter by birthdate. Born between 1984 and 1990."

"Twenty-one. With this few, I can check the parents' names for a match. There's no way to filter it with the search engine. Hang on."

There was a long pause as her fingers flew over the keyboard. Finally, she said something emphatic under her breath and looked up.

"Got them. Four brothers. All with colors in their given names."

Blue started typing.

"The parents were killed in a minibus crash on Castle Peak Road in 1990."

"Okay. What happened to the boys after that?"

"This is only public records, so I can only tell you about ID, deaths, and so on."

"We'll do a separate Google search after this. Tell me what you've got now."

"The eldest is Taihong. Red. Born August 12, 1982. Has a current address—updated four months ago when a new card was issued—in Yuen Long. Zee Long Estate."

"I've spent time there," Yeong remarked. "When I was on patrol. Nasty. Triads. Glue sniffing. Heroin if they have money. Despair."

"It fits. He's the right age. Still in the same area."

"Yeong, contact Yuen Long and have them send a constable to the address," Killian said. "If Taihong is there, go and talk to him."

"Yes, sir."

"What's the next one?"

"Next chronologically is Taibak. White. The boy who drowned. Born June 23, two years after the eldest boy."

"Then?"

"Taiwong. Yellow. November 23, 1985."

A memory as faint as a bat squeak echoed in Killian's head. He frowned, thinking.

"Boss?" Blue asked, looking at him with raised eyebrows.

Killian shook his head and focused. "Sorry. Spaced out. What did you say?"

"He was also listed at the orphanage address. And that's still his registered address. But his last card was issued in 2001. He never got the chip card."

"Pretty good chance he's dead then."

"If so, it would have to be overseas. If he died here, that would be recorded."

"We can follow up later, if the rest don't pan out. Go on."

"Next one is Lau Tailuk. Green. October 1, 1990."

"No more after that?"

"No. That's the year the parents were killed in the crash."

Blue put a finger on the screen.

"The youngest brother, Tailuk, came up as a secondary hit. He was adopted in 1992. By Philip and Mary Butcher. Brits living here. His legal name now is Anthony Jason Butcher."

"Wah," Yeong said. "Very *gweilo*."

"Wait a second. There's another entry after the adoption name change." Blue frowned and sat back. "He reappears three years ago. Applying for his first ID card by right of birth."

"So he's back in Hong Kong?"

"Apparently."

"What's his address?"

"Flat 7, Platinum Tower, Barker Road."

"Sounds fancy."

"The Peak. So more than fancy. Crazy money to live there. Millions."

"Do you think the guy living in the Yuen Long shithole knows he has a brother on the Peak?"

"Something else we can ask when we see them. And, Lin."

"Boss?"

"Call the archbishop's office and ask for information about this German. Kunst. There's a smarmy bastard there I spoke to yesterday. The archbishop's secretary. He'll give you ten thousand reasons why they can't help. Go down to the cathedral and sit in his office until he gives us what we want. If necessary, threaten to arrest him for impeding a murder investigation."

"Arrest him? Really, sir?"

"Yes. We must find out what happened to this Kunst. If he was involved—and it's hard to believe he wasn't—that means the killer may be targeting him too. Take Yeong with you."

They turned to leave.

"And, Yeong, don't forget to call Yuen Long about the other brother."

"Yes, sir."

"Blue," Killian said, "let's go to the Peak and knock down some doors."

"You mean knock on some doors?"

"That too."

THIRTY-FOUR

Killian drove as Blue read from her phone.

"Butcher, Anthony. Head of derivatives trading, Coburg Sampson—that's one of the biggest investment banks on Wall Street."

"Thanks, Blue," Killian said. "I do read the papers."

"'Mr. Butcher studied economics at Trinity College, Cambridge. He then received an MBA from the Wharton School of the University of Pennsylvania. He joined the bank's Hong Kong branch two years ago and is responsible for all Asian Forex trading,' blah blah, swaps, cross-currency, forwards, puts." Blue added, "I have no idea what any of this means."

"If they're paying his rent for an apartment in Platinum Tower, it means money. That place must run to sixty, seventy thousand a month. American," Killian said.

The Land Cruiser shifted down as they entered the steep section of Barker Road. This area of the Peak was mostly old colonial houses, once the exclusive domain of the English elite, but had turned into little Shanghai by a tsunami of mainland money.

The tower loomed ahead, unmistakable—the only apartment block this high up on the hill. It was a narrow finger of glass shooting up sixty-five stories, with only one apartment per floor, completely out of place among the one- and two-story houses. Killian's phone buzzed. He fished it out of his pocket and handed it to Blue.

"Can you see what it is? I'm expecting something important," he said.

"Password?" she asked.

"D-I-N-G-A-U," he spelled out.

She typed. "You really love that dog, don't you?"

He grunted.

"Two missed calls. 5858 prefix. That's HQ."

"I know. What else?"

"A text. You're sure you want me to read it."

Killian frowned. "Of course."

"Okay. It says, and remember I'm quoting here, sir: 'You stupid idiot, I told you to take care of J.'"

"Who's it from?" Killian asked.

"It's signed 'Z.'"

He nodded. Zen. Finally. And of course, it was when the case was coming to a head.

"That's it?" Killian asked.

"No. There's more: 'she popped up after three days OTG.'" Blue looked over at him. "OTG. Not sure what that is."

"Off the grid. Go on."

"Um . . . 'three days OTG. Tagged in car with four reds. Do something!'"

"Shit. Shit. Shit."

"What's a red?" she asked.

What had Zen said when they'd talked what seemed like centuries ago? Red meant immediate arrest.

"I'll explain later. Just type a message saying I'm driving and will call him in five."

"Whatever you say, boss."

In the building car park, Killian waved her on. "Go ahead and register or whatever. I'll be there in a second."

Zen didn't pick up the call. Killian typed a message.

Cannot get away. advise
what action needed

He hit send and followed Blue into the lobby.

Getting off the elevator, a Filipina maid in a blue-and-white candy-striped apron met them at the door and then led them down a long, high-ceilinged, dim corridor lined with stone carvings in niches lit by their own spotlights. The carvings were bas-reliefs showing battle scenes and religious ceremonies. Their footfalls were muffled by thick carpet.

"This is like a museum," Blue whispered.

"Or a mausoleum."

They rounded a corner and walked into the living room, a huge space dominated by floor-to-ceiling windows at the far end. The whole of Hong Kong lay spread out below—the harbor, Kowloon, the IFC tower a needle rising above the other skyscrapers, Lion Rock, the outer islands all visible through wisps of mist. On a clear day, Shenzhen's towers must be visible too.

A boy of about seven sat on a couch near the windows, playing a game on his phone, oblivious to the view. He looked up at the sound of voices. Eurasian, with long, light-brown hair falling over his eyes, he bent back over his phone, ignoring them.

"Come on, Nigel, time to get washed up for lunch," a man's voice called.

They turned. A Chinese man in his thirties was descending a circular staircase from the second level of the apartment, eyebrows raised in polite enquiry above prominent cheekbones and a sharp beak of a nose. He wore jeans, a grey hoodie, and was barefoot. The maid hadn't asked them to remove their shoes.

"But Papa, I just got to the demon boss level. My first time," the boy protested.

"You'll get there again. Now run along, please," the man said.

The boy stood, threw the phone onto the couch, and stomped out.

"Are you Anthony Butcher?" Killian asked, switching to Cantonese without thinking.

Butcher shook his head. "I don't speak Cantonese."

"Sorry. You were born here, so I assumed . . ."

"I was adopted when I was three. We left a year later. I hadn't been back until I was transferred here for work. Please, sit." He waved them toward the couch by the window. "Now, Superintendent, you said on the phone this was about my family. It can't be my parents in the United Kingdom—I just spoke to them. And my wife and son are both here with me, so . . ."

He left the question hanging, sitting opposite them, leaning back and stretching his arms along the top of the couch. His eyes were intelligent but hooded. The jeans were ironed. Fingernails manicured, a small gold signet ring glinting on his left pinkie finger.

"We'd like to ask you about your biological family, Mr. Butcher," Killian said. "Your brothers."

Butcher nodded. "Ah, yes. I see. What did you want to ask?"

"Have you had any recent contact with them?"

"Can I ask what this is about?"

"It's a criminal inquiry."

"And they are suspects?"

"Persons of interest. Have you seen them?"

Butcher didn't reply immediately, calculating. "The bank requires us to report anything that might impact business. I'm afraid I can't talk to you without a lawyer present unless I know what this is about."

"It's a murder case," Killian said. "You aren't a suspect, but one of your brothers may know something that would help us catch the killer."

"Murder. Who was murdered?"

"A priest. A Roman Catholic priest."

A flicker in Butcher's eyes. Killian leaned forward.

"Does that mean something to you, Mr. Butcher?"

Butcher looked unsure of himself for the first time, dropped his arms from the couch back, and folded his hands in his lap.

"I suppose I can talk to you. But it's a bit complicated."

"Tell us, please," Killian said.

"After my parents took me back to England, I had no contact with Hong Kong. Or my brothers. I tried searching for them on the internet later. When I was a teenager. But there was nothing. No social media. No news stories. Nothing. When I moved back here, I visited the orphanage, looking for information. They passed me to a retired priest who'd been there when they were kids. He told me that one of my brothers, the younger one . . ." Butcher trailed off.

"Taiwong," Killian interjected.

"Yes. Yellow, right? The priest said he wasn't right in the head. Hadn't been since my other brother drowned. He and the oldest . . ."

"Taihong," Killian supplied.

"Right. They were both there that day at the camp, or whatever it was. The priest said it traumatized them both. Taiwong lost touch with reality, it sounds like. And the older one, he started running away. Eventually, he started stealing, fell in with criminals. Triads. He left the home for the last time when he was fifteen, and the priest never saw him again. But he heard Taihong had been involved in a robbery. Served time in prison."

Killian and Blue exchanged a glance.

"Do you have any other details? When this happened, for example?" Blue asked.

"I think it was the early 2000s. But I wasn't sure either. And there was nothing on Google. So I forgot about it," Butcher said.

They waited.

"Until last month, when Taihong came to see me in the office. The receptionist called me up on the trading floor, said my brother was asking to see me. It was a shock."

"I'm sure it was. What did he want?" Killian asked.

Killian's phone buzzed. Then buzzed again.

"Money, of course. He said the other brother, Taiwong, was homeless, needed money to find a place to live. He said he was barely making enough to survive, living in one of those cage rooms, so couldn't help."

"What did you do?" Killian asked.

"I said I'd help, of course. But I wanted to meet him first. The other brother. Not to say I was being scammed, but . . ." Butcher shrugged.

"Then what happened?"

"Nothing. I never heard from him again. I'd given him my mobile, and he'd said he'd call, but he never did. I was relieved, to be honest. He was a little . . ." Butcher gestured with open hands. "Not sure how to put it. Disturbing? All skin and bone. Big eyes. Haunted."

"You feared for your safety?" Blue asked.

"No, not exactly. But I certainly wasn't going to let him meet my family. He was like a survivor from a gulag. Someone who had learned to do anything to survive."

Butcher shrugged again. "I actually offered him a few thousand in cash, but he refused. I think he was offended. Like I was trying to get rid of him, which I suppose I was, in a way."

He smiled uncomfortably. Killian's phone buzzed again. Another message.

Butcher opened his mouth to speak but was interrupted by the trilling of Killian's phone. A call this time.

"I'm sorry, Mr. Butcher. I have to take this," Killian said.

Butcher lifted his hand, smiling, and waved permission.

It was the same 5858 HQ number. Killian cut it off, then opened the messages. Two were from Zen:

> Call me now.

Then:

> CALL NOW!!!!!!!

Another message was from Lin:

> Kunst arrived HK yesterday.
> Now at seminary.

The last was a general message from HQ, warning that crowds of protesters were gathering in the streets around the Liaison Office ahead of the announcement. All discipline officers should expect to be called up for duty if the situation deteriorated.

Killian stood.

"Apologies. We have to leave immediately," he said.

He called Zen in the lift. Zen picked up on the first ring.

"Where have you been?"

"A murder investigation. I told you," Killian replied.

"Whatever. Your sister and her friends are headed to Tamar. PLA headquarters. They're going to try and pull something there while all the attention is on the announcement."

Zen was using words that would trigger the tracking algorithms. He didn't care anymore.

"You're sure?" Killian asked.

"What else would they be doing there? There are red flags all over the board. You've got to get her on a plane. Now. I can delay recognition for a few hours. But that's all."

"What about you?"

"Don't worry about me. I'm done with Hong Kong."

Zen hung up.

"What is it, boss?" Blue asked.

The doors opened with a ping, and Killian rubbed his temples.

"I . . . Shit," he muttered, shaking his head. Everything was happening at the same time. "Did someone call Yuen Long about the address we have for the other brother?"

"Yes. He moved out two weeks ago. No idea where," Blue said.

"Okay. So that's out. But I've just been told that the priest who was with Chiu when the boys died, is here in Hong Kong. Paul Kunst. Yeong says he's at the seminary. We need to take him in."

"We're assuming that the eldest Lau brother is the killer?"

"We have to."

"Kunst could be the accomplice."

"Agreed. He's by far our strongest lead. You have to go to the seminary."

"Yes, boss. But, I don't understand. You should be there if we arrest him."

"I will be. If Kunst is at the seminary, wait outside until I show up."

Blue looked confused. "What will you be doing?"

"Family emergency," Killian said.

"A family emergency? Your mother?"

"Just go. I'll explain later. Find Kunst. Guard him. If you see anybody who looks remotely like Butcher, call backup immediately and do your best to avoid him."

"Got it. Find the priest. Guard him. Call backup on anyone who looks like Butcher."

"Good."

Blue turned to walk away.

"Blue," Killian called after her.

She swiveled back.

"On second thought, maybe you'd better . . ."

Blue stepped forward and patted him on the shoulder.

"It's okay, boss. Let me do my job," she said.

"Okay. But be careful," Killian said.

"Yes, Mother."

"I'll call Yeong and Lin, tell them to meet you there."

She waved an arm over her shoulder as she walked away.

THIRTY-FIVE

Killian hit the siren as soon as he turned into Barker Road and raced down the winding streets lined by their massive ornate gates, lights flashing red and blue. Rounding a corner he nearly rear-ended a Bentley trundling along at twenty miles an hour, a shiny bald head visible in the back, reading the paper. Killian leaned on the horn. The car started to edge sideways, and he blasted past, clipping the rear fender as he went, the round mouth of the passenger screaming soundless curses.

More bends followed until he finally hit Magazine Gap Road, plunging downward with Central on his right. Cars slowed to get out of the way, but there was nowhere to go—just a rock wall on one side and a sheer hillside on the other. Finally, a lay-by appeared, and he swung out, narrowly missing an oncoming taxi.

His phone buzzed, and he risked a glance downward.

> They are parked at city hall.
> walking to PLA HQ tamar now

The blare of a horn startled him. Killian looked up to see he was in the right-hand lane. A semi-truck had stopped ahead, its high beams flashing.

He swung the car back into the left lane, squeezing between two other descending vehicles.

At last, Cotton Tree Drive came into view. Four lanes stretched ahead, and, finally, the siren worked its magic. Cars scattered in front of him as he barreled down past the Peak tram, the Bank of China tower, and onto the Harcourt Road Expressway, picking up speed. Another buzz.

> General alert going out now.
> I'm done here. over and out

Black Mercedes and Audis crowded together in the lane for the cross-harbor tunnel like so many plump beetles. They refused to move, unwilling to lose their place in line. Killian picked up the microphone and clicked on the loudspeaker.

"Move your vehicle immediately, or you will be arrested."

They moved.

On Wing Lung Avenue, running along the harbor, he switched off the siren and pinned the accelerator, rocketing the last few hundred yards.

The PLA HQ compound came into view, surrounded by high stone walls encircling two city blocks. Killian jammed on the brakes a hundred yards from the front gates. No police were permitted here; the PLA insisted on handling their own security.

He flung open the door, leaving the Land Cruiser with its strobes still flashing. The sidewalk was empty except for a small knot of people approaching the main gate, all of them were wearing hoodies, masks, sunglasses. Only one sentry stood behind the double gate, assault rifle held across his chest, bayonet mounted, finger on the trigger guard.

Killian's breath rasped in his throat as he ran toward the gate, feet pounding. A double-decker thundered past on the highway.

The group reached the gate and fanned out in a semicircle. A single bareheaded protester, curly hair cropped close to her skull, stood directly in front of the soldier, hands raised in the air, holding a long pole with a black cloth wrapped around the top. The protester waved the pole back and forth and a banner billowed out revealing huge scrawled white characters.

光復香港，時代革命!
LIBERATE HONG KONG!

Killian could hear the soldier shouting a warning. He lowered his rifle so the barrel was pointing directly at the protester.

But the figure was bending down, mouth open, shouting something inaudible, before straightening, a tiny flicker of light at their feet, waving the flag back and forth.

Then there was a woof of air and the figure was engulfed in flames, a black cloud of smoke billowing upward.

Fire raced up the wooden flagpole, licking greedily at the cloth.

Killian sprinted on, gasping. Fifty meters away.

Please. Please, please. Not Jun. Not Jun.

The figure sank to their knees, arms stretched out in front as if in supplication—or prayer—the flag still upright, the pole clamped between their legs.

Two soldiers burst out of the gate, each carrying a red fire extinguisher. An amplified voice barked orders.

Two of the protesters filmed the scene on their phones, ignoring the soldiers.

Cars squealed to a stop on the highway. A crash followed by the tinkle of broken glass sounded behind Killian.

Despite the hoodie and the mask, he recognized her from her stance, her so familiar way of bending her right knee slightly, tilting her head to one side as she filmed. The closest protester was Jun. Her companion saw Killian's uniform and fled toward the highway.

"Jun!"

She looked at him, still holding the phone in front of her. She gave a slight nod to Killian, then turned back to the screen.

Soldiers poured out of the gates. On the opposite side of the road from where he had left the cruiser, a white police van screeched to a halt and a squad of constables burst out led by a sergeant barking into his shoulder mic.

The soldiers stopped a meter from the burning body and raised their extinguishers. White powder billowed, enveloping the kneeling figure which toppled sideways, arms frozen by their sides, forearms hooked like claws.

Killian reached forward and took Jun by the shoulder.

"Jun," he said in a soft voice. "We have to go. Now."

Jun turned again.

"She gave up her life for this. I just wanted to make sure we had a full record."

Killian gestured to the body, laying on its side, a ruin of white powder and black, smoking flesh, the smell of barbecued meat in the air.

"You've done what you could. Let's go."

Jun nodded, hit a button on her phone and slipped it into the pocket of her coat. He put his arm through hers as though he was escorting her away under arrest, and they turned to walk to the cruiser.

The remaining protesters had been grabbed by the PLA soldiers and thrown to the ground.

The sergeant from the van appeared, puffing.

"Is everything all right, sir?" he asked.

"I'm taking this protester in for booking. Go take custody of the other protesters. The PLA don't have jurisdiction."

"Yes, sir." The sergeant trotted away.

Two more police vans pulled up as Killian and Jun walked to the cruiser, a stream of constables jogging past them as though they were invisible.

When they got to the cruiser, Killian opened the passenger door and gently pushed Jun inside. She didn't resist, staring straight ahead. Killian climbed in, shutting the door as he dropped the car into gear and punched the accelerator.

A convoy of police vans flashed past on the opposite side of the highway as they entered Gloucester Road. They joined the river of cars crawling toward Central.

"Who was she?" Killian asked.

Jun didn't reply, pulling off the sunglasses and the mask revealing eyes red from weeping. She cuffed away the tears streaming down her cheeks.

"She was my friend." She found a handkerchief and blew her nose. "She was a hero. We drew lots, but I'm certain she fixed it so she would be chosen."

"You drew bloody lots? Are you mad? It could have been . . ." Killian stopped himself, took a deep breath.

They passed the International Finance Center and he slowed, signaling left to exit the highway onto Rumsey Street. He drove past the Four Seasons then up the ramp that led to the IFC car park. Jun didn't speak as he stopped to take a ticket, then navigated the Land Cruiser past the barrier, pulling up next to the lifts that were marked with signs for the Airport Express.

"You have your passport, right? I talked to Ma. She said you took it with you. She thought you were going on a holiday," Killian said.

"Yes," Jun replied.

"Good. Go upstairs to the train. Do not contact anyone. Go straight to the airport. Understand?"

Her chin thrust forward, but Killian raised a hand to stop her from speaking.

"No. Let me speak now. The time for your protests is over. All you'll achieve is arrest and jail in some camp in China. And when they let you go—if they let you go—you'll be old, broken, sick, dreams gone, your friends in jail or dead. This is a machine. Don't break yourself on it for nothing."

Jun hesitated.

"Take the first plane out. Doesn't matter where. Singapore. Tokyo. Manila. From there, you can connect to London."

"I don't want to go. We have a flat we can hole up in until . . ."

Killian could see she was weakening.

"It's not an option, Jun. Hong Kong is too small. They'll find you in hours. A day at the most."

She sighed.

"You can stay in the United Kingdom indefinitely," Killian said. "Ma has money there. You can study. Or work for what you believe in. But from outside Hong Kong."

"When will I be able to come back?"

Her voice was small, frightened, the enormity of what had happened, what she'd done, finally crashing down on her.

"Forget that. You need to go. Now."

Jun reached for the handle, then turned back. "Thank you."

She reached forward and touched his shoulder.

"You're a good man, Gaw," she waved at his uniform, the cruiser. "Despite this."

Killian nodded.

"Don't let them change that," Jun said. "They will want to take that away, make you like them. Don't let them."

"I won't, Jun. Don't worry." He leaned forward and they embraced awkwardly. "Now go, would you please?"

Killian watched her walk toward the lifts, hunched over as the doors opened, her slight figure disappearing inside, the doors closing with an awful finality.

Killian put the car in gear and headed for the exit.

There was no charge at the barrier. His stay had been less than fifteen minutes.

It had begun to rain, the downpour increasing from spattered drops to a lashing storm of water in seconds, a fusillade beating against the windshield like fists on a door.

Killian imagined the rain washing away the ashes of the protester outside Tamar, black rivulets flowing into the gutter.

So brave.

So futile.

His phone buzzed. Blue.

At nunnery. priest inside.

Killian picked it up and typed.

On my way.

* * *

As he crested the rise leading to the valley, Killian's phone buzzed for the fifth time. He hadn't dared to pick it up before, fully concentrated on guiding the cruiser through traffic at full speed. He looked down the long road sloping into the valley and saw it was empty, then picked up the phone and barked into it: "Lin. Are you at the nunnery?"

"No, sir. I'm at the station. TSW," Lin replied.

"What the hell? I specifically . . ."

"Deputy Commissioner Tsang called, looking for you. He said he's called you many times and you're not picking up."

"And?"

"And he ordered me to stay here. Said the commissioner himself is shutting the investigation down. You're off the case. The archbishop's secretary didn't like being threatened with arrest."

Killian snorted.

"Seriously, sir. The DC is out for blood," Lin said, his normally steady voice tinged with fear. "He said the case has been taken over by the mainlanders. Ministry of State Security. I didn't even know they could do that, take over a . . ."

"*Diu!*" Killian growled, throwing the phone onto the passenger seat and stamping on the accelerator. "Shit. Shit. Shit."

★ ★ ★

When Killian rounded the corner to the nunnery drive, he saw the maintenance van was still parked in front of the building. Its rear doors were shut, and a neat pile of bricks lay stacked beside it. He glanced at the van's passenger cabin as he passed. It was empty. Then, next to the van, sprawled on the ground with one arm draped over the pile of bricks, was a body.

It was Blue.

Killian jumped out of the car and ran to her. She was breathing, a slight snore escaping her lips, her eyes closed. Blood streaked the side of her head. Killian placed his forefinger on her neck. Her pulse was strong. He gripped her shoulder with one hand and hooked two fingers through the belt loop of her uniform pants with the other, rolling her into the recovery position. He supported her chin as her head lolled forward, lowering it gently until her cheek rested against the ground.

Her gun was still holstered, the safety strap buckled. She'd had no warning. Blood matted the back of her head, and as Killian parted the hair, he saw a raw wound at the base of her skull. The bleeding was slow, and the wound seemed superficial—clearly aimed to incapacitate rather than kill.

Killian loped to the Land Cruiser and grabbed the mic. "Dispatch, this is Car AM6530. I need an ambulance at the old nunnery, Seminary Road, Fu Tei San. Officer wounded and needs urgent assistance. I repeat, officer needs urgent assistance."

"Copy that, AM6530. Officer needs assistance. Dispatching ambulance."

"I also require backup in the vicinity, Special Duties Unit if possible. I have a potential hostage . . ." A piercing shriek rang out from above.

Killian's voice hardened. "I have a hostage situation. Suspect armed and extremely dangerous."

The dispatcher replied, but Killian had already dropped the mic. He scrambled in the glove compartment, retrieved his Glock, racked the slide, and sprinted toward the nunnery. His arm hung loose at his side, his finger resting on the trigger guard.

Ascending the stairs to the first floor, Killian stopped to listen. The building seemed empty except for shouting from the floor above, one voice full of rage, the other pleading. The words were muffled. He climbed to the next flight, his footsteps light and deliberate.

The shouting voice grew louder, frantic. "No! No! No!" The sound swelled into a scream of pure terror, then morphed into a guttural, animal howl of pain that reverberated through the corridor.

Killian approached the door to Room 203. From inside, a whimpering voice cried, "Oh God. Oh God. God help me."

Another voice answered, low and menacing, "He's not going to help you. Just like he wasn't there to help all those boys you killed, was he?" A heavy blow followed, accompanied by a sharp cry of pain. "That's because he doesn't care. About them or you. Does he, Father?"

Killian stepped through the doorway, gun raised. A man in blue overalls stood with his back to him, bent over another man seated in a chair. The man in the chair, pale and naked, had spindly legs splayed awkwardly, his head lolling to one side. His eyes fluttered open and shut as the man in overalls swung a hand, delivering a sharp slap.

"Wake up! You're not going to escape that way," the man growled. He had the same sharp nose and prominent cheekbones as Butcher, Killian saw. Strong genes. But this face was blotchy and sagging, ravaged by time. And rage.

In the man's other hand was a steel cleaver, its blade streaked with dried blood. Crimson puddles pooled beneath the chair, streaking the legs.

Killian shifted slightly; a floorboard creaked under his foot. The man in overalls glanced over his shoulder. His eyes narrowed, then darted back to the priest as he circled behind the chair. He hooked his right arm around the priest's neck, pressing the cleaver blade under the man's chin.

"I knew you'd come for your lady, police," the man sneered.

Killian took a step forward, his gun still raised. "Put the knife down, Mr. Lau. Then we can talk."

Lau ignored him, tightening the blade against the priest's throat.

"You came to see justice done, eh, policeman? No one else would do it. Not the Church," Lau spat, "the Church that protected him. Not the police. No one."

"Put the knife down first, Mr. Lau," Killian repeated.

Lau's eyes sharpened. "You know my name."

"I've been talking to your brother."

"My *gweilo* brother. Did he tell you what this man did?"

"No. He said there was some trouble at a . . ."

"Trouble! Trouble!" Lau's voice rose to a shriek. "This man—this priest—fucked my brother to death. That was the trouble."

"If he did, then he'll be charged, Mr. Lau. I promise you. But please . . ."

"We were hiding in the closet and saw it all—heard it all. And then they killed the other boy, Mak. Strangled him. They put their bodies in bins. Like rubbish." Lau's voice broke, trembling with rage. "And that's where he's going too."

Killian stepped forward. "We have evidence. Videos. Photographs. Enough to convict him a hundred times over. The world will know what he did. Don't you want that?"

Killian heard the sound of steps behind him, but didn't take his eyes off Lau.

"Do you want your brother's killer convicted or not, Lau?"

Lau paused, the pressure on the priest's neck slackening slightly. His eyes darted to Killian's Glock, then to the two newcomers—civilians in black suits—who had stepped into the room behind Killian.

Who were they? Killian wondered. Not backup, that was for sure.

Lau gestured with his chin to one of the men.

"Tell them to back off, or I'll kill him."

He pressed the cleaver closer, blood welling along the knife's edge, staining the priest's pale skin. Kunst's eyes bulged, and he tried to say something, but produced only a choking gurgle.

"Don't shoot," Killian barked to the men, his eyes still fixed on Lau. The suits ignored him, the one on his left counting down in Mandarin.

"San, er . . ."

"I said don't shoot!" Killian shouted. "He's going to . . ."

"Yi!"

Two deafening shots rang out. Blood sprayed across the walls as Lau crumpled, half his face gone. The cleaver clattered to the floor. The priest sagged forward, unconscious.

Killian spun to protest, but an arm swung toward him, a pistol butt aimed at his temple. A burst of light, then everything went black.

The Standard

TWO KILLED IN NEW TERRITORIES HOSTAGE TAKING

By Tam Chi-ming

A hostage standoff in the New Territories ended in tragedy yesterday when an apparently mentally unstable man killed himself and his victim after being confronted by Police Special Duties Unit officers.

The standoff at a former nunnery in Fu Tei San ended with the deaths of the two men at around 2:20 P.M. and left a police officer in the hospital. According to a police spokesperson, Chief Inspector Choi Lam Tin had been tracking Lau Taihong as part of a separate investigation and confronted the man at the nunnery, where he was employed as a handyman. Lau attacked Choi with a brick, leaving her with a serious head wound.

"Despite being seriously wounded," Senior Superintendent Sheung Li Mei told *The Standard*, "the chief inspector managed to radio for help before passing out."

SDU officers arrived at the scene to find Lau had appropriated Choi's service weapon and was holding a priest, Father Helmut Kunst, hostage in a bedroom at the former nunnery, which now serves as a dormitory for visiting clergy. When he realized he was trapped, Lau shot the priest, killing him instantly and then turned the weapon on himself. Both men were pronounced dead at the scene.

"Tragically, Father Kunst seems to have been in the wrong place at the wrong time," said Senior Superintendent Sheung.

"He had just arrived in Hong Kong from the Philippines where he lived and had no connection to Lau, who we believe had developed a vendetta against Catholic priests as part of a psychotic breakdown."

Chief Inspector Choi is recovering from her head wound at the Tin Shui Wai Hospital, Sheung said. Her condition was described as stable.

"The chief inspector's investigation led her to attempt to interview Lau at his workplace. Unfortunately, he attacked her without warning before she was able to confirm his identity."

Police sources said that in recognition of her conduct Choi would be put forward for a SAR Silver Medal for Bravery.

THIRTY-SIX

When Killian walked out the front doors of Prince of Wales Hospital, he was surprised to find almost no cars on the street. Even the Sha Tin Expressway, which ran in front of the enormous hospital complex, only had a few vehicles moving on it. He tried to think what day of the week it was and realized he didn't know. He'd been in the hospital for four days when he woke up. The nurse had told him that. And it had been another week since then, a time during which he had fought the doctors and Mother to be allowed out. That meant eleven days since the MSS goon had pistol-whipped him. Maybe.

"You may experience some memory issues," the surgeon had said. He'd apparently developed a subacute subdural hematoma after the blow from the pistol butt. They'd had to do a burr hole surgery and he had been kept in an artificial coma until the operation. "That was mostly precautionary because of the length of your unconsciousness," said the surgeon, a brisk man named Ngee who seemed barely Killian's own age. "That's why we kept you here too."

So he'd stayed in the hospital. Until today.

He'd call Mother to tell her he was coming home, though no doubt she'd say the least possible on the phone. Like everyone in Hong Kong, she was getting used to the shock of having the National Security Law passed. When he asked her about Jun when she visited him in the hospital, she'd nodded her head and given a thumbs up, then put her finger to her lips and said, "Just concentrate on getting better, Ah Gong. The hospital is the best place for that."

A row of shops caught his eye. He walked into a 7-Eleven and picked up a copy of the *South China Morning Post.* Monday, July 2. Of course. The day after Handover Day. It was a made-up public holiday.

The front page headline read:

HONG KONG CELEBRATES RETURN TO THE MOTHERLAND

PARADE, FIREWORK DISPLAY COMMEMORATES 24TH ANNIVERSARY

NEWLY APPOINTED CHIEF EXECUTIVE AND POLICE COMMISSIONER PRESENT

Beneath the headlines were two photos: fireworks exploding over the harbor in red and yellow and a march past a reviewing stand lined with VIPs, all of them saluting. In the center of the crowd, between a figure in police blue and a bewigged judge, was a man wearing a grey suit and a bow tie:

CHIEF EXECUTIVE SUN GUANGWEN (SUEN GWONGMAN), CHIEF JUSTICE JIANG SHENYUE (TSEUNG SAMJOEK) AND COMMISSIONER OF POLICE, ZENG BIN (TSANG BAN) REVIEW THE PARADE

Killian stared at the photo. No wonder Eddie had sounded so cheery. He had called on the eighth day or maybe the seventh. Told Killian he was expected back at HQ as soon as he was fit. That the station at Tsim Bei Tsui was officially closed and his exile over. His things had been collected by a couple of constables and were being stored for him. No need to go back.

No mention of Killian violating orders and continuing to investigate the murder. Instead, he was praised for solving the case. All was forgiven, apparently, just as Blue had predicted.

Killian absorbed this, still feeling slow, groggy, then said, "Did they find a dog?"

"A dog? Did you say a dog?"

Eddie sounded as if he thought the effects of the blow were still slowing Killian down.

"Yes, sir. I kept a dog with me at the station."

"No. No dog. Nothing but dust and empty San Miguel bottles I'm told. Tsk, tsk, Killian. Luckily for you I'm in a good mood."

"Thank you, sir. And what about the two MSS men who assaulted me? Will they be prosecuted?"

Silence. Then a sigh. Disappointment.

"It's over, Killian. The murderer was killed. The priest died of his wounds. Case closed."

"Yes, sir, but . . ."

"You had no official role in the investigation, did you?"

"No, sir."

"So Chief Inspector Tsui gets . . ."

"Choi. Chief Inspector Choi, sir."

"Chief Inspector Choi gets the credit. I'm sure you don't mind sharing the glory with a young, upcoming officer, do you?"

"No, sir, of course not."

"Excellent, I'm glad we understand each other. Better to just move on, Killian. Put it behind you, concentrate on the future. You do understand that we are in a new Hong Kong now that the National Security Law has been passed, don't you?"

"Yes, sir."

But even then, he could hear the doubt in his own voice. He wondered if Eddie hadn't been the one who ordered him to be kept for a few extra days in the hospital, "for observation."

He looked down at the newspaper in his hand again.

Police Commissioner Zeng. They had used the Mandarin spelling for his name first. It was, after all, the official language of the People's Republic. How long would it be before they banned people from speaking Cantonese?

But Eddie had finally gotten what he'd been working toward all these years. However they spelled his name. And Suen had made it to chief executive.

The memory of Suen's cold, pitiless eyes came to him. He shook his head wearily. Poor Hong Kong.

"Wai."

Killian looked up. A spotty clerk at the checkout counter was pointing at the newspaper.

"No reading. It's thirty-five dollars."

Killian dropped the paper back onto the rack.

"Thanks. I've read enough."

* * *

A taxi was idling at the bottom of the ramp leading out of the Tin Shui Wai MTR station. The driver flicked his cigarette out the window as Killian climbed in.

"Tsim Bei Tsui police station, please."

The driver swiveled around, frowning. "It's closed."

"Just take me there, please."

The driver shrugged.

"It's your money."

* * *

His keys still worked. That was a blessing. The patrol car was still parked in the side bay too.

He paused at the front door, his key in hand, a wave of unease washing over him. Shaking it off, he inserted the key and pushed the door open.

The smell of dust and mold. Of failure.

The place had been cleaned out, much of its furniture removed. His steps echoed as he walked to the sergeant's desk. He punched in the code for the steel key locker, finding it still operational. Inside, the rows of interior keys hung neatly on the rack, alongside the patrol car keys.

The kitchen was bare, its drawers emptied, refrigerator unplugged. The rest of the station showed similar signs of abandonment.

No sign of Gau. Even his metal bowls were gone.

Perhaps he had found a way to get out. If so, he was long gone. Looking for food. And shelter. Not one to hang around and mourn.

In the main room, Killian opened a sideboard and reached into the back. The cleaners had missed the whisky. He retrieved a glass from the bathroom, poured himself a drink, and carried it back to the observation room.

Facing the sergeant's desk, he raised his glass in silence. He drank. The whisky burned as it went down, warming him. But it felt hollow.

He turned toward the observation windows, gazing out at the falling evening. Across the water, Shenzhen's lights were winking on. The Zeiss binoculars still sat on their tripod, alongside the radar. The nightscope was gone. The radio remained, dark and silent.

Killian scanned the coastline, his gaze passing over the corrugated iron fence to the rocks and mangroves. Thunder rumbled in the distance, and black clouds loomed to the west. Shenzhen's towers blazed with light, their brightness contrasting with the dimming, storm-tinged marshes on the Hong Kong side.

A solitary egret, luminous in the encroaching gloom, stepped carefully through the bog. A dog barked—a high, frightened sound, nothing like Gau—before falling abruptly silent.

Killian downed the last of his whisky, grimacing. Another rumble of thunder echoed as he turned to leave. Then he froze. A flash of light among the trees. Someone was out there.

* * *

The patrol car rolled into the lot, where a large tourist bus stood parked. The driver smoked a cigarette by the open doors. He glanced at Killian, who stepped out wearing jeans and a T-shirt.

"Police? Or did you borrow it?" the driver quipped.

Killian sketched a smile. "Funny. Do you want to see my police ID?"

The man raised his hands in an exaggerated gesture. "Oh, no. Wouldn't dare ask that. No right to ask anymore. You'd probably arrest me for even thinking of asking."

"Have it your way."

"Can't take your picture either. Or film you, can I? A year in jail." The driver ground his cigarette underfoot.

Killian shrugged

At the viewing platform—a small pagoda—tourists crowded the railings, snapping selfies against the backdrop of the Shenzhen skyline. Dusk was creeping in, and the world hung between light and darkness. Most of them were mainlanders.

Killian pushed through the throng. "*Duibuqi. Duibuqi. Duibuqi.*"

Sorry. Sorry. Sorry.

Finally, the last two women moved aside, one grumbling in a thick Sichuan accent, "*Aiya! Xinggang ren zhen mei limao.*"

Killian smiled faintly. She wasn't wrong—Hong Kong people weren't known for their manners.

Stepping over the railings, he made his way to the path, now clearly marked and recently used. Ten meters to the right of the pagoda, it led into the trees.

The smell of wood smoke hit him first. A dry branch cracked underfoot, and moments later, movement stirred ahead. A familiar shape emerged, loping toward him.

"Gau. Din Gau," Killian called softly.

A pause, then a single, joyous bark, and Gau was upon him. He buried his face in the dog's neck, grinning like a fool, hugging him close.

Eventually, he disentangled himself and stood.

"Let's see how your benefactor is doing."

The clearing was the same as the first time Killian had visited: the string of salted fish hanging from the line, the vegetable garden, the sweet shit stink, the fairy lights. Even the skewed stack of plastic chairs.

Wong was there too, squatting by the fire, the flames highlighting the hollows under his broad cheekbones, the sharp nose. Strong genes indeed.

Lau Taiwong. The other brother. The fisherman. How much did he know? Or understand?

There were probably scores of makeshift camps along this desolate stretch of coastline. It was a strange coincidence that Lau had camped so near to the station. But no stranger than everything else to do with this case.

Lau looked up at the sound of his step.

"You're back, Mr. Policeman."

"Hello, Mr. Lau."

"Call me Ah Wong." He smiled. "You haven't come for a fish, I don't think."

Killian smiled. "Not fish, no."

"So why then?"

"I was looking for him." Killian pointed to Gau, who had taken up a position next to Lau and was swinging his head back and forth as they spoke, watching.

"You took your time," Lau said.

"I was unavoidably detained. How did you find him?"

"Heard the yowling coming from the station. For a quiet dog, he can make a racket when he wants."

"Just as well. How did you get in?"

"A police station is still just a house, especially when it's empty. And, anyway, some fool had left a back window open."

Killian smiled again. "Some fool indeed."

"I suppose you'll want some coffee?"

"Yes, thank you." He pulled one of the chairs out of the stack, placed it opposite Lau, and sat.

Lau flipped open the lid of the cooler and reached inside. Rooting around, he finally gave a grunt of satisfaction and pulled out the coffee pot. Next came a packet of coffee and a bottle of Watson's water. Red-and-silver packet. Illy coffee. Where did he get that?

"Station's closed. But you're still policing?" Lau had added coffee grounds to the pot and placed it on the fire.

"Not clear."

"Holiday?"

"Maybe. Thinking of taking a break. I might travel. To England. I have family there."

"Family's important."

"Yes, it is."

"And the shooting, the riots, all that's finished now, is it?"

"Yes. More or less."

"That's a good thing then, isn't it?"

Killian shrugged. "It's complicated."

Lau nodded, then reached into the cooler again and pulled out a carton of milk. Still ParknShop. Next came a Tupperware, inside a bag of Taikoo Sugar. Then he reached over and picked up the pot, which had been making agreeable burbling noises.

Lau retrieved two enameled blue mugs, closed the cooler, poured coffee from the pot into each one. Then he tipped two spoons of sugar into each mug and handed one to Killian.

He stared at the coffee for a while. Then he sipped.

"I'm sorry," Killian said finally.

"Sorry for what?"

Lau regarded him, waiting politely for a response. When none came, Lau took a sip of coffee and turned to scratch Gau's head with his free hand, smiling and making a low clucking sound that set the dog's tail wagging.

"For everything that happened," Killian said finally. "That your brother was killed. I was trying to persuade him to turn himself in."

Lau sipped his coffee, then shook his head. "He never would have agreed. Anyway, you don't have to worry about me. I'm happy." He smiled. "And my brother, he couldn't help himself. It was a sickness inside his head. I didn't recognize him at the end. Or trust him. That's why I came out here."

Lau took another sip of coffee.

"He was crazy with anger at those two. The priests."

"You made the right decision," Killian said.

Lau nodded. "It is lucky he didn't try to get the other one too."

Killian frowned, puzzled. "The other what?"

"The other man who was there that day." Lau put down his cup on the cooler and pointed to the container behind him. "It's in the newspaper."

Lau stood, walked over, picked up the top two papers, and slid a copy out from underneath. Marching troops and fireworks on the front page. It was the same paper Killian had read in the 7-Eleven: July 2.

Lau put his forefinger on the photo, the nail rimmed with black.

"I thought you knew. He was there too." His finger rested below the beaming face of the chief executive of Hong Kong, Suen Gwongman. "My brother said he didn't do anything. Just watched. But he was in the room."

Just watched, Killian thought. Just watched two ten-year-old boys being raped and murdered.

Suen was there. Guilty at the very least of complicity in rape and murder.

Killian heard himself gasp as the implications sank in.

"Mr. Policeman?"

Killian took a step back, then another, hand on his head.

How could he have been so blind? This was why the MSS had shot the priest and Lau's brother.

It all began to click into place, one door opening after another.

The MSS thugs hadn't just appeared out of the blue. They had been tracking this case. Beijing would have known for weeks or even months that they would appoint Suen as the new CE. And as soon as that decision was made, he became one of the *lingdao*, the sacred party leaders whose reputation had to be protected at all costs.

The MSS would have gone to the commissioner and demanded access to anything "sensitive" that could mar the image of the incoming chief executive. And of course, a spectacularly gory murder would qualify.

They must have seen the forensics reports . . .

Another door swung open: Chan. They would have had him review all the evidence and report anything incriminating to them. There must have been something in the objects recovered with the arm that linked Suen directly to the victim. A photo of the two of them together. Or a letter. It didn't matter what it was. The MSS knew their job was to expunge any links between the *lingdao* and a nasty murder.

Hell, Chan had tried to warn him during the phone call that there was other evidence. But Killian had ignored him, thought the man was delirious with exhaustion.

They'd probably ordered Kwok to frame Ngai too, so they would have a culprit handy if the story got out. But then Killian had sunk that plan by forcing Zen to release the video of the waterboarding.

Even then, HQ, Eddie, the commissioner, they wouldn't have been unduly worried. After all, they knew there were no good leads except the bloody rosary. And they knew Killian was desperate to get back into active duty. Back to his old life.

Even after Killian had identified Deacon Chiu as the victim, they hadn't been worried enough to intervene beyond calling him repeatedly. Because they had every reason to think he would close the case, which would have buried it forever.

And it would have too. Except for Poon. Poon had paid for the head reconstruction on his own and not informed HQ.

But the MSS were different: They answered to Beijing only. Maybe they knew something about how serious the threat to Suen was. Probably not. It didn't matter. They knew their job was to erase anything that connected Suen to the murder.

They must have been following him when he and Blue went to the Peak. And then to the seminary. He had led them straight to the priest. And the murderer, both conveniently in one place so they could shut down any possibility of a leak. Forever.

What a blind idiot he'd been.

A chill of fear swept through him: Did they know about Jun? Had she been tagged at the immolation?

But no. She'd been wearing a mask, hoodie, sunglasses. She must have fooled the face recognition software. And they would have lost the video feed when he drove into the IFC carpark to drop her off.

Anyway, if they really had ID'd her, or even had any suspicion she was involved, they would have eliminated Jun, living in London or not. A car accident. Something like that.

And they would have arrested him too, sent him to some camp in Gansu. Or put him up against a wall and had him shot. They never left loose ends when *lingdao* were involved.

All they cared about was the leaders. The *lingdao*. Not some random figure in a hoodie. But they must have been laughing as they followed his progress via the traffic cams and all the other surveillance, chortling as he nosed along like a mole, digging and digging without knowing he was being watched the whole time, giving them everything they wanted. A useful fool.

"Mr. Policeman?"

Killian stood and put down his coffee cup.

"I've got to go."

Lau, still holding the paper, smiled. "You are always welcome to come back. Especially if you aren't police any longer."

"You must never tell anyone about this, Mr. Lau. You do understand that? It would be dangerous for you. Very dangerous."

"No one to tell."

Killian started to speak again, but Lau held up his hand.

"Our family escaped from the mainland. I understand what the party does to its enemies."

Killian nodded and turned to go.

"What about him?" Lau pointed at Gau, lying next to the cooler, head on his paws. "Will you be taking him back with you?"

"I'll leave him here, if that's okay. I have something to take care of."

"No problem, though I think he's sick of fish by now. Fish and rice. Not much variety here."

"Thank you. I'll be back soon."

THIRTY-SEVEN

The flat was empty and dark when Killian returned. He walked over to the front window and pulled back the curtains.

When the family moved into this flat, they'd had an uninterrupted view of the harbor and Kowloon, sweeping from the container port and Stonecutters Island on the western approach to the tip of the old runway poking out in the east. Now, a forest of apartment buildings blocked almost everything, only a tiny slice of the harbor was visible though a gap between two buildings, red-and-blue neon reflecting off the swaying water.

He smiled. If they ever sold the place this would be advertised as having "a harbor view." Only in Hong Kong.

Hong Kong.

Home.

A hard city for outsiders to love sometimes. Crowded, expensive, her people brash, unapologetic capitalists, entrepreneurs, strivers, and seekers, the children and grandchildren of refugees who had built something magnificent on top of a barren rock. It was a spectacular, unique city, but they'd also built something more: A community of shared values like decency and fairness and the rule of law, values that a new generation had wanted to preserve, build on.

All that was gone now, or would be soon.

He looked up. The sky was darkening, the light of the day almost gone, the tops of the buildings silhouetted against a dim band of blue and orange, darkness sweeping in from the east.

It was going to be a long, long night. But Hong Kong would survive. And thrive. And be free again. Maybe not this year, or the next. But one day soon.

He had to believe that, or what was it all for?

Killian turned to drop his keys on the hallway table and saw Mother had left two letters there, both addressed to him and marked ON GOVERNMENT SERVICE. He picked them up and walked to the window, using a ballpoint pen to open the first one.

It was from the Complaints Against Police Office board and consisted of only a single sentence between the salutation and the signature:

> The case brought against Superintendent Tong is dismissed for lack of evidence.

The second letter was from the shooting tribunal, and was nearly as brief:

> This Tribunal finds that Superintendent Tong carried out his duties in an exemplary fashion. It further finds that the video evidence and testimony of witnesses suggest that a protester wrested Superintendent Tong's service pistol from him and discharged the shot that wounded Mr. Shek.

More lies. Even when you weren't one of them anymore, they protected themselves.

The party. The Force. The Church. They were all the same. Closing ranks. Protecting their own. The honor of the institution could never be put at risk. It was justification to commit any crime, however terrible.

They thought they were untouchable. Invulnerable.

Maybe some were. For now.

Some crimes could never be righted, but the suffering of the victims should be acknowledged. And blame admitted by the guilty.

Killian walked through the living room, tossing the two letters into the rubbish bin as he passed.

In his old bedroom, he sat down at the small desk, reaching over to turn on the lamp and opening his laptop. He had work to do.

* * *

Two days later, just after 6:00 P.M., Killian arrived at Saint Joseph's. The Saturday evening Mass, popular with young people and families who wanted to have their Sundays free, started at 6:15.

The church was almost full when he walked in through the main entrance, a few latecomers hurrying their children along, taking places in the rear pews. He made his way down the left aisle, heading for the side entrance through which the priests entered.

The evening sun streamed in through the high windows, diffused to soothing blue, red, and orange by the stained glass. The wooden pews were full, most of the worshippers looking toward the altar, little talking, just an expectant quiet, the occasional high child's voice quickly hushed.

As Killian pushed through the doors to wait in the hallway outside, he noticed a young Chinese priest standing in front of the altar, saying something. A moment later, the congregation started singing.

It was as familiar to him as his own face, a hymn he must have heard for the first time when he was only weeks old. He listened now, his mouth set in a thin, hard line.

The darkness deepens, Lord, with me abide,
When other helpers fail and comforts flee,
Help of the helpless, oh, abide with me.
Help of the helpless.

In his head, he heard the boy on the tape screaming for help. No help came for him. Only suffering and death.

Killian closed his eyes and breathed.

A hand on his shoulder. He turned.

"Killian!"

Father Dec stood there, in full Mass regalia—a heavy green gown, a gold cross stitched into the front.

Astonishment, then consternation flashed across the priest's face before it was instantly wiped away, replaced by a blossoming smile.

"You're alright, Killian. Thank the Lord. We were worried." Father Dec moved forward to hug him, the robes enveloping him in the smell of incense and stale sweat.

Killian recalled the names of the vestments from his altar boy days. Amice, alb, cincture, chasuble. He used to hand each one to the priest, waiting as the appropriate prayer was recited.

He had memorized the prayers too, even though he hadn't understood them.

The cincture. A cord around the waist.

Gird me, Oh Lord, in thy cincture of purity and quench in me the fire of concupiscence, that the virtue of continence and chastity may remain in me.

He kept his arms by his sides, stiff, immobile. Father Dec stepped back, frowning.

"Is something wrong, my boy? You've a face like death. What did they . . ."

"I need to ask you some questions, Father."

The priest frowned and looked at his watch—the same stainless steel Rolex he had worn for decades. A gift from a parishioner. "My only indulgence."

"I'm to say Mass in a few minutes, Killian. Can't it wait?"

Killian didn't reply.

"Saturday evenings are my best crowd, you know." Father Dec smiled. His famous self-deprecation.

"I need to ask now, Father. It will be quick." Killian waved over his shoulder toward the church. "They can talk to God while they're waiting. It's what they're here for, isn't it?"

They regarded each other for a long moment. Then Father Dec reached forward and touched him on the shoulder. "Very well. Come."

In his office, Father Dec sat on the couch and waved him to sit in the armchair opposite. Killian remained standing.

"Now, my boy, what is so urgent that it takes precedence over God?" The priest raised his eyebrows and smiled that familiar grin. But his eyes were wary.

"Was Suen Gwongman at the Po Toi Island camp that day?"

"What? I don't understand. At what camp, Killian?"

"Please don't pretend, Father. You know exactly what I'm talking about."

A pause.

"I remember that terrible day, of course," the priest said finally. "If that's what you mean. Those poor boys."

Those poor boys. Those lovely boys. Killian kept his voice even with an effort.

"And was he there? On the island?"

"Of course he wasn't, Killian."

"How do you know?"

"I don't know why you're asking these questions, Killian. No one has ever said he was on the island. He volunteered there, yes. But he wasn't there the day the boys drowned."

"How do you know?"

The priest looked at his Rolex again.

"I know you have been in the hospital, Killian. So I am going to excuse this—this obsession—and answer your question. I know because the Chinese came and asked for our records before he became CE. They can't have a trace of scandal, of course. So they vetted him. Gwongman was here at the church that night. First at mass, then at a meeting of the Youth Club."

"And you, Declan O'Shea, where were you that night?"

"What are you saying, Killian? Are you asking if I'm a pedophile?"

"No, Father. I know you're not a pedophile. I'm asking about a sin of omission, not of commission."

"What does that mean?"

"It means you are lying. I never mentioned anything about pedophilia. And yet you brought it up. You knew all along. You changed those records to cover up everything that might make the Church look bad. And please stop saying they drowned. The boys were murdered. Raped and murdered."

Father Dec shook his head. "This is madness, Killian. Fantasy."

"I know about the cover-up because I have spent the last two days talking to people who were there," Killian said slowly. "The old priest who ran the orphanage was kind enough to give me a list of the other boys who were at the camp. Four of them were willing to talk about what happened. No one had ever asked before. And they all said Suen was there. They also said they had been assaulted by Kunst and Chiu. Sometimes just touching. But two of them were made to perform fellatio."

"Are you saying I knew about this, this disgusting crime, about murder, and covered it up, Killian?" Father Dec's face turned ashy pale, and his large, freckled hands resting on his thighs began to tremble. He saw Killian looking and clenched them into fists, the knuckles turning white.

"You were the cardinal's assistant, weren't you?"

"I was, but I don't see what that has to do with this."

"One of the letters I found in Deacon Chiu's trunk was from the cardinal reassigning Chiu and Kunst to a rural parish in the Philippines. The cardinal's name was on the letter, then the words 'Per Procurationem.' That means signed by someone else. The scrawled signature wasn't the cardinal's. It was your signature, Declan O'Shea. You signed it for the old man, didn't you?"

Father Dec gave no response except a slight lowering of his head.

"The letter also said that any further evidence of misconduct would result in defrocking. And you knew perfectly well what 'misconduct' meant, didn't you?"

The priest shook his head. "How can you suspect such things, Killian? After all the years I have known you, that I would . . ."

Killian held up his hand.

"I'm sure you convinced yourself over the years that it was simply a drowning. That you'd done the right thing to protect the Church. Or maybe you forgot all about it. Until I called and asked about Chiu. Did it all come flooding back? Did you know then that you'd condemned scores of other boys to abuse? To death?"

The priest stared down at his shoes.

"I have the tapes. And the letters. And the witnesses."

Father Dec looked up, a gleam of defiance in his eyes. "None of this means anything. The case will never be prosecuted in Hong Kong. You can't touch Suen."

Instead of anger, Killian felt a wash of exhaustion. A hollowness in his chest. He was tired. So tired.

He reached forward, put a hand on the priest's shoulder, and saw the flinch. He pulled his arm back, dropped to a squat, and locked eyes with the older man.

"No, this will never come to court. But it doesn't have to. If I put it up on the internet it will be the end of you. And for many, many of your parishioners it will be the end of your precious Saint Joe's too. They'll never be able to trust their children at your schools. They'll stop going to Mass. Contributing money. The Church will survive, of course. It always does. But for Catholics in Hong Kong it will be cataclysmic. As it should be."

Father Dec passed a hand across his brow and looked away.

"What do you want of me, Killian?"

"I want you to leave Hong Kong. Resign your priesthood and go away. It doesn't matter where. And when you're on your own, I want you to think about what you've done, the lives you've destroyed. The awful suffering you caused. And I want you to think about Hell, Father Declan O'Shea. I hope you still believe in Hell. And I hope that the thought will torment you every second until you die. Because if it does exist, you will surely be spending all of eternity there."

No response.

"It's your choice."

Finally, the priest spoke, his voice low, exhausted. "You've become very hard, Killian. Life isn't black-and-white. There were . . ."

"Do you agree to my terms or not?"

The older man sighed. He seemed to have aged years in the minutes they had been in the room, his face mottled with red patches, the flesh rubbery.

"I agree. For the good of the Church."

"For the good of the church?" Killian repeated, almost hissing. "Still the same excuse? You disgust me, Declan O'Shea."

Killian stood and walked to the door, then turned back. Father Declan sat immobile, head bent, a white bald patch visible amid the grey curls. He looked up and spread his hands.

"I did what was best, Killian. You have to trust me on that."

Utter conviction, again. Was it still a lie if the old priest had convinced himself it was the truth?

"No, Declan O'Shea. I don't have to trust you ever again. You have a week. Don't make me come back."

Killian walked away, leaving the old priest sitting on the sofa in his gaudy robes, hands on his knees palms up as if in supplication, out through the church's side entrance and into the warm, diesel-scented embrace of the Hong Kong night.

ACKNOWLEDGMENTS

City on Fire was originally conceived while I was living in Hong Kong several decades ago, a time when the police still agreed to do briefings for prospective crime novelists. A young inspector took great relish in showing me gruesome crime scene pictures from a murder in which the unfortunate victim had been dismembered in the bath of a tiny apartment. That's about all that's left of the briefing, but I remain grateful for the start.

I did try and get in touch with the police again when I went to Hong Kong in 2019 to research this book, but got no response to my queries. The police had other things on their minds, I guess.

The protesters though were more than willing to talk at length, always anonymously, often while still wearing their gas masks or assembling Molotov cocktails. What I heard on the streets astonished me. Even though I was born and partly raised in Hong Kong, I had internalized the widely accepted trope that the city's residents were crude, money-grubbing materialists.

But the young people I talked to were among the most idealistic I have ever met. And they were also perfectly aware of the futility of their struggle. And yet they persisted. It was both deeply inspiring and extremely depressing.

That said, I must of course stress that all the characters in this book are born from the writer's imagination, and that any resemblance to actual persons is entirely coincidental.

Books, like children, take a village. This one is no different.

I'll have to miss most of the villagers, but a brief shout out must go to my readers, without whose criticism and support this book would still be a pile of pages in a lower desk drawer. First among these, chronologically and otherwise, is the inimitable Ed Gargan. He was followed by other long sufferers: Freddy Balfour, who rode a bike with me on my first visit to Tin Shui Wai; Bob Sherbin (twice!); my own daughter Naomi; my sister Victoria; the ever supportive Paul French; Adrian McKinty; Sonia Land; Howard Schweber; Bill Schwartz; Amy Pershing; and all the others I have omitted, for which apologies.

I'd also like to express thanks to my agent, Peter Rubie, whose patience in the face of my sillier vaporings has been astonishing.

To Victoria Wenzel and Claiborne Hancock at Pegasus, thanks again for an editing process that was somehow both acutely detailed and remarkably smooth.

In the traditional last but absolutely most important of all position, my wonderful wife, Yoke Ling, without whom this book wouldn't be a few pages in a desk drawer, it would be some ashes in a grate. Thank you, my love.

And, of course, to Naomi and Nicholas, to whom this book is dedicated. Thank you for your love . . . and ever-skeptical eyes.